Also by Jessica Cunsolo

She's With Me

Stay With Me

PENGUIN BOOKS

Still With Me

Still With Me

JESSICA CUNSOLO

PENGUIN BOOKS

PENGUIN BOOKS

UK | USA | Canada | Ireland | Australia
India | New Zealand | South Africa

Penguin Books is part of the Penguin Random House group of companies
whose addresses can be found at global.penguinrandomhouse.com.

www.penguin.co.uk   www.puffin.co.uk   www.ladybird.co.uk

Penguin
Random House
UK

Published in Great Britain by Penguin Books in association
with Wattpad Books, a division of Wattpad Corp., 2022

001

wattpad books

www.wattpad.com

Printed and bound in Great Britain by Clays Ltd, Elcograf S.p.A.

The authorized representative in the EEA is Penguin Random House Ireland,
Morrison Chambers, 32 Nassau Street, Dublin D02 YH68

A CIP catalogue record for this book is available from the British Library

ISBN: 978-0-241-58480-4

All correspondence to:
Penguin Books, Penguin Random House Children's
One Embassy Gardens, 8 Viaduct Gardens
London SW11 7BW

To my dad, Bruno Cunsolo. Thank you for your unwavering support, and for wholeheartedly believing there's no limit to what I can achieve.

Prologue

When I was in elementary school, I thought being normal was the worst thing I could grow up to be. Maybe I was six or seven. We had to imagine ourselves as a grown-up, pick a career from a preapproved list, and then do a project. There wasn't an option I wanted, so I picked doctor and went straight home to complain about it. My dad was thoroughly confused when I explained that I didn't want to be a doctor or lawyer or teacher, but wanted to be a hairdresser exclusively for gorillas, who also juggled part time while in a traveling ukulele band.

He tried throwing logical facts at me but I was undeterred by the fact that gorillas probably didn't need hairdressers, or that I didn't know how to juggle or play ukulele, and that no one even wanted to see a juggling ukulele band in the first place.

Then he hit me with the that's not a normal career path speech. I replied, in my cutesy, little-kid way, that being normal sounded boring, and I'd much rather have interesting things happen to me, even if they made my life harder. Looking back now, I would do anything to slap six- or seven-year-old me silly and eat my words out of existence.

My dad wanted me to have a normal, boring life without hardship. I scoffed at the idea. It's ironic how in the end he was the one who set into motion a chain of events that ensured my life would never be completely normal again.

There have been multiple attempts to end my life made by two different men, all within in the last year. There's Tony, the man who's quite possibly a real psychopath, and the reason I've had to move three times and change my identity each time in order to keep myself safe.

Then there's my boyfriend Aiden's biological dad, Andrew Kessler, who's ruthless and clearly has no problem getting someone to murder a teenage girl in order to send a message to his estranged son, who'd threatened to blow the whistle on his true, shitty past and ruin his chances of becoming governor.

My mother is having an affair with the father of one of my best friends, and I have no idea if or how I should tell Mason. Plus, there's the whole Mason's most likely in love with me thing that I really don't even want to think about addressing right now.

Annalisa's half brother, Luke, is going to stand trial for murdering Aiden's stepfather, which he claims he doesn't remember doing because he wasn't sober at the time, and Annalisa is just now realizing that she can't bear to not have Luke in her life.

Noah and Chase are in a weird we're friends but not really stage because Chase walked in on Noah in bed with the love of Chase's life, Charlotte, who really doesn't know if she even likes either of them as more than friends.

My middle (and favorite) finger is dislocated from punching Ryan, Aiden's now ex-stepbrother, in the face. My nose is swollen and bruised from walking into Mason's elbow, and there are a bunch of cuts and bruises on my body from Aiden's dad's attempt to *murder me*.

And to make all of that worse, I'm being relocated as soon as the agents assigned to my case finalize our new location and identities. King City is the one place that feels like home, where I have friends I adore and a *boy* I love. But Aiden already knows all about me, and I decided to break *some* small rules so that I don't have to completely give him up—namely the no contacting anyone from your old life rule. But what my mom and the agents don't know won't hurt them, and I'll be supercareful. When the time comes to leave, I won't feel like my heart is being ripped out; I'll still have Aiden.

But in the meantime, while I'm still here in King City, not only do I have Kaitlyn and Ryan trying to make my life miserable, but my best friends are all in the middle of their own dramas, and I *still* have two grown men trying to kill me.

Nice.

Honestly, Julian's the only one in this group who has his shit together and is living a relatively normal life—except for the fact that he hangs out with all of us.

After the accident when Aiden and I were run off the road by Harvey, Andrew's right-hand man, Aiden and Mason gave the cops a pretty convincing story about what had happened, mostly sticking to the truth but omitting any mention of me or Julian. As far as I know, the detectives don't see any discrepancies in their story.

Harvey, the man who ran Aiden and me off the road and tried to shoot me, wasn't found, but "Aiden" didn't deliver a kill shot, so authorities believe Harvey is injured. They ran the prints on the knife that he held to Aiden's throat and they were matched to a Harvey Vedenin, who, to no surprise, has been arrested before. It's also not a shock that Harvey Vedenin is a known associate and bodyguard of Andrew Kessler, which gives validity to Aiden's story. Of course, there's no evidence that actually proves Andrew Kessler was behind Harvey's actions, but we know the truth.

Aiden and Mason stayed at the beach house for an extra week to sort everything out, and the rest of us returned home, Noah driving Jason and Jackson back to Mason's house. During that week they stayed back, I didn't dare go to school. While I couldn't really afford to miss any more of it, I felt guilty returning to school and pretending everything was fine when it was anything but.

Aiden did end up speaking to Vivienne Henfrey, the reporter who'd made it clear she was not a fan of Kessler's, and who'd practically begged Aiden to go on air. I watched Aiden on the news from home, my heart exploding with pride at seeing his handsome and determined face as he shared a part of his life that I knew he'd rather bury so far inside of him that his subconscious didn't even know it was there. I know how hard it was for him to share his past, but he was confident as he told the world about how he is the son of Andrew Kessler. He explained how Andrew left when his mother was sick and pregnant, and how he hasn't tried to contact his family since she died.

He was the same Aiden as usual—cold, stoic, and deadly beautiful, looking even more intimidating with the bruised jaw and ten stitches on the side of his forehead. And the world couldn't help falling in love with him, right then and there. That's the thing about Aiden. He has that presence and charm—even on camera, even when he's not trying—that just makes people gravitate toward him, that makes people like him, makes them want *him* to like *them*, even when everything about him screams don't mess with me.

Vivienne took Aiden's story and old family photos and ran with it, destroying Kessler's platform and family-friendly agenda with it. She basically proved that Kessler is the biggest hypocrite on the planet and doesn't actually care or live by any of the issues he campaigned on. Obviously, Kessler denied everything. His team worked quickly and efficiently at his response and recovery from this new revelation, and as far as I know, he has no plans of dropping out of the race for governor.

We were all together when we heard Kessler say as much, and Charlotte asked, "He'll never recover from this, right? People will think he's an awful person or a phony or a hypocrite and won't elect him if he chooses not to drop out? Right?"

Annalisa snorted as she replied. "You never know—worse people have done worse things in this country and have still been elected to high places of power, so . . ."

We all deflated a bit after that, knowing it was true, but at least Andrew's under more public scrutiny and won't make any attempts to take my or Aiden's life anytime soon.

Hopefully.

1

No matter how many times I've seen my face and body all bruised and scraped up, I've never gotten used to it. Even though it's been just over a week since Aiden and I were in the car accident, I feel like the bruise on my cheek is taking way too long to go away; like it's stubbornly remaining just to mock me, to remind me of what I've been through. My nose has healed from the accidental elbow to the face Mason dealt me at the beach house, but the rest of my bruises are taking their sweet time. Aiden's injuries were worse than mine—I didn't need stitches, at least—but every glance in the mirror reminds me of Harvey, of Andrew, and of how they're still out there, getting away with their crimes, with their attempt to kill us.

A few days after school started, while I was stubbornly refusing to attend until my friends could join me, Makayla Thomas, Kaitlyn's best friend, saw me at the grocery store, still banged up and bruised from the accident. She told everyone that my face is fucked up from botched plastic surgery, and I couldn't help but roll my eyes when Charlotte told me about that rumor going around the school. This means everyone's going to try to get a look at me when I return today with Aiden, but that's nothing in comparison to what he's going to face when he steps in the building.

He doesn't normally open up—it was a miracle when I got him to tell me even the most insignificant detail about himself, and he *liked* me. Having a bunch of stupid teenagers knowing your business and openly staring at you and stage-whispering as you walk by isn't something he'll especially enjoy. I haven't seen him since the accident because he and Mason just got back last night, but I wouldn't have blamed him if he'd decided to skip the next few days. But he's not; he's going to meet me at school, and while I missed him and am so excited to finally see him properly after a week apart, I'm also dreading it, because it'll start the countdown to when I leave. Technically, the countdown started last week when school started, but I can't bring myself to think about that, about how I wasted a week of my life here in King City before I'm relocated without Aiden, without my friend group. I don't know how much time I have left before I'm forced to leave and become someone new, but I know I don't want to throw away another single second. I'm going to make the most of it, even if it means going back to school and facing the gossip mongers who have nothing better to do than gawk and stare at us.

As I walk into the school for the first time since the break, I already feel the stares on me. I fidget with the necklace that Aiden got me for Christmas, feeling calmed by its weight. The necklace with a secret button to release a hidden blade has been around my neck since we left the beach house. Obviously, I know I shouldn't be wearing it to school, but I can't bear to take it off now. Besides the fact that Aiden got it for me and that its presence is comforting, I didn't wear it the night Aiden and I went to meet with Vivienne Henfrey, and we were run off the road and almost killed. I could've really used it then against Harvey, so I'd much rather have it on me now, just in case. Besides, it doesn't *look* like a switchblade, so I'm sure I won't get in any trouble since no one will know. Either way, I keep it tucked under the collar of my shirt when I'm not fidgeting with it.

I meet Annalisa in the front hall, and she holds her head high as we walk, a scowl on her face as she stares down the people who gawk at us without shame until they bow their heads in submission. If I wasn't her friend, I'd be terrified of her. We round the corner to get to my locker and I stop short. Leaning on my locker with his arms crossed, looking perfectly at home but still managing to appear menacing, is Aiden. Talking on the phone and FaceTiming this last week hasn't done him justice; it's nothing in comparison to him in person. A sense of peace washes over me at seeing him standing there, waiting for me, looking at me with hunger and impatience. Everything fades away as I walk over to him. Aiden pushes himself off of my locker and studies me as we approach him.

"How's your face?" is the first thing he says to me once we're close enough.

Wow. He's so romantic. The corner of my lip turns up. "Not as bad as yours."

He smiles at me as he shakes his head and immediately pulls me in for a hug. I melt as he rests his chin on the top of my head.

Yes, FaceTime cannot compare to being in his arms, to feeling the tight muscles in his back. It cannot compete with the feeling of my head tucked into his chest, with hearing his steady heart beating in time with mine beneath my ear, with the feeling of safety and assurance that comes with being in his arms. I can say with absolute certainty that nothing can substitute for the feeling of actually being with him in person.

"Are you okay?" he whispers.

There's something about sharing a traumatic, life-threatening experience with someone that brings you immediately closer to them. When you think about it, Aiden and I kind of saved each other's lives. Actually, not kind of. We did. After the car crash, when Harvey's gun was pointed at me and he pulled the trigger, the shot went wide because of Aiden's quick thinking. And when Harvey started slicing Aiden's throat, he only stopped when I shot him. I'm so grateful my aim was good that day. Being with Aiden now, I instinctively know that no matter what happens in my life, he'll always be close to my heart.

"Yes. Are you?"

He pushes a piece of hair behind my ear and pulls back to meet my eyes. "I'm better now."

My heart flutters, and I remember when he said something similar to me after we got separated at the Tracks when the cops busted the races, which seems like forever ago, even though it's only been about a month.

Annalisa clears her throat. "I wanted to know how you were, too, in case you were wondering."

I laugh and separate myself from Aiden so Annalisa can have her turn with him.

"I'm glad you're okay," she says when they stop hugging.

Noah and Julian come around the corner and grab Aiden into one of those bro hugs.

"I knew we'd find you here," Julian says to Aiden with a quick glance in my direction.

"But would it kill you to answer a text message every once in a while?" Noah complains as he gives Aiden a shove.

Aiden steps aside so I can open my locker.

"Hey, how are the twins handling all of this?" Annalisa asks. "Have you explained everything to them yet?"

Aiden runs his hand through his hair, which is getting kind of long. "Just like with the whole finding Greg dead outside our house thing, I didn't exactly tell them *everything*. But they know who Andrew Kessler is now, and they don't really care for him. So since we're staying at Mason's for a bit, Brian and Natalia have been really good with keeping them occupied and getting them ready for back to school."

Ever since Aiden's arrest, Mason's dad has had legal custody over him and his brothers, Jason and Jackson. Once Aiden turns eighteen this week, he'll file for custody. I'm guessing the current situation's working out pretty well for now—since Aiden's been dealing with a media frenzy, it's helpful to have actual adults you can depend on around.

The warning bell rings so we all start moving toward class. As we walk, Aiden grabs my hand in his bigger one.

"Hey, just a heads-up, don't make plans this Friday." Noah grins, not so innocently.

Aiden sighs, apparently already knowing what Noah's talking about. "I told you, I don't want a birthday party."

"You're turning eighteen in two days! You're getting a birthday party! My. House. This. Friday. Be. There," Noah says.

"Noah, the last time you threw a party, you ended up in the hospital," I point out, and I know none of us wants a repeat of that. Especially right now.

"You can't just stop trying to live because something bad

happened," Noah says thoughtfully. "We're just gonna pull up our big-boy and -girl pants and throw the best damn party that Aiden deserves. And *no one* is going to talk me out of it."

It's Aiden's party, so really, he gets the final say. He mumbles something that sounds like "Fine, whatever," under his breath, making Noah cheer triumphantly.

Bad things happen in life—especially mine lately—and we can't let that stop us from living. I am going to get through senior year and have a normal life if it kills me, which it honestly just might. With my new resolution coursing through my veins, I feel more determined than ever to not let the bad things bring me down; to make the most of my time here in King City with my friends.

"What classes do you have after lunch, again? History, spare, then math with me?" Aiden asks me as we walk up the stairs.

"English, spare, then math. Why?"

"We have a sub for math." His eyes light up mischievously. "What do you say we get out of here after English and go do something?"

"Like what?" I ask. Alone time with Aiden? Don't have to ask me twice! We haven't had any real alone time since before the accident.

"Your choice."

"So if I wanted to get pancakes . . . ?"

"Then you're getting pancakes," he replies, making my heart squeeze.

"Then how can I say no?" I'd never say no. Who knows how much time I have left with him?

"Good. I'll meet you at your locker after fourth period." He kisses my forehead quickly, an act that for some reason feels so much more intimate and sweet than a kiss on the lips, and leaves in the opposite direction with Julian.

Noah and I have the same subject, and we'll drop Annalisa off along the way, continuing along to room 341, the class that started all of this, these friendships that mean so much to me.

"Well, damn. I've never felt more like a fifth wheel in my life," Noah grumbles. "Anna and Julian were on one side of me making out, and Amelia and Aiden were on the other side of me making out. But no one's over here making out with me before first period."

"We were not making out." Annalisa and I defend ourselves at the same time.

"Yeah, yeah." He dismisses us. "Maybe it's time I find a nice girl and settle down. Any suggestions?"

"Kaitlyn," Annalisa says flatly.

We both swing our heads over to look at her.

"That's not even funny," I deadpan.

"No, I'm not talking about Noah," she explains, tilting her head in the direction she was looking. "I meant Kaitlyn is coming."

Sure enough, the she-devil herself is marching right in our direction.

I can practically feel the excitement coursing through Kaitlyn's veins at getting to pick a fight with me. She must have gone stir crazy over the break without having me to annoy the shit out of. She and Makayla stop in front of me and cross their arms over their chests in what seems like practiced synchronicity, barely even noticing Annalisa and Noah at my side.

Kaitlyn has the same icy, blue eyes and permanent scowl etched on her face as always, but she looks different somehow.

"I'm glad you tried to fix your face over the break, it needed a lot of work done." Kaitlyn sneers at me. "But I thought people get plastic surgery to make themselves look *better*, not worse. You should consider suing your doctor."

Back at it again. Is it bad that I'm almost excited to trade insults with her? This feels somewhat normal, innocent even—at least in comparison to what we've just been through. "You must've sued the shit out of your doctor, then, Kaitlyn. I mean, I'd be pissed if my face came out like that."

"Kaitlyn's face came out great!" Makayla jumps to her defense, earning her a glare from her friend and an amused eyebrow raise from Annalisa, Noah, and me.

"I didn't get plastic surgery, dumbass," Kaitlyn hisses at her second-in-command before turning back to me. "Either way, that monstrosity you call a face is distracting everyone here. I could get you a paper bag to wear if you'd like?"

I narrow my eyes at her. "My face was good enough to steal your man."

Ohhhh shit.

Boom.

Mic drop.

I didn't actually steal Aiden from her, he's made that abundantly clear. But *damn*, that felt good. I swear her eye twitches and a vein in her forehead pops, but she does a good job trying to remain calm and unfazed. Wow, maybe her New Year's resolution is to try not reacting explosively. Annalisa's laughing beside me, and Noah is practically glowing with pride.

"Ryan is twice the man Aiden is."

Doubt it. "Not that I don't thoroughly enjoy our time together, Kaitlyn, but is there a reason I'm spending my morning talking to you?"

Her blue eyes laser focus on me. "I hate you. I more than hate you, I despise you. You've had a good first semester, running around thinking you're the queen of the school. But that ends now. This is my school. I'm running the show."

She takes a step closer to me, and I force myself to square my shoulders and stay where I am, to not back down. The shadows under her eyes that she's concealed with makeup are more prominent this close, and she seems different. Older, maybe. But still the same, entitled attitude.

"Ryan thinks there's something off about you, more than in the sense of you being a stupid little bitch, and I agree. Andrew Kessler is going to ruin Aiden's life, and we're going to ruin yours." She gets even closer to me, if possible, and this time I do step back. "Secrets don't stay secrets forever. Stay out of my way."

I open my mouth to lob back one of my patented snarky comebacks, but my mind draws a blank. Honestly, I'm a bit rattled. All the time she's spent hanging out with Ryan has clearly changed her. She seems more focused and calculating, less likely to explode. She's always been kind of scary, but now she seems more threatening, if possible.

Something on my face must give away how much her words affect me, because Noah steps in and gently pushes her away from me. "Lay off, Kaitlyn."

She gives him a calculated look. "Don't act like I killed someone. *I'm* not the one who has a murderer for a brother, am I, Annalisa?"

Oh. No. She. Didn't.

Annalisa's head snaps over to Kaitlyn so fast *I* get whiplash. "What?" she asks lowly, almost as a warning.

"Ryan said the Luke Montley who's going to rot in prison for killing his dad comes from your white-trash family," she basically sings, loud enough for the whole hallway to hear.

Annalisa and Luke have different last names, so when his came out in the news, no one harassed her since they didn't know he was her brother. Even though Annalisa doesn't have the greatest relationship with her brother, we all know how much this is affecting her, and how bothered she is by her brother being in this kind of trouble. I put a hand on Annalisa's arm, warning her not to react the way Kaitlyn wants her to.

"Does your brother get his jollies from killing innocent old men? Is that what you do in your spare time, too, Anna?"

Suddenly, whatever was holding me back before disappears from my mind since it's no longer me Kaitlyn's threatening, it's my friend. Brushing past Noah, I get so close to Kaitlyn that I can count each eyelash.

"Tread very carefully here, Kaitlyn," I warn, my voice low, making sure she understands every word I'm saying. "I know your mom's the principal and you think you're untouchable, but I promise you, push the wrong buttons and nothing's stopping us from pushing back."

"I'm just stating facts," Kaitlyn says confidently, no fear in her eyes at all.

Annalisa moves around Noah, assuring him she won't do something stupid, and I step back so that she can stand in front of Kaitlyn. It takes Annalisa a great deal of strength to stand so near Kaitlyn and be somewhat calm. I can tell she's fighting every instinct in her body that tells her to destroy Kaitlyn.

"Talk about me or my family again, and I will find you, and I will make sure that no amount of reconstructive surgery will be able to fix your face."

The tone that Annalisa uses sends shivers down my spine, and she's not even talking to me. To Kaitlyn's credit, she looks completely unfazed by Annalisa's promise. It's probably something she's heard plenty of times before from Annalisa. Kaitlyn actually smiles, as if she just won some game that Annalisa and I weren't even aware we were playing.

"Just stay on your shitty side of town and we won't have a problem."

Satisfied, she turns around and struts off, shoving a freshman out of her way and into a locker without a thought as she continues down the hall, Makayla at her side.

"Whoa, someone took an extra dose of their evil psychopath pill this morning," Noah says as Kaitlyn disappears around the corner.

I don't hear what Annalisa replies, my brain focusing on what was just said. *Secrets don't stay secrets forever.*

Here I was, excited to trade insults with Kaitlyn like the good old days and feel back to normal in our routine, our *simple, safe* routine in comparison to murder attempts and political scandals, but obviously Kaitlyn's stepping up her game. Does she know something? Is she close to exposing me? If she doesn't already know and digs deep enough, she's going to stumble onto a secret that's much bigger than she, or anyone, could've ever imagined.

2

As I go through my morning classes it's impossible to keep Kaitlyn's words out of my mind. I don't know how much time I'll have at this school before I'm relocated, and even though it hasn't all been pleasant, I'm going to miss it. I'm going to miss the shrieking toll of the bell, the beige color of our lockers, the fading Go Lions! mural in the hallway, and as I walk through the halls after English and spot Aiden leaning against my locker, I know I'll miss that sight most of all.

"Did you drive this morning?" he asks when I'm near enough, pushing off the locker.

"Nope, my mom's home today so she dropped me off."

"Perfect. I'll drive then," he says as we walk to the parking lot instead of to our next class.

"You got your new car already?" I ask.

Aiden's beautiful Challenger was destroyed when Harvey ran us off the road. They wrote it off, which I know is heartbreaking for Aiden because he loved his car.

"No, my new car won't be ready for another week or two. I'm driving a rental right now," he answers, not quite looking at me as he adjusts the collar of his shirt.

I frown at him as my mind goes crazy trying to figure out what kind of car Aiden would pick out as a rental. Something fast, for sure. And definitely something pretty.

We exit the school and weave through the parking lot. "Where is it?" I ask, looking around for the fast and pretty car I'm imagining.

We've been walking for quite a bit, and we're almost at the end of the parking lot. He stops walking and points to the automobile right in front of us. I look at the car and back at Aiden with wide eyes, then burst out laughing.

It's a *minivan*.

"Aiden Parker, street-racing champion and all-around cool guy is driving a minivan? And not even one of the nice ones!"

I really don't even have anything against minivans, but Aiden is just not the kind of guy you'd imagine getting out of one.

"Yeah, yeah, it's the only car they had," he murmurs, but there's a ghost of a smile on his lips.

"This is why you parked all the way in the back, isn't it?" I tease as he opens the passenger-side door.

"Just get in," he grumbles adorably, and I laugh as I do. The seats aren't leather like his Challenger, and I don't see a bum warmer button anywhere. It's not a stick shift either. Do they even make stick shift minivans? This must be killing him.

"Are you still craving pancakes?" he asks as he starts the car, scowling when it quietly purrs to life, decidedly lacking the customary roar of his Challenger.

It's definitely killing him. I try not to laugh. "With strawberries. No, with Nutella. *No!* Strawberries and Nutella."

"Where do you think we're going to find a breakfast place open at 1 p.m. on a Monday?" he asks, as if trying to stump me.

Grinning arrogantly, I hold up a list on my phone with the location of at least thirteen breakfast places in the area.

"I did some research instead of paying attention in calculus." I pass my phone to him to check out the options.

He raises an eyebrow but doesn't look surprised. "Maybe that's why you're failing calculus."

"Maybe I'm failing calculus because I have an awful tutor," I joke.

We may tease, but Aiden actually has helped me pull up my calculus mark so far. For a minute, I wonder if he'll help me with calculus over the phone once I move to my new school. I need to pass to graduate, and like everything else, he's a good tutor. He passes my phone back to me and pulls out of the parking lot.

"Not only do you have the greatest tutor to walk this earth, but he's also funny, charming, and ridiculously good looking."

"You left out incredibly humble."

He nods. "Yes, that too."

I laugh, staring at him as if I can memorize the details of his profile. "Simmer down. You're not that great."

He takes his eyes off the road. "Aren't I, though?"

Maybe.

He turns the radio on and raises the volume when he realizes it's a song from my favorite band, Siren of the Heart.

Okay, he definitely is.

He reaches across the center console and grabs my hand, the warmth instantly making me feel at peace. It suddenly feels like *so long* since I've seen him, since I've really *talked* to him—not about the shallow stuff, but about the heavy stuff. The *real* stuff. It hits me all at once how much I missed him. As the lead singer of Siren of the Heart sings in the background about needing to be closer to his love, the tightening in my chest tells me I feel the same way. He's sitting *right here*, right beside me, touching me, holding my hand, but for how long? How much longer will I get to be with him, to touch him, to feel his arms around me?

"Pull over," I say.

"What?" Aiden's eyebrows draw together as he scans me, but he pulls over easily since the road isn't busy, and engages the parking brake. "What's wrong?"

I can't unbuckle my seat belt fast enough.

"Thea?" he asks, and my real name on his lips sends shivers down my spine.

Instead of answering him, I attempt to climb over the center console. Pain radiates from the crown of my skull when I bang it on the roof of the minivan. It's more spacious compared to the Challenger, but I may have overestimated just how spacious.

Aiden's eyes are wide. "What are you doing?"

I grumble as I unsuccessfully attempt to clear the center console. "I'm trying"—I bang my foot on the glove compartment—"to be cute and spontaneous"—I slip off my shoes, which are too bulky for what I'm attempting—"but I'm failing miserably."

The expression on Aiden's face changes as he realizes my intention.

"Don't laugh at me!" I huff, and he doesn't bother hiding the amusement on his face.

"I'm not. Here." He reaches beside his seat and the seat slides back, giving me space. "Better?"

I flop into his lap with as much grace as I can manage and straddle him on the seat. His hands come to my waist under my leather jacket and my hands grip his shoulders, the earlier awkwardness gone in an instant and replaced with an intense longing. Leaning closer, I press against his chest, my heartbeat speeding up with each breath he takes, with each glance at my lips. His are mere inches from mine, hovering there, teasing me. He's *so close* I can feel his shaky mint breath against my skin.

"Much," I whisper when I can't stand the miniscule distance anymore and bring my lips to his. As soon as his lips meet mine, the unsettled feeling in my chest lifts, and every nerve in my body awakens. It's rough and desperate and I know he missed me as much as I did him. There's a deep groan from the back of his throat and his hands slip under my shirt and up my back, pressing me even closer against his hard chest. I can feel him everywhere, invading all my senses. The softness of his hair as I run my fingers through it juxtaposes the hardness of his body, and the warm earthiness of his cologne mixes with something that's entirely Aiden. As he kisses me, all my worries and problems melt away as I lose myself to everything he makes me feel.

>> <<

Sitting across from Aiden now at an all-day breakfast place not too far from my house, stealing not-so-subtle glances at him, I'm glad we have some alone time to talk things through. I told him about what happened this morning with Kaitlyn, but he assured me that she and Ryan combined didn't have two brain cells to rub together, never mind be able to uncover my secret identity, and it put me at ease.

"How's everything between you and Mason?" I ask between bites of Nutella smothered pancakes. "He barely said a word at lunch."

"We're good. We just kind of pretend that night didn't happen, which is fine by me."

He doesn't need to clarify which night he's referring to: the one at the beach house when Mason basically told Aiden that he's an asshole who doesn't deserve to be with me, right before everything with Harvey went down.

"Have you guys talked since?" he asks me.

"He called me to apologize for the hundredth time about my nose, and we talked a bit, but not about that night. I guess we're going to pretend it didn't happen too. I didn't get a chance to talk to him in first period."

Mason knows how I feel about Aiden; all our friends know. So even though he technically didn't come right out and tell me that he has feelings for me, Aiden and I know the truth, and I'm sure our friends aren't oblivious to it, even if they haven't outright said anything. Mason is my friend, and I'd never want to hurt him, but I love Aiden, and Mason deserves more than trying to fight a battle he knows he already lost.

"How are you feeling about everything with your dad?" I ask, and Aiden's jaw twitches. Every time I asked about it on FaceTime he would brush it off and ask me how *I* was coping with everything.

"You mean Andrew?" he corrects, and takes a sip of his coffee. "I'm fine. I haven't heard from him since before New Year's Eve, and it's cool with me if I never hear from him again, unless it's about him being arrested for ordering a hit on you."

I hesitate. "And what about . . . everything else?"

"You mean the death threats from random people on the internet? As long as they leave my brothers alone, I don't care."

After Aiden's interview exploded on the internet, he became semifamous. In addition to the whispers from kids in the hall, which didn't faze Aiden at all today, he's receiving both support and death threats from strangers. He doesn't like talking about it, but my friends and I know it's happening.

"Have they been getting worse?"

He shrugs, seemingly unaffected. "I've been trying to stay off social media. People can get really aggressive and I have other things to worry about."

Being "Amelia," I don't have social media, but even I know the kinds of things people are saying about him and to him.

"Were these pancakes everything you ever wanted and then some?" he asks, biting into his crispy bacon.

I take his cue and we change the subject, continuing the conversation with lighter topics. We don't talk about the past or anything that happened at the beach house. I think we may just need an afternoon where we don't stress and can pretend everything is okay in our worlds. I'm not leaving him soon, and he's not receiving death threats on the internet. We're just two normal teenagers skipping sixth period, sharing a plate of pancakes.

"It's still early, what should we do?" he asks me once the bill is paid and we're making our way outside to the minivan.

"We can watch a movie at my house until you have to pick up the twins from school if you want?"

Aiden alone in my house? *Please say yes, please say yes.*

If he's reading my mind, he doesn't give me any indication. "Only if I can pick the movie."

"Deal!" I agree and jump into the passenger seat. *Geez, Amelia. Can you at least try not to look so eager?*

3

My house is quiet when I unlock the door and step over the threshold, Aiden following close behind.

"Mom?" I call as we close the door and take off our shoes and jackets. "Hello?"

No response. Guess she went out. I resist the urge to look at Aiden and let him see the excitement all over my face. We're home alone.

"Did you pick a movie yet?" I ask Aiden as we walk down the hallway.

"Of course. But I'm going to keep it a surprise." I already know it's going to be a movie that scares the shit out of me.

"You set it up, I'll grab some snacks."

"We just ate," he calls after me, but I ignore him. He'll be the one who eats most of the popcorn, I already know it.

After I pop the popcorn and dump it into a bowl, I grab some drinks and find Aiden on the couch. As I suspected, the screen is full of movie options that all look terrifying.

"Admit it, you're picking a scary movie so you can put your arm around me, aren't you?" I tease as I settle beside him on the couch.

"I don't need a scary movie as an excuse to put my arm around you," he says.

Aiden puts his hand under my jaw and tilts my head up as his eyes draw me in like quicksand. They're unguarded and readable, which is a treat from Aiden that I can't get enough of. You can tell that he's happy. He's genuinely and truly happy, and that makes my heart soar.

He leans in and brings his lips to mine, and even though we spent a good chunk of this afternoon kissing, the way I feel when he kisses me still takes me by surprise. We can't get close enough. The taste of his lips is addictive, and so are the shivers that run up my spine as he deepens the kiss and parts my lips, running his hands up my back under my shirt. My fingers tangle in his soft hair, so at odds against the rest of him since nothing else feels that way. He eases my shirt collar over to expose my shoulder and trails kisses across my neck, making me melt into a pile of nothingness at his touch.

The front door swings open, and my mom's distinct laugh rings through the house before it's suddenly cut off.

Aiden and I jump a foot apart on the couch, my heart racing frantically as I rearrange my clothes and make sure my hair doesn't scream that we were making out. Why does Mom need to be home right now of all times?

As we glance into the hallway, toward the front door, my jaw drops to the floor. My mom is aggressively *kissing Mason's dad* as she hops around and throws her heels haphazardly onto the floor. Mason's dad just pulled my mom's shirt off.

I'm going to puke.

Jumping up, I run into the hallway, making my presence known. "*Mom!*"

Brian Evans and my mom jump apart in surprise and stare at me, both breathless from earlier.

Gross.

"Oh . . . Amelia. Shouldn't you be in school?" Mom asks, reaching down to find her discarded shirt on the floor.

Aiden comes to stand beside me, his expression neutral and not giving anything away, and I've never been as envious of his ability to hide his emotions as I am right now. My shock and horror are definitely written all over my face.

Aiden and I both know about my mom and Mason's *married* dad, but they don't know that we know. And we certainly haven't ever witnessed them groping each other. That's something I never, ever, ever want to see again. Ever.

Mom pulls her shirt back on and looks pointedly at us. "You skipped school to fool around with your boyfriend?"

"I'm not the one with my shirt off." I provoke her with narrowed eyes.

"School ended about twenty minutes ago." Aiden tries to smooth over the situation, but his steely eyes are locked on Mason's dad. Brian took Aiden and his brothers in. He's known Aiden for years. I wonder if he feels guilty now that Aiden, his son's best friend, knows about his infidelity to his wife, who, from what I can tell from my only interaction with her before our vacation, is one of the sweetest women I've ever met. I try to fix my face to be neutral like Aiden's.

"Yes, he's right, Caroline. Time must have gotten away from us," Brian says, adjusting his blazer and addressing my mom by her fake name, the one they gave her when I became Amelia.

Brian is a good-looking man, like an older version of Mason, with tanned olive skin and dark hair. I'd be proud of my mom if not for the fact that he's married. He's literally still wearing his wedding band as he's cheating on his wife, the mother of one of my best friends.

"Listen kids," Brian says, "I'm sorry you had to find out like this, but it's complicated, more so than it may seem. Sometimes things just happen, and they need to be kept a secret for a reason. We wouldn't want to start a lot more trouble for everyone unnecessarily, would we?"

Aiden and I stare at each other with the same *is this guy for real* look.

"We're not five, Brian, don't talk to us that way." Aiden takes a step closer to him, this man, who before all this, was basically our hero. He stepped in when Aiden was arrested and got a lawyer for him. He managed to get custody of Aiden and his brothers so they wouldn't be separated in the system when their stepfather, Greg, died. He suggested we get away for the break to de-stress from everything that went on and found us a beach house for free in the town Aiden suggested. He never gave us reason to doubt him—at least, not until I walked in on him with my mom when I forgot my sleeping pills. But I never told anyone about that, only Aiden.

Aiden continues, "You're asking us to keep our mouths shut and forget what we all know. Mason is my best friend. I'm basically living with you and Natalia until I'm eighteen. You want me to lie to her for you?"

Brian locks eyes with Aiden, probably trying to decide how best to get his way. Before he can say anything to make this situation much worse, I exhale the breath I've been holding and look between my mom and Brian.

"We've both known for a couple of weeks and didn't say anything," I admit. "If you're trying not to get caught, at least do a better job hiding it."

It's hard to keep the venom laced in my words hidden, and Mom opens her mouth then closes it again. They both look genuinely taken aback.

"You were spying on us?" she asks incredulously.

"As I said, you should do a better job hiding it," I say flatly, then look over at Brian. "And you have a family. Your son is our best friend. The only reason we didn't tell him yet is because we didn't know how to do so without destroying his world. You need to figure your shit out, Brian."

"I'll have to take that into consideration, Amelia," Brian says.

"This secret has been weighing on my conscience for two weeks now. I could barely look at Mason without wanting to puke the entire time we were in Torywood Springs. It's not my place to say anything, but I will if I have to. I can't keep living like this, running away every time he breathes in my direction because I can't take the guilt. He deserves better. So—I'm going to say this once—either you tell him, or I will."

Brian puts his hand on my mom's lower back. "Like I said, this situation is . . . complicated. You're right, Mason and Natalia deserve better, and it's not our intention to hurt anyone. I'll have to take some time to think about the best thing to do. Don't say anything to Mason, I'll figure out the best course of action."

Aiden and I exchange a glance. Is he buying this? Am I?

Brian straightens up. "I should get going now. Good-bye, Caroline. Amelia. Aiden, I'll see you at home later."

He gives my mom a quick kiss and then turns to leave. Mom watches him go, then turns back to me and Aiden, trying to assume the Responsible Mom role instead of the Mistress one.

"I don't think I like the fact that you two were here alone, doing goodness knows what. That's not very responsible of you, Amelia," she says, frown lines marring her mouth.

"And I don't think I like the fact that you're fucking my best friend's married dad, so I guess we both can't get what we want, can we?" I reply with as much attitude as I can.

Her mouth drops, and even I'm a little surprised. I guess to hell with a brain-to-mouth filter? But we *did* just catch her shirt-less and making out with Brian, so she really can't stand here and lecture me about being responsible. Such a hypocrite. We stare at each other in a standoff, our shoulders squared and eyes challenging the other to say something.

"I should go pick up the twins from school," Aiden says. "I'll call you tonight?"

Aiden slips out quickly to avoid the fight that's about to happen. I don't break the staring contest I'm having with Mom.

She's the first to break. "I don't think I want you seeing that boy anymore."

"Who? Aiden?"

She turns and I trail after her into the kitchen, where she pulls some vegetables from the fridge and places them on a chopping board. I face her from the other side of the island.

"Yes, Aiden. You spend a lot of time with him. What if you slip up and tell him our secret?"

For a split second, I consider telling her that Aiden already knows, and that he's more supportive of me than she's ever been, just to spite her. But I don't, because I'm trying to be logical, and telling Mom that a boy she doesn't particularly like knows our life-changing secret wouldn't go over too well.

"I've been doing this for over a year now, I think I know how to keep a secret," I lie, since I *can't* keep a secret from Aiden. "We're leaving soon, so it doesn't even matter, does it?"

I add, "Plus, you've been spending a lot of time with Brian. What if you slip up and reveal everything?"

"Oh, we don't do much talking when we're together." She laughs.

I make a general sound of disgust and take a seat at the island. "Mom, for real."

"Relax, I was joking. I know how to keep certain information from people. But can you?" She pauses from chopping vegetables to raise an eyebrow at me.

"Are you asking me if I'll keep your affair a secret from my friends?"

"Well?"

"Depends," I answer nonchalantly, stealing a carrot that she just sliced.

"On what?"

"Are you going to keep seeing him?"

A corner of her lip turns up. "Depends."

"Mom, come on. I'm happy you're not moping around after Dad and are getting back out there, but with a married man? And he's my friend's dad! He's going to end up finding out, one way or the other. It's not going to be pretty."

She puts down the knife and studies me. "Why does everyone always go after the other woman? I'm not the one lying to my family and cheating on my wife. I'm not breaking my family. I'm a grown woman and can make my own decisions, and so can Brian."

She makes a valid point, but this is Mason's family we're talking about here. "But you know that he's married. You're choosing to be a part of possibly ruining his family. *And* we're leaving soon, so you're a part of all this drama and it's not even worth it in the end."

"I don't need an ethics lesson from my daughter." She picks up the knife and starts chopping again. "And it's different with Brian. He means more to me than just a fling, Amelia."

"What . . . what do you mean, Mom?"

"I haven't felt this way in a long time. Maybe since your father and I started dating."

"Mom," I whisper. Does she know what she's saying? What the weight of her words means?

She brushes her brown hair out of her face. It's the same shade mine used to be. Would I feel more like myself if I hadn't decided to dye mine? "Life is unpredictable, Amelia. We of all people should know that. With everything going on, we need to make the most of it."

Those words coming from her lips are funny, considering she hasn't been quiet about the fact she disapproves of Aiden and me, but I don't want to keep fighting. It's been a long day, and I don't want to get into it even more with her. I get up to leave. She's my mom; I can't tell her what to do.

"Amelia?" she calls just before I leave the kitchen, and I turn to look at her.

"Yeah?"

"You're not going to tell Brian's son, right? You'll wait for Brian to figure it out himself?"

I shrug and leave the room, not even knowing the answer to that question myself.

4

By Wednesday, the bruise on my cheek is finally starting to slowly fade, and so is everyone at school's fascination with it. I know people still wonder about Aiden, though, whispering in the halls when we walk by, as he's being used as the main focal point in the anti–Andrew Kessler for governor campaign, but only a few brave souls have dared to ask him anything about it.

Aiden officially turns eighteen today, and we bring him a cupcake-cake for lunch. We couldn't get a cake knife in the cafeteria, and a bunch of cupcakes iced over to look like one cake is a lot easier for us to divide.

"I told you not to make a fuss." He sinks into his seat, looking like he wants to disappear as Annalisa lights the candles on the cake, completely ignoring him.

"No singing," he orders, staring directly at Noah, who immediately inhales and belts out at the top of his lungs, "*Happy Birthday to you . . .*"

We join in as Aiden looks mortified, making us all sing louder, which annoys Aiden to no end. He blows out his candles as quickly as possible and we all rip a cupcake from the tray.

Aiden leans over to me as I devour my cupcake. "Jason and Jackson want you to come over after school. They want to make me a cake but don't want me to see it, and I don't let them mess around in the kitchen without supervision ever since I let them make a smoothie and they got chunks of fruit all over every square inch of it. So they want you to help."

I try not to let it show on my face how happy it makes me that his brothers chose me over Mason or Julian or any of our other friends to come over and help them with their surprise cake.

"Sure. I didn't know you were allowed back."

The rest of the table continues their own conversations, not listening to me and Aiden. Across the table, Noah and Mason shove a whole cupcake each into their mouths and try to grab the last chocolate cupcake before anyone else.

"The police cleared the crime scene and collected whatever evidence they need. I've been allowed back a couple of times to get clothes and stuff, but the twins haven't been back yet."

"They didn't want to make the cake with Natalia?"

He shakes his head. "They specifically wanted to do it with you."

This time I can't stop the thrill from reflecting on my face. They want *me* to help, and now I need to make sure we make the best damn cake that has ever graced this world. "I'll pick up some ingredients and be there after school."

When I show up at Aiden's later, Jason and Jackson have pulled out every bowl, spatula, and kitchen measuring instrument they own. After we kick Aiden out of the kitchen, they help me unload the ingredients from the car and we get to work.

"Do you need help cracking the eggs?" I ask Jason as I mix the icing.

"Nope! I got it," he replies, focusing intensely on the task at hand. His tongue sticks out in an adorable way as he selects an egg from the carton.

"Make that a yes. He always gets the shell in the bowl." Aiden waltzes into the kitchen like he wasn't banned by the three of us just thirty minutes ago.

Jackson shields the bowls and pans laid out on the counter with his body. "No peeking!"

"I already know you're making me a cake," Aiden says as he leans against the door frame.

"Yeah, but you don't know what kind," Jason retorts, matching Aiden's stance with his arms crossed over his chest.

"Okay, you heard them, out of the kitchen." I shoo Aiden into the hallway and away from spying on our baking attempt.

"I don't like feeling useless." He pouts, which only draws more attention to his perfect lips.

"I know, I know. You like taking care of everything. But it's your birthday, let me be the responsible adult for once."

He puts an arm around my back and draws me closer to him. "I'm eighteen today. I'm technically the adult here."

"Then go do your taxes or iron your clothes or do whatever it is adults do. I got this." I use every ounce of willpower to untangle us, but he just holds me closer and brings his lips to mine.

Like every single time I kiss Aiden, I melt into him. I can feel the heat emanating from his body as I wrap my arms around him and pull him closer to me. This is what a normal life with Aiden would be like. Yes. This is all that I want.

"Shit!" a voice exclaims from the kitchen, and Aiden and I push apart.

"Language!" Aiden scolds, heading into the kitchen to see what happened before I stop him.

"I got it," I intervene, stopping him from venturing into the kitchen any farther. "Responsible adult here, remember?"

"Fine." He steps back and it looks like it takes some effort. "I came to remind you guys that everyone is going to be here in an hour and a half."

"Oh wow, time flies! Okay, no big deal, we got this." I turn back into the kitchen and find Jason and Jackson hunched over the bowl, fishing around in the chocolate batter with forks.

"What happened?" I ask, looking into the bowl.

"I think I lost, like, half an eggshell in the batter," Jason sheepishly admits. "Maybe more."

He thinks? A quick glance at the clock tells me there's no time to start over. "Let's just see if we can find it, or as much of it as we can."

"What if we don't find it all?" Jackson frowns. He wanted this cake to be perfect.

"It'll add . . . texture to the cake. No big deal," I reassure him.

An hour and forty-five minutes later, the table is set and the cake is iced, and our friends have arrived to celebrate Aiden's birthday.

He demanded that we not get him any presents, but obviously we did. Before the winter break, we all pitched in and got him this super-high-tech barbeque that he and Julian have been drooling over for the last couple of months. Even though it's January and kind of cold outside, the guys were so excited to use it that they brought over a bunch of meat and we had a barbeque birthday feast.

We sing happy birthday to Aiden again as he sits looking extremely uncomfortable, even more so than earlier today at lunch, and blows out his candles as quickly as possible. We sit in the family room to eat the cake, with a movie on in the background that no one's really watching.

"Is it supposed to be crunchy?" Julian asks.

Jason and I look at each other, and his eyes are wide as he mouths "Eggshell" at me. I try not to laugh as I hold my finger to my lips and wink. It'll be our secret.

"Um, yeah . . . we wanted it to have some texture. Right, Amelia?" Jackson says, casually putting down his own half-eaten cake and pushing it away. Jason and I do the same.

"That's absolutely what we were going for," I reply confidently, ignoring Aiden silently laughing beside me.

As the rest of the conversation carries on, I turn to Aiden. I don't want to ruin his day, but he hasn't said anything else about Andrew since we ate our pancakes together on Monday, and I keep itching to ask. They couldn't possibly have just moved on and decided to leave us alone. We're not that lucky. So when is the other shoe going to drop?

"Hey, have you heard anything else about Andrew or seen Harvey? Do you think they kind of forgot about us? Is that just wishful thinking?"

His facial expression turns grim, as if just the opposite is true.

"What, Aiden? What's wrong?"

His face is blank. "Nothing, Amelia."

I've gotten so used to Aiden not hiding his emotions from me that at this point, a blank face is his biggest tell that something's wrong.

Placing my hand on his strong jaw, I force him to look at me. "Aiden?"

He studies me intensely, a debate happening behind his gray eyes. I can tell when he's made his decision because he runs his hand through his hair and curses under his breath.

He stands up and pulls me with him, grabbing my arm and practically dragging me out of the room.

"I know where they're going! Rhymes with shmirthday smex!!" Noah calls out after us with a laugh, immediately followed by a thud and an "*Oomf!*"

Someone, I'm guessing Annalisa or Charlotte, must've thrown a pillow at him. I follow Aiden up the stairs.

The last thing I hear is one of the twins expressing their disgust since they "Know what rhymes with 'shmirthday smex,'" before Aiden closes the door to what looks like his office. It's a small room, with a desk with a laptop sitting on it, as well as a big leather chair with wheels on the bottom.

"I didn't want you to worry," Aiden starts, opening a drawer to his desk and digging around. "You've been through so much and already have one madman to worry about, I didn't want to stress you out."

He pulls out an envelope and closes the drawer, turning to face me with clouded eyes. "But I'm not going to make that mistake, where I keep you in the dark to protect you."

Hesitantly, I take the envelope from his outstretched hand. Is this the shoe that's dropping? My throat tightens as I open the envelope and pull out . . . a birthday card?

This doesn't make sense, and it certainly doesn't warrant Aiden's warnings, but his expression gives nothing away.

I've faced much more powerful, violent, and smarter opponents than you, Aiden, and I always come out on top. Keep the things most precious to you close, because this isn't over until I've won. Send "Amelia" my regards.

Happy Birthday, son.

Aiden leans against the desk and crosses his arms. "It came this morning."

"Have you shown anyone?" I read the card again, the words truly sinking in.

"Just you."

"'Keep the things most precious to you close,'" I read aloud. "He's threatening the twins?"

His gaze burns as he looks at me. "And you."

I freeze, staring at him as his words sink in.

"Anyone who looks at me knows I'm in love with you," he continues. "He already went after you once."

My eyes snag on my name and the quotes that are around it. Why are those quotes there? What is Andrew implying? And there's the thing about him saying my name all weird and suspicious at the fundraiser. What does he know? What is he going to do with that information?

I slump into the big office chair as I set the card on the desk. I already had to worry about keeping my identity a secret to stay hidden from Tony, but now Andrew is specifically going after me to get to Aiden.

At this moment in time, I wonder which one is going to get to kill me first.

"Hey." In one fluid motion, Aiden scoops me up as if I weigh nothing and sits down in the office chair, setting me down on his lap. "You know I won't let anything happen to you, right?"

He's reassured me of this countless times since New Year's Eve, when everything went down. I rest my head on his solid chest and think back on all the times that Aiden's been there for me. When he got Ethan Moore to take down the video he posted of me on the internet. When he dealt with my car after Kaitlyn and Ryan slashed my tires. When he drove an extra four hours so I could get my sleeping pills. When he pulled me out of an upside-down car and then saved me from being shot.

"He's trying to get you to stop talking to the media and ruining his 'good name.' I can't believe he's not above trying to *kill* a teenage girl to get the message across."

"He's always been a crooked guy, and he's finally gotten what he wanted most in the world: wealth and power. He's not going to let me take that away from him like I did when he got my mom pregnant and was forced to have a shotgun wedding. So far, he's tried to bribe me, pay me off, and then kill me. I don't know if he'll ever stop. But I won't let him hurt you or my brothers."

It's impossible to be frightened here with Aiden, his muscled arms around me, my ear against his chest, the steady beat of his heart calming my own. "We're not going to let him win. He's in the spotlight now, I don't think he'll try anything."

His thumb under my chin gently forces my head up to look at him. "Still, we should be careful, just in case. I'm not going to let him hurt you."

"I know," I reply, genuinely meaning it.

Today was so nice, Aiden and me just being ourselves without having to worry about drama or other issues. I want to get back to that. I *need* to get back to that. It might be my fault, because I *did* ask him about it, but he would've told me eventually. I'm making a promise to myself, right now, that I'm going to live out our remaining time together as normally as possible before I'm forced to move and we have to switch to long distance. I'm going to be with Aiden like a normal teenager and I'll be damned if I let Aiden's father ruin that.

5

Noah was not joking about throwing Aiden a huge party at his house. Even though people are mostly intimidated by Aiden, there are a lot of people here.

Noah somehow convinced his parents to go on a romantic three-day stay at some fancy hotel a few hours away, so he transformed his house into the ultimate place to be on a Friday night. Earlier today, Annalisa, Charlotte, and I threw streamers and balloons all over the place to make it more festive, and the guys were in charge of setting up the keg. Chase got one of the guys from school to bring his equipment and DJ the party for us, and now the music is so loud the walls are practically vibrating. Everyone here is someone that we (or at least the Boys) know; we're all talking, hanging out, drinking, and dancing, and there has been a total of zero party crashers. So much more fun than the last party we all attended.

Aiden's not really a drinker but he's having fun hanging out and talking to people. The moment he catches me staring from the other side of the room, he shoots me an arrogant wink. I roll my eyes even though the sight of him having fun sparks the butterflies. Look at us at a house party, making eyes at each other from across the room like regular teenagers.

Turning my attention back to Charlotte, I throw my hands up in front of my face. "Oh my God! Char!"

"Sorry. Forgot you're all camera shy." She puts down her phone and stops recording. "There's just this new app, S-Live Time, that lets you live stream videos to your followers and save all the videos to your feed! I'm so obsessed with it."

"Maybe just don't get me in any videos, okay?"

"Fine." She exaggerates her sigh. "But you know you're, like, the weirdest teenage girl ever, right? You're going to need to get on social media sooner or later."

"Maybe later," I reply absentmindedly as my eyes wander over to Aiden, who's talking animatedly to some guys I don't recognize.

"Things are really good between the two of you, huh?" Charlotte states more than asks, almost wistfully.

"I can honestly say I haven't been this happy in a long time." I hope it lasts when I move.

"I'm so happy for you. You guys are perfect for each other," she says.

"Thanks. What about you? What's going on with the whole Noah and Chase situation?" *Also known as the time Chase walked in on the two of them in bed together at the beach house and got into a fistfight with Noah, revealing to everyone who already didn't know that he's in love with Charlotte.*

She swirls the cup in her hand to mix up the drink. "Nothing, really. Noah doesn't like me like that. It was just a heat of the moment thing. And it's not like we slept together . . . I mean, we would have, but either way it's not a big deal. I like having him as my friend."

Noah is talking to Mason and a couple of pretty girls I recognize from history class. I know what she means. I like having him as my friend, too, as well as Mason.

I miss Mason. It's so weird now. Our friendship used to be fun and free and playful, but now it feels strained. I want nothing more than for us to go back to normal, but every time I look at him I'm reminded of his father's affair with my mother, and I don't even know what he's thinking every time he looks at me.

I want to tell him about his dad but don't want to be the person who destroys his family, who ruins his image of his father. If I tell Mason, it might ruin my relationship with him forever. But not telling him might do an equal amount of damage. Either way, I lose. Brian needs to do the right thing and tell him, and hopefully Mason won't hate me too much for knowing and not saying anything. Aiden is strongly on team Mason needs to know. We got into a heated debate about it the day after Mom and Brian walked in on us. If I were Mason, I'd want to know too. But how can I tell him that *my* mom is the other woman? I don't care what anyone says, people *always* shoot the messenger, and I'd like to stay bullet-free for now. If it comes to it, I'll tell him, but I just need some time to fix our relationship first.

"What about Chase?" I ask Charlotte, bringing my own red Solo cup to my lips for a drink. The cranberry juice with a light splash of vodka is refreshing.

"I don't know how I should feel about Chase. He's my best friend and I love him, but it's not the kind of love he wants me to feel."

"Hey, no one can tell you how to feel," I say.

And it's true. Coming into this I wasn't supposed to make friends, never mind fall in love. And despite everything, I fell in love with Aiden.

Hard.

No one can tell Charlotte that she should fall in love with her friend, just like no one can tell me not to fall in love with Aiden.

"I just . . . I don't get it." Charlotte finishes the rest of her drink. "He told me he loves me, but all through high school he's been out with other girls, sleeping around. Not that I'm judging him or the girls, but if he was in love with me the whole time, why didn't he just tell me? If he really cared about me like that wouldn't his actions reflect that? Wouldn't he tell the person he was closest to instead of sleeping around? How could he possibly love me if he's always with other girls?"

I know why Chase didn't tell her but that doesn't mean I agree with his reasoning. "What if he was scared you didn't feel the same way and that would ruin your friendship?"

"That's stupid. I'm not a mind reader. What if I did like him back?"

"Do you?"

She studies her empty drink. "I need a refill. Kitchen?"

I follow her through the hallway to grab another drink. We pass a couple of rooms on the way, and in one of them is Chase, making out with Aliyah from our chemistry class.

Charlotte looks at me and raises an eyebrow, as if to say *See?*

The kitchen isn't as packed as the rest of the house, which is odd, because this is where to find the booze. Charlotte and I put our cups on the counter and fill them with our preferred liquors and juices, making small talk with the people already in the kitchen.

As we're about to leave, two girls come into the room, and they catch my attention because they're talking about Annalisa. I stop Charlotte and we stand in the corner of the kitchen, casually eavesdropping.

"Did you see how hot Julian looks tonight?"

"He *always* looks hot, Becki. I'm going to go talk to him later; work my magic." She winks at her friend and they both giggle.

"Oh wait." The excitement drains off Becki's face. "He's still with that girl. Anna."

"Ugh." The friend sighs. "I'll probably still talk to him anyway. Maybe change his mind."

"No, Sara. He's dating *the Anna*. You know? The one everyone's talking about," Becki emphasizes.

Everyone's talking about Annalisa? Charlotte looks just as confused as I am.

This apparently means something to Sara, because her eyes widen and her face turns solemn. "Wacko Anna White is Julian's girlfriend?"

Wacko Anna White?!

"Yeah, the one who told Kaitlyn she'd put her in the hospital if she even breathed in Julian's direction, for no reason at all. Like, Kaitlyn was just in the hall with Makayla Monday morning, minding her own business, and Anna went off on her. She had to be restrained!"

What?!

There is so much wrong with that statement it's not even funny. First of all, when has Kaitlyn *ever* minded her own business?

"And then"—Becki pauses dramatically, knowing full well basically everyone in the kitchen is listening to her—"she told Kaitlyn that her brother's the one who killed her boyfriend's dad, and that she's not afraid to murder someone too! She said, and I quote, 'We're a family of killers.'"

Family of killers?!

My blood is practically boiling. What is wrong with people? Who says that?

I'm about to step in and tell them exactly what I think about their family of killers when some other girl in the kitchen beats me to it.

"That can't possibly be true," the girl says to Becki and Sara. "You know how Kaitlyn is."

Yes! Thank you.

"No, no." Becki rushes to back up her claim. "Aliyah was there and heard it all! She's the one who told me."

Everyone gasps, even the other people in the kitchen. A collective acceptance settles over the room, as if Aliyah is the fucking oracle of truth and if she said it, she *must* not be lying.

I can't take it anymore. "That is not what happened. I was there. People like to twist the truth to make things more dramatic when they're telling a story." The girls in the kitchen stare at me.

"My friend Riley was there too," some other girl pipes up, "and she told me that Anna almost knocked Kaitlyn out for no reason when they were talking."

"*Everyone* has a reason to want to punch Kaitlyn out. Come on now, you guys are being dramatic," I say. "Anna is not a murderer! I can't believe I actually have to say that out loud."

Just then, Annalisa enters the kitchen, and everyone stares at her with wide eyes. Perfect, she can settle these stupid rumors.

"Anna, would you honestly kill Kaitlyn? Like, straight-out murder her?" I ask, prompting her to reassure everyone that she's not part of a "family of killers."

Annalisa shrugs. "If she pissed me off enough, sure."

Murmurs spring up around us, and everyone rushes out of the room to apparently get as far away from Wacko Anna White as quickly as possible.

"She's just joking! She doesn't mean that! Come on, guys!" I call after them, then turn to face Annalisa, who's unfazed by everyone running away from her. Soon it's just Annalisa, Charlotte, and me left in the kitchen.

"You're not helping here!"

"What? It was a joke." She pours herself some vodka and cranberry juice.

"Yeah. *We* know that, but they're just going to use that to add more fuel to the rumor mill."

Annalisa shoves a chip in her mouth. "What rumors?"

Charlotte and I tell her what we heard Becki and Sara saying. Annalisa's face is normally pretty pale, but it gets even paler as we get to the family of killers part. Her fist smashes down on the bag of chips, turning the snack into little pieces of dust.

"Where's Aliyah?" she manages through gritted teeth.

"Anna, if you beat up Aliyah it's just going to make things worse." Charlotte warns her.

"I'm not going to beat her up, I just wanna talk." Annalisa pulls the multiple rings off her fingers and shoves them in her pockets, then strides from the room.

"Then why did you take off your rings?" I shout as Charlotte and I scramble after her.

This is not good, and Charlotte knows it, too, as we weave through the kids in the hall to catch up to Annalisa. She marches through the hallway with an angry purpose, stopping suddenly and causing Charlotte and me to practically run into her. She charges into the dark room where we last saw Aliyah; she's still making out with Chase. She's on his lap on one of the couches, and they look like they're thoroughly enjoying each other's company.

Annalisa walks right up to her, grabs her arm, and before I can stop her, roughly pulls Aliyah off of Chase, the force causing her to land on her ass on the floor.

Chase, who's already pretty drunk, looks confused when the girl on his lap suddenly disappears. Charlotte must be the first person he sees, because he says her name almost reverently, as if hoping she was jealous and pulled a girl off his lap.

"Do you want to tell me what you've been saying, Aliyah?" Annalisa fumes at the girl sprawled on the floor. The other people in the room halt their conversations to watch the unfolding scene.

Chase looks at Charlotte sadly, probably realizing that it was Annalisa who interrupted his make-out session. "What the hell's your problem, Anna?"

Annalisa's dark smoky makeup makes her narrowed eyes look all the more intimidating. "My *problem* is that Aliyah is going around talking about me and my family, saying that we're a bunch of murderers!"

Aliyah clambers to her feet in an instant.

"Your brother *is* a murderer!" Aliyah has to yell over the loud music to be heard.

"Anna, this isn't helping with the whole Wacko Anna White thing," I whisper.

She brushes off my concern and glares at Aliyah, who shifts uncomfortably on her feet as Annalisa's gaze grows more and more heated.

"And all that stuff about 'Anna's going around telling people she comes from a family of murderers'? Where'd you get that one, Aliyah?"

"Fiona heard you say it, a couple others did too," Aliyah says.

More than a couple of people are watching now, whispering and pointing at Annalisa. Some have even ventured in from the hall to see what the commotion is all about.

Annalisa looks like she's going to snap, and as I mentally run through ways to de-escalate the situation, something seems to click behind Annalisa's eyes, and the hostility in her posture deflates. "Just go, Aliyah."

Aliyah looks wistfully at Chase, who still looks confused. "But—"

"*Get out of my face!*" Annalisa yells loudly.

Aliyah jumps up and scrambles out of the room, passing Julian on the way out.

"Anna . . ." I start.

"There's no point. The rumors are already out there. People are going to say whatever they want to say anyway. It's fine." She aggressively shoves her rings back onto her fingers, contradicting her last statement.

"Were you just yelling at Aliyah?" Julian asks Annalisa when he reaches her.

"Yeah. Because I'm Wacko Anna White and that's what I do!" She shoves past him and marches out of the room.

"What . . . ?" Julian looks at the space where his girlfriend has disappeared into the crowd.

Chase stands up. "Honestly, I only understood half of what happened, man. But you should probably go after her. It looked bad."

Julian moves easily through the crowd of people to find

Annalisa, who is definitely more bothered about this than she wants us to know.

"Should we go after her too?" Charlotte asks me.

"No, we don't want to bombard her. We'll talk to her after."

"Does one of you want to tell me what just happened?" Chase asks.

Just then, some guy from school comes up to Charlotte and starts talking to her, making Chase narrow his eyes at him.

"Come on, Chase. Why don't we go somewhere quieter and I'll tell you," I say, attempting to guide him from the room before he makes a drunken scene over nothing. Again.

Charlotte giggles at something the guy says, and Chase's nostrils flare.

"You were literally just making out with Aliyah three minutes ago. You're not allowed to be jealous," I inform him, practically dragging him out of the room.

"Whatever. I'm going to get more beer." He shrugs me off and walks to the kitchen.

Okay, so I guess he doesn't want to know what just happened with Annalisa? I'm left standing awkwardly in the hallway for a full three seconds before Mason barrels into me.

"K-bear!" he half slurs. "What're you doin' in the middle of the bathroom?"

The surprise at the resurgence of my nickname only lasts a millisecond as I look around at the hallway, which is clearly *not* the bathroom. Mason stumbles and I steady him and move us over to the side. A part of me is so happy to hear him call me by my nickname again—it's been a while since I've heard it—but the other part of me is concerned he's got alcohol poisoning.

"How much have you had to drink?" I ask him.

His eyes are unfocused and he looks like he can't decide to look at me or the second me he's seeing.

"Yeah, you're right. It is hot in here."

He reaches up and pulls off his T-shirt, throwing it on some random guy walking by, who's also apparently too drunk to notice the new addition hanging over his shoulder.

Okay. That happened.

"Why don't we go sit down? Get you some water?"

"You're so smart, k-bear. So, so smart. Way too smart for me," he rambles and leans against the wall.

Oh no.

"I miss you, k-bear. Why aren't we friends anymore?" He leans his head against the wall. "Are you mad at me for elbowing you in the face?"

"Mason, of course we're friends! And I've told you a thousand times I'm not mad at you. It wasn't your fault."

A couple of kids walk by livestreaming on that stupid app Charlotte's obsessed with, and I turn my head as they walk by so I'm not in the video. Somehow, even though he thinks we're in the bathroom, Mason notices.

"You can't even stand being seen with me! You do hate me!" Mason's normally happy face completely falls. He leaves, stumbling down the hallway.

"No, Mason!" I run around so that I'm standing in front of him again. "I don't hate you! I super–pinkie promise!"

I hold up my pinkie finger, waiting for him to take it. He stares at it intently.

"You know if you break this promise I'll have to break your pinkie. That's what a pinkie promise means."

I shake my little finger impatiently. "I know, I know. I promise I don't hate you."

He locks his pinkie with mine and holds our hands together.

"K-bear." He locks eyes with me, his brown eyes studying me intensely as his other hand reaches up and pushes my hair out of my face. "I lov—"

"Ohhhhh-kay." I cut him off quickly and back away, letting his hands fall to his sides.

He was about to say the L-word, I'm sure of it. He's never said that to me before and I'm not ready to hear it, not right now. He cannot tell me he loves me, especially not while he's hammered. We both want things to go back to normal, and that's not going to happen if Mason goes and says the L-word in an *as more than a friend* kind of way.

"Why don't we go see where Aiden is?" I ask, hoping the name of his best friend will remind him who I'm actually in love with.

Mason doesn't respond. His eyes are closed, and he's fully slumped against the wall.

Oh my God. Did he just fall asleep standing up?

"Mason?" I get closer to him and poke his shoulder.

The poke is all that is needed to throw him off balance, and almost like in slow motion, his body tilts backward. Scrambling, I race around to catch him before he bashes his head on the floor, and wow, he is *heavy*. Holding on to him from behind, I lean him against the wall and listen to his breathing.

Yup. He's sleeping.

Damn it, Mason. Control your drinking.

I can't just leave him here in the hallway with a bunch of people, and need someone to help me. Maybe I can set him down and find Aiden. No, there are too many people in here; they're going to step on him. I guess I'm just going to have to drag him upstairs to a bedroom.

"Mason." I shake him, trying to wake him up.

"Hmmm?" His head lolls to the side.

"We're going upstairs, can you stay awake for, like, ten more seconds?" I move so that his arm is around me and I'm supporting the vast majority of his weight. He makes some noncommittal sound with his eyes closed. His body weight is crushing.

Okay, great.

Thankfully, the stairs are very close, and I don't have to go too far carrying him. With some prodding, Mason manages to ease up the stairs with my support. I drag us to the closest door and open it, and it looks like Noah's room. *Perfect.* He'll be Noah's problem now.

I deposit Mason on the bed and he lands on the end of it, half of his body hanging off the end. He groans and I take a big, well-earned breath of air and try to catch my breath. I honestly broke a sweat; getting him here was not easy.

"Mason?" I ask, and he makes some noncommittal sound. "You're going to fall off the bed like that."

He makes no move to fix himself and I sigh. With a knee up on the bed for leverage, I try to maneuver him so he won't slide off the mattress, and grab his arm to pull, but it's all useless. He won't budge. I switch to pushing him up on the bed and finally make small progress. It would be a lot less awkward for me if he was wearing a shirt, not that the view is bad. With one final, big push, I finally get him in the middle of the bed, but I slip and land with a heavy thump on top of him, banging my head on the low headboard in the process.

"Damn." I rub my head and take a second to get over it.

Having a fully grown teenage girl land on top of him must've woken Mason up, because I feel his hands land on my waist.

"Amelia?" he asks groggily.

"Amelia?" comes a second voice from the entrance of the room.

Standing with his hand on the doorknob is Aiden, the prince of perfect timing, taking in the scene in front of him. Me, lying on top of Mason, who's shirtless and has his hands on my waist, in bed.

"This isn't what it looks like!" I exclaim, trying to roll off Mason and the bed.

Aiden stands there with his face blank, then cocks his head to the side as if listening to something.

"Stay here," he says emotionlessly, then backs out of the room, closing the door behind him.

"What?" With zero grace, I flop off of the bed and scramble to my feet, staring at the closed door. A quick glance at Mason shows he's passed out again.

I start toward the door, but my conscience tugs at me, forcing me to turn around. Cursing under my breath for wasting precious seconds, I cross back over to Mason and roll him into recovery position so that he doesn't choke if he throws up, which hopefully he won't. Satisfied Mason's taken care of, I rush out the door, close it behind me, and run down the stairs to explain myself to Aiden.

6

As soon as I get into the hallway, I realize something's wrong. The air's thick with a tension that has no place at a party, and the feel-good energy that permeated the house before has been replaced with a sense of foreboding. The music has been cut off and there's shouting coming from downstairs. I follow the loud voices into the main room.

Ryan, Kaitlyn, Dave, Makayla, and some other people who weren't invited have crashed the party. Not just crashed it, but ruined it. They're standing off with Aiden, Noah, and Julian, who are refusing to let them venture any farther into the house. Annalisa must've been talked into not leaving the party earlier, because she and Charlotte are there as well, albeit a bit off to the side, but all my friends appear relatively sober. The rest of the partygoers are standing around with undisguised excitement, watching the scene unfold.

"Come on, Ryan. We're just trying to have a good time here, no need to start problems," Noah insists, trying to guide them to the door to leave.

"And like I asked before, I'm not invited to my own step-brother's birthday party?" Ryan shoots back, his eyes dark and calculating.

"No," Aiden asserts, with authority in his voice. "And you're not my stepbrother."

I'm about to push through the crowd to stand with my friends when Aiden's sharp eyes meet mine. He gives his head a discreet shake, accompanied by a stern look I know all too well by now: Stay out of it.

A lot of people have their phones out and are filming on that stupid app S-Live Time in anticipation of a fight breaking out.

I'm torn between wanting to back up my friends and needing to stay off social media. In the end, needing to stay off social media wins, because keeping Tony away from me means keeping that monster away from my friends.

"Why don't we ask my dad to settle this disagreement like he used to when we were kids?" Ryan pauses. "Oh wait, we can't. *Her* white-trash brother *killed him*." He gestures to Annalisa, and people in the room reflexively take a step away from her.

There's something different about Ryan. He looks like he's taken the death of his father really hard. He had just gotten Greg back from prison, and then he was killed. Ryan barely got to reunite with him, and it's obvious that's affecting him. Even though I hate Ryan, I can sympathize with him. I also lost my dad at a time when our relationship was strained, and even with everything that went on after, his loss still hits me. I don't know what Ryan's relationship with his father was like, but it's obvious he cared about Greg, and I get it.

Ryan's face is unshaven, and looks tired and drawn, but at the same time hardened. His hair, which is usually styled in a short ponytail at the top, looks rushed and messy, and the sides that are usually shaved have grown out. His normally hostile brown eyes are ice cold. Maybe the last shreds of kindness within Ryan were buried with his father, and all that's left are the parts that hate everyone with a burning passion.

Julian steps closer to Ryan.

"You watch what you say to her," he threatens in a low voice.

Ryan all but ignores him. "Where's the other little bitch who's always here?" He directs this at Aiden.

Who's he calling little? I'm five foot six in three-inch heels!

Ryan looks into the crowd and I shrink back, not wanting phone cameras turned on me. "You know, the one with the big mouth that I'd like to stick my d—"

Aiden surprises everyone, and maybe even himself, when he reaches out and grabs Ryan by the throat. Ryan doesn't squirm, so Aiden must not be pressing that hard, just enough to get the message across.

"Finish that sentence and we'll see just how far we can get my boot down *your* big mouth," Aiden growls with barely restrained rage into Ryan's ear. He releases his grip and steps back, leaving Ryan to rub his neck.

"Get out of here." Aiden crosses his arms across his chest, accentuating the muscles we already knew were there.

Around me, people are whispering about Aiden's reputation, about how they wouldn't want to be the one messing with him.

Ryan gestures at Annalisa. "I'll leave when the murderer's sister steps outside to have a little chat with me."

Annalisa shoves past Julian and Aiden, getting up close and personal with Ryan.

"You think *I'm* scared of *you*?" She practically yells in his face and points at Kaitlyn. "Ask your girlfriend here—apparently, she's telling everyone I've got the killing gene in my blood."

Murmurs of "Wacko Anna White" make their way around the crowd, and I clench my fists to remind myself to stay out of it. Kaitlyn stands with Makayla, a frown on her face, like she doesn't care what happens either way.

"Your junkie brother wanted to get high and killed my dad when he told him he wasn't selling anymore!" Ryan insists, spittle flying out of his mouth.

"Bullshit!" Annalisa yells. "You think your dad was clean? What did the coroner's report say, Ryan? There was heroin in his system when he died! Your dad's a piece of shit in life and death!"

If the vein pulsing in Ryan's neck is any indication, Annalisa's really pushing his buttons now. The crazed look in Ryan's eyes has been getting more intense the more she talks.

"Shut the fuck up right now!" he yells, whipping out a large pocketknife and pointing it at her. "Shut the fuck up *right now!*"

Aiden and Julian both hadn't foreseen this new turn of events, and Noah pushes Charlotte behind him. I'm glued to the spot. Aiden and Julian both try to push Annalisa away, but she's unfazed. She stays right where she is, knife pointed at her and all.

"My brother didn't kill your asshole father!" she yells right back at Ryan, with so much conviction that her belief in her brother is undeniable to everyone.

I look around. Everyone has moved back but no one is doing anything about the *knife* that Ryan's *pointing at one of their classmates.*

Ryan and Annalisa continue to yell at one other. Aiden and Julian keep trying to get between the knife and Annalisa but she's persistent, and keeps shoving them away, her icy, blue eyes laser focused on the boy insulting her and her family.

I can't get in the videos, but I have to do something to break this up before Annalisa says something that makes Ryan *really* snap.

Thinking quickly, I run up to some random kids, trying to look frantic and confident. "The cops are here! They're arresting anyone who's underage drinking! We've gotta get out of here!"

Racing through the party, I do the same thing to everyone I see, and soon enough other kids are doing it, too, until people are running around yelling "Cops," and everyone's scattering, tripping over each other trying to get out of the house as fast as they can. As the crowd disperses, I'm satisfied that all the cameras are off, so I run up to Annalisa and pull her back, allowing Aiden and Julian to step between her and Ryan.

As Ryan's friends take notice of everyone frantically trying to get out of the house before the cops come, they pull him back. All the while he's shouting at Anna, promising that he's not done with her.

"Bring it!" Annalisa screams back.

Finally, Ryan and his friends leave Noah's house, along with the rest of the crowd. Soon enough, it's just Noah, Charlotte, Aiden, Anna, Julian, and me left in the house, plus Mason sleeping upstairs. Who knows where Chase is.

"Shit, we gotta get rid of the keg." Noah starts toward the kitchen before I stop him.

"Relax, there's no cops. I made it up because that situation was escalating to a place we wouldn't be able to come back from," I say.

Annalisa huffs and crosses her arms. "Should've let him stab me. That way everyone would've had it on video that I killed him in self-defense."

"No one's stabbing anyone," Aiden declares.

Annalisa storms from the room and this time I follow her, leaving the guys and Charlotte to go through the house to make sure all the partygoers have left. I find her in the kitchen, angrily dumping out half-full Solo cups.

"He had a knife pointed at you, and you were still purposely aggravating him," I comment, helping her with the cleanup.

"I told you. I wanted him to stab me," she deadpans, and I can't decide if she means it or not.

I stop picking up cups and study her. "Do you really think Luke's innocent?"

Annalisa stops as well, resting her hands on the counter. "I don't know. I just feel it in my gut, you know. Luke's done some pretty bad things, but I *know* he wouldn't do *that*. He doesn't even remember that night! How do you kill a guy then not remember?"

I don't point out that not long ago, Annalisa was telling everyone that Luke killed her mother. She's come a long way from hating his guts to being his biggest defender.

"We have to do something. I can't just let him rot in jail." She looks down, blinking back tears.

As long as Ryan's convinced Luke killed his father, he's never going to leave us alone. He's going to threaten me and my friends, and make sure he makes our life as hard as possible. I can't have him ruining my chances of staying here with my friends and living out a normal senior year for as long as I can. I can't have him devoting all his time to hating us; devoting so much time that he might stumble upon my secret.

"Okay, Anna."

"Okay what?"

"We're going to prove that Luke's innocent."

How we're going to do that, I have no idea. But as a wise goof once said, it's time to pull up our big-boy and -girl pants.

She rushes me and engulfs me in a hug. "Thank you, Amelia. You're a true friend, you know that?"

The pang of guilt in my heart shouldn't take me by surprise, but it does. I wonder if she'll look back at my time here and remember me as a good friend or hate me for disappearing without a trace when the time comes.

"Of course, Anna," I say, ignoring the tightness in my chest.

I hear Aiden's voice from somewhere in the house, and the pit in my stomach intensifies. For all he knows, he thinks I was cheating on him with Mason. My heart races as panic sets in. I need to find him and set the record straight.

"I'll be back later." I leave Annalisa in the kitchen and search the house, hoping to find Aiden. He must know it was purely a coincidental incident he walked in on. He didn't seem mad when he told me to stay out of the fight, but then again, who really knows with Aiden.

I find him alone in the basement, throwing empty cups into a garbage bag.

"Aiden . . ." I start, my throat dry. His gray eyes focus on me and I lose all words. "What happened up there . . . it wasn't what it looked like."

"You mean Anna didn't tell Ryan to stab her?"

"Well, no, I mean, that did happen, but I'm talking about me and Mason. And the bed thing? I know that looked really bad but—"

Aiden puts down the garbage bag. "Thea, I know what Mason looks like when he's blackout drunk. I saw you hauling him up the stairs and came to see if everything was all right."

Relief washes over me. "You're not mad at me."

He strides over to me and my heart automatically speeds up with each step that brings him closer. He puts his hands on my waist and tugs me to him, forcing me to look up at him. My body acts on its own accord and my hands clasp behind his neck.

"I *know* who you are, Thea," he whispers, his words reaching my soul.

"Plus," he adds with a smirk, his thumb drawing lazy circles on my back, "I know your tendency to get yourself into awkward situations."

"You know me, always trying to keep it interesting."

"Honestly, I'm more surprised that you actually listened to me for once than I am at finding you on top of Mason."

"What are you talking about? I'm a great listener." I bite my lip. "But just to clarify, which specific case are you talking about?"

"I'm *talking* about up there, just now. I told you to stay out of the fight, and to my complete surprise, you actually did." His hands tighten around my waist.

"Well, I didn't listen to you about staying put upstairs with Mason, so I figured I'd make it up to you," I joke.

"No, really, Thea." He grows serious. There's no space between us at all now; I'm pressed right up against him, feeling the contrast of his hard, sculpted body against the softness of my own. "The last thing I ever want is for you to get hurt. And I know you like to just jump in without thinking about it, but there was just something in Ryan's eyes. Plus, everyone had their phones out and—"

"I know, Aiden," I say, my heart squeezing and tightening at his words. "I know I need to start thinking things through. I don't want to jeopardize my life here. I'm making the most of whatever time we have left."

His face darkens. He doesn't like thinking about it, and neither do I, and just knowing that makes my knees weak. I rise up on my tiptoes and Aiden's already reading my mind because he brings a possessive hand to my face, his lips meeting mine halfway. The pressure of his mouth against mine is perfect and heat spreads through my body. Aiden gently guides me backward until I feel a wall press against my back, our kiss deepening until I am consumed by all things Aiden. My hand slides down his chest, feeling the contours of his body. It slips under his shirt, and his abs contract at my touch. I love that I can cause that kind of reaction from him.

"Put your clothes back on, we're coming down!" Noah's voice carries to us from upstairs.

With excruciating effort, we pull apart, catching our breath as Noah, Annalisa, Julian, and Charlotte make their way down the stairs. I fix Aiden's hair since I messed it up, and we step apart just as they come into view.

"Why did you assume we had no clothes on?" I ask, hand on my hip.

Noah plops down on one of the couches. "Aiden was down here, then I saw you come down here. So naturally that means the two of you were probably getting it on."

I open my mouth to deny it, but nothing comes out. He was right, gotta give him that.

Aiden ignores Noah's statement and sits across from him. "Is everything okay upstairs?"

"Yup," Julian answers. "Mason and Chase are passed out, the house is mostly clean, and Joey packed up his DJ equipment."

"I want to visit Luke," Annalisa randomly blurts out.

We all turn to look at her, and she looks uncharacteristically nervous.

"I just—I haven't seen him since that day. He put me on his list of approved visitors, all of us, actually. I never considered visiting, but I think the first step in proving his innocence is just talking to him. If we can really dig, we can maybe find out what really happened."

"You think he's innocent?" Charlotte asks.

"We're going to prove that he's innocent?" Noah asks at the same time.

Annalisa looks at me, almost as if in confirmation, and I nod to reassure her.

"Yes. Yes to both of you. I mean, if you'll help."

"Of course we'll help." Aiden confidently reassures her, and everyone else chimes in their assurance.

If I can do one thing for Annalisa before I leave, at least it'll give her some closure between her and her brother, and hopefully clear his name. It would be one step closer to reconciliation and healing between the two of them, and Annalisa deserves that, so after a bit of searching, we figure out jail visiting hours. Luke must have put us on the list thinking Anna would send us to talk to him on her behalf or something, but either way, it works out for us. Bright and early in the morning, we'll drive the three hours to visit Luke.

7

Even though we're exhausted from staying up late and waking up early this morning, Charlotte and Annalisa have a great time roasting Aiden when he pulls up in front of my house in his new, albeit temporary, ride. I can only giggle at his discomfort when Annalisa asks him where the soccer team is, causing Aiden to huff and shake his head, then get in the minivan and wait for them to run out of jokes, an annoyed expression on his face.

The jovial mood dies down quickly as Aiden turns onto the highway and we head south, toward where Luke is being held. Annalisa wraps her arms around herself and stares out the window at the passing trees, and even Charlotte doesn't have any comforting words to offer her. I try to channel my inner Noah and think of a joke that will break the tension, but my mind comes up short. Instead, we settle into a quiet that's punctuated only by the soft music playing on the radio.

Two hours into our journey, Aiden, looking in the rearview

mirror at Annalisa and Charlotte, asks softly, "Do you think they're sleeping?"

I twist in my seat. "Anna?" She doesn't stir and neither does Charlotte. "Yeah, I think they're sleeping."

Aiden nods, and I take the silence as an invitation. "Do you think he's innocent?" I ask.

"I guess anything is possible. Doesn't look too good for him, though."

I know Aiden's glad that his stepfather's dead, and as long as he's not the one who killed him, he doesn't especially care who did.

Eventually, we pass a sign for the jail, and I turn around to wake Annalisa and Charlotte up as we near it. When Aiden parks, we hop out to stretch. Annalisa looks paler than usual as she stares up at the imposing building.

"You ready for this?" I ask her.

Resolution settles over her face. "Let's prove my brother's innocence."

We sign in and go through security checks, but eventually we have our visitor passes and are ready to go see Luke.

One of the guards tells us it's two at a time only, and Annalisa grabs my hand without hesitating and pulls me forward. We follow the guard into a big room with a bunch of metal tables with metal chairs attached, armed guards at strategic positions around the room.

He points us to an empty table, and we sit. I shift in my seat, trying not to look too uncomfortable. Something about this place just gives me goose bumps. I feel like everyone's looking at us, though I doubt anyone actually is.

I fidget with the visitor's pass hanging from a lanyard around my neck. People are talking to their loved ones in soft voices all around us. At the table beside us, a woman who looks like the inmate's mother sobs as she holds his hand across the table.

Annalisa's leg is rapidly bouncing up and down as her foot taps the floor anxiously.

"You okay?" I ask.

"Peachy," she replies.

I lift an eyebrow at her and she sighs.

"The last time I saw him, I stormed over a table in the middle of an ice-cream parlor to get away from him. I don't know how he'll feel about seeing me." Yeah, that was when he contacted us and told us that he thought he'd killed Greg but didn't remember doing it, and begged Annalisa's forgiveness but she wasn't having any of it. It feels like forever ago but it's only been a couple of weeks.

"He put you on his visitation list. He wants to see you."

She pouts, so I continue, "All he wants in this world is his sister back. He's going to be so incredibly happy to see you. He'll be even happier that you want to prove his innocence and get him out of here."

Her leg is still bouncing.

"He doesn't even believe his own innocence."

"That's what we're here for," I reassure her.

Her leg stops bouncing and her intense blue eyes are focused on the other side of the room. Luke's behind the door opposite to the one we came in from, staring at us as the guards remove his handcuffs.

His expression is a mixture of hopefulness and disbelief, but there's a weariness there as well. He looks mostly the same as the last time we saw him, but older, if that's possible. He looks tired, the dark circles under his eyes giving him a haunted look.

The guard moves to the side of the room, and Luke stays standing on the other side of the table, as if unsure whether to embrace Annalisa or not. A guard makes that decision for him by yelling "*No touching!*" at another group two tables down from us, startling all three of us.

Annalisa gives nothing away, looking him over with a blank face. After a few awkward seconds, he sits down in front of us.

"You look like shit," Annalisa says, breaking the tension.

"Yeah. Jail does that to you." He rubs the back of his neck with his hand.

"You still look better than you did when you were using," she deadpans.

I stay quiet, almost afraid to make a noise and draw attention to myself. Maybe Annalisa should've done this without me. I feel like I'm intruding on a private family matter.

"They didn't tell me who my visitor was." He changes the subject. "I hoped it was you."

Annalisa shifts uncomfortably in her seat, as if the thought of talking about her feelings makes her sick.

"You *are* my brother," she says finally.

Luke hesitates, treading carefully. "Yes. But I thought you wanted nothing to do with me?"

Annalisa's hand clenches into a fist, and I can just imagine the feeling of her long, black nails digging into her palm.

"I may have been . . . overly mean." She pauses, considering her words. "But I'm *not* apologizing. You fucked up when you walked away when mom died. You fucked up when you chose drugs over me. And you definitely fucked up by landing yourself here."

Luke opens his mouth to say something but she beats him to it. "*But* you were trying. That day at the Tracks was the first time I saw you sober in a long time. You wanted to make it right between us."

She looks away from him, the muscles in her jaw working as she clenches it. I know that face; she's trying to stop herself from crying.

"And I think I do too," she admits quietly.

Luke's eyes light up at the admission, hopefulness settling over his expression as he takes in her words.

"Yes," he says, almost too quickly. "I'll do anything, Lise. I swear, I'll do whatever I can to make it up to you, even from in here. I'm sorry I'm such a fuckup. I'm sorry I'm in here instead of out there, doing what I can to be there for you. And I'm especially sorry that I let you down, again." He boldly reaches across the table and grabs Annalisa's clenched hand. "Even if I'm in here for life, I'll never stop trying to be the brother you deserve."

I bite my lip. *Don't you dare cry. Don't you dare cry! This is* not *your moment to ruin.*

I keep chanting this statement in my head, but a lone tear escapes anyway. I discreetly swipe at it, trying not to draw any attention to myself.

Annalisa yanks her hand out of his grasp and bangs it on the table. "You are *not* going to prison for life. It's bad enough you're stuck in here while you wait for trial."

A guard comes over at the commotion. "Hey, keep it down here."

She nods to placate him and the guard goes back over to his position.

"Lise, I'm looking at twenty-five to life," Luke warily reminds her.

"Not if you're innocent," she states.

"It's not looking that way . . ." He deflates, the earlier hopefulness and confidence gone. "Besides, I don't even remember what happened. There's nothing I can do."

"To hell with that!" Annalisa proclaims, earning her another warning from a guard.

She apologizes and returns her attention to her brother. "Of course *you* can't do anything from in here, but we can. We're going to put together what happened that night."

"But you can't even—"

"Just shut up and trust me," she cuts him off, all evidence of her previous vulnerability gone with the return of her normal, confident demeanor.

Luke closes his mouth and waits for her to continue.

"I need you to tell us what you remember from that night."

He shrugs. "I told you guys what I remember already when we met at Sweetie's that night. That's all I remember."

"Just go over it again!" she demands. "Maybe you forgot something."

He repeats the same story as before, about feeling down about himself and breaking his sobriety by going to an old bar. About running into some old friends who told him his old drug dealer was out of prison. About finding Greg and getting into a fight with him, but not remembering where he found Greg or how he woke up at home the next morning.

"And that's everything, I swear. I've been racking my brain for weeks trying to put together the missing pieces, but it's a big blank."

"And you're sure you weren't high that night too? There was heroin in his system when he died," she grills him.

"*Yes, I'm sure*," he says emphatically. "I'm not going back down that road, ever. Plus, even if you don't believe me, they gave me a test the night I was arrested, and it came back clean."

Annalisa rubs her temples with her fingers. "I—I don't know where to go from here."

"Why don't we search Luke's apartment?" I suggest. "Maybe we can find some clues the cops overlooked as to where he was that night? A receipt or something?"

They agree it's a good start and a guard comes over to tell us our time is up.

Luke quickly tells us his address and where we can find a key to get in as the guard hauls him up. Almost as if before she can change her mind, Annalisa stands up and rounds the table, wrapping her arms around Luke and hugging him close for what might be the first time in years. Luke looks almost as shocked as Annalisa is at herself, but he hugs her back just in time for the guard to order them apart.

Annalisa steps back, toeing the floor awkwardly. The guard leads Luke away, and he looks back at Annalisa the whole time, as if trying to drink in the memory of her while he can, like she'll never come back. We stay there watching as they lead him out the door and handcuff him, until we're forced to leave the room. That probably took more of an emotional toll on her than she let on.

"How do you feel?" I ask as the guard collects our visitor passes.

"Okay, I guess. I think I needed that," she says. "Thanks for being there with me. I don't know if I could've done that alone," she admits with vulnerability in her voice.

"Hey, I barely said a word. You practically did it all by yourself. I felt like I was intruding on something that should've been private."

She puts a hand on my arm to stop us walking, and stares right into my eyes with her piercing blue ones.

"No, really. There's no one I would've wanted there more than you. You're one of the most genuine people I know."

Yeah. *Supergenuine*. I tug at the collar of my shirt. It's not like I'm hiding a life-changing secret from you or anything. Or planning on ditching you and never speaking to you again in a few weeks.

8

It's Sunday, the day after visiting Luke. Annalisa, Charlotte, and I are standing in the hallway of his apartment building, trying to find the hidden key to his apartment, which is on the first floor of a sketchy apartment building in a part of town that's not the greatest or particularly known for its safety. Apparently, his rent has been paid for the next couple of months, so no one's been here to pack up his stuff and kick him out.

"Remind me why we couldn't wait until one of the guys was free to come here again?" Charlotte asks, eyeing the end of the hallway with suspicion.

"Because we're strong, independent women who don't need to wait for a man to get shit done," Annalisa reminds her with a straight spine, seemingly right at home.

"This strong, independent woman wants to get the hell out of here ASAP," Charlotte mumbles, wrapping her arms around herself.

This place gives me the creeps, so I don't blame her. The hallway is dimly lit and smells like cigarettes. The fluorescent light in the ceiling above Luke's door is flashing on and off in no particular pattern, giving the hallway an especially eerie feel. The remnants of police caution tape dangle in front of Luke's door. What we'll find here that the police haven't already, I'm not sure, but at least we can say we tried. We walk to one of the potted plants in the hallway and Annalisa lifts it up to look underneath.

"There are five keys there. What a stupid hiding place, why would everyone just leave their key here?" Charlotte wonders out loud as Annalisa grabs one at random.

"Maybe no one here has anything worth stealing?" Annalisa suggests, trying the key in the door to no avail.

She tries all five keys, and none of them work.

"What the hell? He said it was in the plant. This is the apartment he said, right?" Annalisa asks me, annoyance creeping into her tone.

"Wait—he did say *in* the plant." I grimace.

Annalisa groans with disgust as she rolls up her sleeve and sticks her hand in the dirt, fishing around for the apartment key.

"I swear, if I'm doing this for no reas—found it!"

She pulls out a key and brushes the dirt off it, then off of herself. She tries it in the door and we hear a click. Nervously glancing around the sketchy hallway one more time, we push the door open and pile into the apartment, shutting the door and locking it behind us.

I don't know what I was expecting, but Luke's apartment isn't too messy. It's small, with a little kitchen, an eating area, and a TV area together in an open space, and two doors near the back, which I'm assuming lead to the bathroom and his bedroom.

"I guess we're looking for anything that proves where he was that night?" Annalisa says, sounding unsure of our less-than-solid plan. "Time of death was around 6 p.m., so look for around that time."

We look around aimlessly, splitting up to sort through Luke's stuff, opening cupboards and moving dirty dishes into the sink to check the counter, hoping that whatever it is we're looking for will just jump out at us.

Annalisa finds Luke's laptop, which luckily wasn't taken by the police, and plugs it in so she can turn it on and see what she can find. Charlotte's going through the various papers scattered on his table and counter, so I venture into his bedroom. Anything useful has probably already been brought in as evidence, but we're not looking with the assumption he's guilty, we're looking for clues of his innocence, and I hope that gives us an edge on finding information that may have been overlooked.

Clothes are thrown in a pile in the corner of the room, and the bed is just a mattress on the floor. It isn't made, either, and the pillows aren't even covered with pillowcases. The gray paint is peeling from the walls, and other than a small desk with a couple of drawers and a folding chair, the room is bare. The desk, however, looks promising. It's a dark-brown wood, and has an ancient-looking, gray printer sitting in the corner.

The papers on top are mostly just bills and take-out menus, same as in the kitchen. Sitting in his chair, I open the first drawer, which is just various chargers and office supplies. I try the drawer beneath it, which has a bunch of papers strewn about and some video game boxes.

None of the papers seem to be important. This whole thing feels weird to me, like I'm spying on Luke, and as I push past an open pack of condoms, it's getting harder to ignore the fact that

I'm totally invading his privacy. I mean, he gave us permission, and we might find something to get him out of jail, so it might be worth it in the end.

This is pointless. I want to help Annalisa and prove her brother's innocence, but maybe he really *did* do it? What can we possibly find to prove his innocence when the police haven't found anything? What was I thinking in agreeing to this? Now all she's going to remember about me when I leave was that I got her hopes up and disappeared without actually doing anything to help.

I stand and shove the chair back under the desk, turning around only to almost trip over Luke's tangled bedsheets. For some reason, the unruliness of it all makes me feel itchy. It's not my room or my bed, but the longer I stare at it, the more anger bubbles in my chest. It's just a stupid bed, and I don't want to touch the covers, because who knows when he last washed them, but it's sitting there, all innocent looking, taunting me, looking just as out of control and unkempt as my life and my current situation. My life may be out of my control, but I can fix how annoyingly messed up Luke's bed is. Grumbling under my breath, I grab Luke's sheets and yank them up, only to spot a flash of something on the bed before the sheets fall into place. Throwing the covers all the way off the bed, I find a manila folder in the middle of the mattress, some papers scattered around it, like Luke was looking at it in bed before he got distracted and left to do something else. Or the officers found it and regarded it as nothing of importance in their search. Either way, I'm curious, so I grab the folder and open it to reveal the documents inside. As I make sense of what I'm looking at, a certain page causes me to go still. This can't be right. I pick it up and realization slams into me as my heart stops.

What?

I feel the blood drain from my face and I can barely remember how to breathe.

Why?

I flip to the next page, the room closes in on me.

How?

My brain can barely process what I'm seeing. My throat tightens.

What? Why? How? The words are on repeat as I hastily shuffle papers around to get a better idea of what I'm looking at, trying to find logic, trying to make sense of *this*. I stumble through paper after paper, my hands shaking, my breathing coming out fast and shallow, my heartbeat too loud in my ears.

This is not right. I am not seeing this. There's some kind of mistake.

"Hey, guys! I think I found something!"

Charlotte's voice brings me back to earth, causing my head to snap over to the door, which is only open by a sliver.

I hastily cram every single paper back into the file and shove it in the bottom drawer of Luke's desk. I push it down deep, deeper than anything else in there, willing it to go away, to pretend I never found it, to push it out of existence.

Slamming the drawer closed, I straighten but the room spins. I remind myself to breathe.

In and out. In and out.

When I'm convinced I appear normal, I leave the room and go to where Charlotte and Annalisa are standing. They're holding a crumbled receipt, carefully smoothing it out.

"It was in his jacket pocket," Charlotte explains, pointing to a part of a receipt. "And it has the same day on it, with a time stamp of 5:16 p.m."

"Howard's Convenience. Where's that?" I ask, praying my voice doesn't sound as shaky as I feel.

"There's an address on the top—"

A high-pitched, shattering noise cuts Annalisa off, and we instinctively shriek and duck for cover as glass rains over us. A heavy object flies through the air with a flash of red.

Suddenly I'm somewhere else. The edges of my vision blur. I don't dare breathe. A white room. A doll with a knife shoved through it on the bed. Tiny pieces of glass slicing my arm. A brick with a death threat. Tony.

"You fucking coward!" Annalisa's yelling; she's standing at the now-broken window.

Get away from the window, Annalisa! The words are stuck in my throat.

I move into action, my limbs weak, practically falling over myself to crawl over to Annalisa, to get her away from Tony.

He'll kill us!

"Anna!" My throat is dry. It doesn't even sound like I'm talking.

This is it; it will be my fault my friends died. And they won't even know why.

"That man is psychotic!" she rambles, staring into the parking lot. She doesn't even know she's in real danger.

My body finally catches up to my brain, and I stand up, running over to Annalisa and Charlotte at the window.

I'm about to tackle them, to tell them to get down, when Annalisa exclaims, "I fucking hate Ryan!"

I stop midtackle.

Ryan?

There it is. A very distinct red Mustang, speeding out of the parking lot.

》 《

Annalisa's sitting on the couch, turning the note over in her hands, trying not to tear it apart. It was attached to the brick Ryan threw through Luke's window, like a page right out of Tony's playbook.

Still a bit shaky, and not really knowing what to do, we did the most logical thing. We called Aiden. Just hearing his deep and reassuring voice made me feel better, but more than that, Aiden always looks after us. He's the one to go to when you need help. He asks us if we're okay, then snaps into fix-it mode, asking questions about the mess and the window and promising to be here soon.

Annalisa leaves a message for the building manager about the broken window since he isn't working today, and Charlotte and I carefully clean up the shattered glass. The January air that seeps in from the broken window makes the room so much colder than it already was, and I zip up my leather jacket to keep the chill out. Not long after we've gotten the glass cleaned up and have settled down on the couch, there's a knock on the door, and Aiden and Julian are here, hugging us, checking us for injuries.

"We're fine." Annalisa pulls out of Julian's embrace, then shoves the note in his face.

"This was attached to the brick he threw through the window. What is wrong with him? Why does he have nothing better to do than harass us?" She glares at the brick now sitting harmlessly on the counter, as if trying to make it explode with her mind.

"'Rot in hell with your white trash, murdering brother,'" Julian reads, before passing the note to Aiden. "What is with him and his fascination with saying white trash? Clearly some of his own insecurities are manifesting here."

Annalisa rips the note from Aiden's hands, crumpling it up for the hundredth time and throwing it on the floor. "I don't care! How are we killing him? I vote slowly."

There's another knock at the door, and we open it for Chase and Noah. Chase looks worriedly between us before his gaze finally lands on Charlotte. "Hey, are you guys all right?"

Charlotte looks away and fidgets with the hem of her sleeve.

"We're fine," I tell him. "Where's Mason?"

"He's coming. He stopped to pick up some food for everyone," Noah says, taking in Luke's apartment for the first time.

"We have some plywood in the back of my truck." Julian analyzes the broken window. "It should be the right size. Let's get this window covered up then figure out the rest."

Annalisa's anger is still palpable but simmering down a bit, especially now that Julian, her voice of reason, is here. She hugs Julian before he leaves and as he kisses her forehead sweetly some tension leaves her shoulders.

"You sure you're okay?" Aiden's standing right in front of me, concern in his cool eyes and a double meaning in his tone.

He remembers. I know it deep in my gut, know it better than I know my own name. He remembers the story of how Tony threw a brick through my window. He knows this bothered me in more ways than one. He knows what memories this brings up.

I grab his solid hand and give it a reassuring squeeze, my eyes softening as I look at him. "I'm okay."

He studies me. I don't think he's totally convinced but he lets it go anyway, dropping my hand to follow the guys outside.

While they go grab the tools and wood from Julian's pickup,

Annalisa, Charlotte, and I sit still on the couch. It's a good thing the guys thought to do that. I honestly wasn't processing anything other than "It's not Tony. You're not going to die."

"I don't understand how Ryan knew we were here?" Charlotte wonders. "He wasn't camping out in front of this apartment until he saw someone familiar walk in the building."

"Maybe he was following us?" I suggest, glancing at the boys as they come back in the apartment, this time with Mason, who drops brown paper bags in front of us.

"You guys okay?" he asks, his eyes lingering a bit too long on me. I bite my lip, memories of the last time we were together at Noah's party rushing back to me.

"We're fine. I'm pissed." Annalisa answers for us, then returns to our conversation as we dig into the fries and chicken nuggets Mason brought. "Was he stalking us?"

Charlotte raises an eyebrow. "Don't you think he has something better to do with his time than follow us around all day?"

Annalisa scoffs. "Clearly not. He had time to come to Luke's apartment, figure out which one was his, get a brick, attach a note to it—"

"We get it, we get it." I cut her off. "But how—?"

"Um, it might be my fault."

We all look at Chase. He's got a french fry half raised to his mouth, his face growing red as we stare at him.

"What do you mean? How could it possibly be your fault he's crazy?" Annalisa asks.

"No, not the crazy part, but the *how he knew you were here* part." He finishes the fry and awkwardly dusts off his hands.

Everyone turns their full attention to him. Julian, Noah, and Aiden pause, too, holding the plywood in midair.

Chase takes a breath. "I ran into him at the gym earlier. And you know him, running his mouth, being annoying, and talking about how I hang around with white trash, etcetera, etcetera."

Julian raises an eyebrow at us at the white trash part, as if to say *See? He's manifesting.*

When Chase doesn't continue, Annalisa prompts him. "And?"

He looks sheepish. "And I may have told him that you girls were here at Luke's to prove his innocence."

The room explodes with disbelief and exhausted choruses of "Chase!" and "Why?!" and "Seriously?!"

"I'm sorry! I'm sorry!" He defends himself. "Ryan just gets under your skin, you know?"

"And you guys thought I was the one who's bad at keeping secrets," Noah mumbles.

"You still are," Mason replies.

"Nuh—"

Mason cuts off Noah's denial. "How about the time you told our freshman homeroom class that I asked out Tammy Klied but she told me she'd rather eat dirt than go out with me."

Whoa. Tammy Klied's rude.

Noah tilts his head as if thinking. "Okay, that's fair. But to this day, I've never told anyone that you believed in Santa Claus until you were, like, fourteen. I'm taking that to my grave."

"Noah!" Mason exclaims.

"What? I didn't . . . ohhhh." Realization dawns on Noah, and he starts laughing. "Okay, but come on. That's hilarious."

Mason mutters some insults and throws a crumpled-up take-out menu at Noah, who's still laughing.

"*Anyway*," Annalisa draws the conversation back. "What are we doing about Ryan?"

"I thought we were done starting wars with Ryan and friends?" I jump in quickly.

We *cannot* keep escalating things. We cannot give him more fuel to look into us, into *me*. We cannot let him keep ruining the time I have left with my friends.

Annalisa folds her arms across her chest. "We're not the ones starting a war! We're just gonna be the ones finishing it."

I look helplessly at Aiden, who's already looking at me, as everyone throws out suggestions.

"Why don't we finish it by focusing our energy on getting Luke out of jail?" he proposes.

The room quiets down as it sinks in that Aiden's right.

"Did you guys find anything?" Julian asks, walking around the tool bag to stand next to Annalisa.

We show them the receipt we found from Howard's Convenience.

"Maybe they have cameras? Maybe he was still there when it happened?" Mason suggests, looking up the location of the store on his phone. "It's closed now."

"Okay. Why don't we worry about fixing this window for now and we can check it out tomorrow after school?" Aiden reasons, nodding at the broken window.

Annalisa still doesn't look satisfied but reluctantly agrees. There's nothing we can do until tomorrow.

9

The school day goes by smoothly. A lot of people come up to us (mostly to the guys) to tell them how great Aiden's party on Friday was. It's hard to imagine that Noah threw Aiden's birthday party just a couple of days ago, but it was, and apparently everyone had a great time.

No one mentions the fact that Ryan pulled a knife on Annalisa.

I manage to ignore Kaitlyn and friends for the day, even if we do share some classes. I especially know it takes Annalisa a lot of personal strength not to confront Kaitlyn and yank out a clump of hair. We don't need to add more fuel to the rumor mill. We don't need more people talking about Wacko Anna White.

After school, I run into Annalisa by the stairs.

"Hey, you ready to head out?" she asks. "I think everyone's by Julian's truck."

"I'll meet you by the cars. I'm just going to grab some stuff from my locker."

She doesn't object and I continue to my locker, passing Aliyah on the way, who shoots me a dirty look. I guess she's still upset about the whole being yanked off of Chase's lap mid-make-out session thing.

After grabbing my books, I leave through a side door since it's closer to where Julian's parked, and spy a red Mustang.

Something takes over my mind. My vision narrows until I see nothing but Ryan's car. The feelings of fear and helplessness from yesterday come rushing back. The memory of my chest tightening and throat closing is so vivid it's like it's happening all over again. He's the one who made me feel like that. He's the one who goes around tormenting people for fun. He's the one who made me think I was going to die.

Before I even realize what I'm doing, I'm marching over to the car, determination settling over my bones, blood rushing through my veins.

The car idles as he waits for Kaitlyn to get in.

"Hey, asshole!" I yell, getting his attention.

A small part of my brain, the rational side, is telling me that I'm dumb, and remembering that this guy literally almost stabbed my friend a few days ago. But the majority, the part that loves jumping into fights, the part that hates feeling helpless and refuses to take shit from bullies, ignores it. He emerges from the car, a look of mild amusement on his face.

"Your boyfriend isn't here," he replies as I get closer.

"You think it's funny to throw a brick through a window?" I stop just inches from him, my anger like electricity between us. "What if you hit one of us?"

He shrugs, only slightly interested. "A life for a life."

My jaw drops. "Oh my God. You're legitimately insane."

Kaitlyn's watching the scene with a mostly bored expression like she did at Noah's on Friday, like she's heard it all before. Who is she? What happened to the girl who always has something to say? "I know that you have issues, too, but why are you with this guy? I'm sure even *you* can see that he's psychotic."

"Why are you so obsessed with us?" she asks.

That *really* takes me by surprise. It takes me a couple of moments to get over my incredulity and find my voice.

"*Me?* Obsessed with *you*?! *I'm* not the one crashing your parties! *I'm* not the one who spends every waking moment thinking about you. *I'm* not the one following you around and throwing bricks through windows and trying to hit you with them!"

Kaitlyn raises an eyebrow at Ryan. "They were there when you threw that brick?"

He scoffs at her as if that was the dumbest question he's ever heard. "Obviously. Otherwise that's just a waste of a brick."

I take a step back from him. I'm talking to a monster. I wonder if he's on something?

Kaitlyn's lips purse thoughtfully and she steps closer to him. "But what if—"

"Just get in the car," he orders, as if over this whole conversation.

"But—"

He grabs her wrist, and it looks like a hard grip. Painful. "I said. Get in the car."

My reaction is automatic, even if it is Kaitlyn. "Hey! Let go of her!"

"Mind your own damn business!" he spits back at me, yanking Kaitlyn toward the car.

It's obvious. You can see it in her face that she's in pain, and that's not okay with me. I reach out to him. To do what? I don't know. But before I can do anything he grabs my wrist. Now he has Kaitlyn in one hand, and me in the other. And I was right. His grip *hurts.* I try to push at his shoulder with my free hand, but it does nothing. His grip tightens. Panic rises in my throat.

"I told you to mind your own. Fucking. Business," he growls at me, his dark eyes swirling with hate.

Kaitlyn's eyes meet mine, and for a second, everything melts away. She is me and I am her, and we wear matching expressions of fear. A tremor runs through my body and my breath comes up short. I fucked up by coming out here to confront him. What did I think I would accomplish, anyway? What could I possibly have done to make a difference?

But then I remember. I remember who I am. I remember what I've been through. My spine straightens and I look him directly in the eye. I'll be damned before I let a kid with a *man-bun* manhandle me into submission.

Everything happens quickly, way too fast for him to react. I bend my knees a bit and spread my feet out to get a good, solid base. Instead of trying to pull my arm out of his grasp, which is basically impossible, I angle myself a bit closer to him. Then I swing the elbow of the arm he's holding so it hits his forearm, drawing that hand near my shoulder. It's a fast action, and the movement uses his grip against him. Since his wrist physically can't bend that way, I break out of his grasp, relishing the feeling of freedom, and shove him away from me. It takes him by surprise, so I guess his grip on Kaitlyn slackens, and she pushes out of his grasp.

"Don't do that again!" she barks at him, her voice shaky, then opens the passenger-side door and gets in, slamming it closed. She's still going with him?

He's about to say something when Kaitlyn starts honking from inside the car, trying to get his attention, to force him to get in and drive her home.

"Your time will come," he says ominously, and then gets into the car.

I stand there as they drive off, trying to ignore the bad taste his words leave in my mouth.

My wrist is sore as I rub it, watching the car recede into the distance, knowing there's going to be a bruise there tomorrow. A bruise that's going to match Kaitlyn's.

10

After that confrontation, I don't really feel like going with everyone to Howard's Convenience to play detective. I just want to go home and put on sweatpants and eat a Nutella sandwich. Maybe curl up in bed under the thick covers and pretend my life isn't spiraling out of control.

I text Annalisa a quick apology and tell her to go without me, and to let me know what they find. I'm opening my car door when a deep voice calls out to me. Aiden's jogging toward me, and even though I'm pretty sure a bruise won't be starting to form so soon, I quickly reach into my car and throw on a jacket I was too lazy to put in my locker this morning.

"Hey," he says when he reaches me. "Everything okay?"

I have to stop myself from unconsciously tugging down the sleeve of my jacket, even though it's already covering everything.

"Yeah, fine. Why?" He didn't see me talking to Ryan, right? He definitely wouldn't be this calm if he did.

"Anna said you weren't going with them. Are you sure you're okay?"

"Yeah, just tired. I figured you didn't need all eight of us to ask a couple of questions." I shift from one foot to the other, in a totally unsuspicious way.

He pauses for a minute, the only sounds between us the slamming of car doors and tires on asphalt as the last remaining kids hightail it off school property. "I'm torn between wanting to give you some space and needing to find out what you're hiding from me."

"Why do you assume I'm hiding anything at all?" I defend myself, but my voice comes out a tad too high, and just a little too quick.

I'm a great liar, just not to Aiden, damn it. His gray eyes stare right into the depths of my soul.

"Thea." His voice softens, concern edging into it. "I can't help you if you don't tell me what's wrong."

My heart squeezes. I hate lying to Aiden, but I can't tell him what happened with Ryan. He'll freak out and do something stupid, like slit Ryan's throat, and then we're back to square one.

I bite my lip, trying to figure out how best to play this situation. He already knows something's wrong, and he won't let up until I tell him something.

Actually, something else *is* bothering me that I *want* to tell Aiden about.

"Did everyone leave already?" I ask him suddenly.

Aiden's confused by my change of subject, but answers nonetheless. "Yeah, I told them to go on without me."

"Perfect. Meet me at Luke's apartment," I tell him, throwing my bag into my car and getting in.

He puts his hand on my door to stop me from closing it.

"Why?" he asks, studying my face.

"You want to know what's bothering me? Meet me at Luke's. Go straight there."

His lips press into a straight line as he contemplates my words, then he steps back and lets me close my door. What I've found at Luke's has been in the back of my mind all day. I need to tell someone, and there's no one I trust more than Aiden.

Even though I leave before Aiden, he beats me to Luke's apartment, and I park beside his minivan.

"When are you getting a new car?" I gesture at the rental as we walk into the apartment.

Aiden glares at it like it's personally offended him. "Insurance money should be coming in soon."

I laugh at his obvious distress at being seen in that car, but my mood turns sour when we get to Luke's apartment. I hurry over to the gross plant, desperate to get out of the creepy hall with the fluorescent light that wants to die but manages to cling to life anyway.

With a grimace, I stick my hand in the soil and fish around. We voted to keep the key in the same spot instead of Annalisa keeping it, in case someone needed to get in. God, I wonder how many drunk people have peed in this plant. I finally find it and brush my arm and the key off, then open the door and close it behind us quickly.

The place looks the same as when we left it last night, but it's both darker and colder due to the plywood covering the broken window.

I ignore Aiden's questions as I grab his hand and lead him into Luke's bedroom.

Aiden takes in the room, then glances at Luke's bed with a raised eyebrow. "You know I have my own house, right? If you wanted alone time in a bedroom we could've just went there. It's cleaner too."

"This is serious!"

He raises his hands and turns his palms toward me, surrendering, a silent cue to carry on. I glare at him one last time for good measure and open the drawer of Luke's desk. The file's still there, right where I shoved it deep in the back. Suppressing an angry huff, I wish I imagined it. I wish it wasn't real, wish I didn't have to go through this on top of everything else.

"I found this when we were looking for clues. I didn't tell anybody about it."

I hand it to him almost mechanically, and step back, waiting for his reaction. He pulls the documents out and piles them on the desk, flipping through them with that guarded expression that never gives away what he's thinking. I study his face intently, waiting for a reaction. All he gives me is an occasional "*Hmm.*"

My heart's beating so fast and loud he can probably hear it from over there. I can't take it anymore. "Aiden!"

He looks up from the file. "What?"

"What do you mean 'what'?! What do you think?!"

"Let's not jump to conclusions."

"What do you mean 'Let's not jump to conclusions'?!" I practically yell.

"Thea, stop quoting me with the preface 'What do you mean.' I mean what I said. Let's not panic, we don't even know what it means."

His voice is calm and his face is unreadable, but that's his tell. He only guards his emotions from me when it's bad.

"I know exactly what it means." I wrap my arms around my chest, trying to keep myself together.

"It can't be as bad as it seems," he says, but it sounds more like he's trying to convince himself, to speak it into existence.

He turns his face away from me and back to the papers, but it's too late: I saw it. It's just a quick, barely there glimpse, but I saw it.

He's scared.

He's trying to be strong for me, to reassure me that my world isn't crashing down around me. He's trying to do what he does best and take care of everything, but it's too late; we both know we're screwed.

We stare at the file: a file full of information on Tony. *My* Tony: The man I've spent a year running away from. The man who locked me in a basement for three days. The man who's trying to kill me. *Tony.*

There are pictures of him, although they look older. Polaroids of him with a bunch of people, dated on the backs to almost twenty years ago. There are other men in the file as well, but none featured as much as Tony, although he's referred to by his real name, Anthony DeRosso, in Luke's notes about him. Does Luke know who I am? Is he looking into me? What could he possibly want with information on Tony?

"What are you guys doing here?" Annalisa's voice cuts through my thoughts, causing me to jump.

She peers into the room from the doorway, a frown on her red lips. We were both so absorbed in our thoughts and worries that we didn't hear Annalisa sneak up on us.

Aiden turns to face her as well, casually sidestepping so his large body blocks the file sitting on the desk, blocks the connection she has to Tony, the man making my life hell.

"I—uh—forgot my house key here last night. This is the last room I searched so I figured it would be here," I answer, praying that it sounds as smooth and believable aloud as it did in my head.

"Oh." She tilts her head, my words turning over in her mind.

"Hey, what happened at the convenience store?" Aiden asks before she can decide that I'm lying.

He walks toward her, and I casually lean on the desk and slide over so that my back is covering most of it.

Aiden's distraction works, and her eyes light up as she explains what happened.

"When we got there the guy said that they do have cameras, but if we wanted to look at them we'd have to get a warrant! A warrant! Can you believe that? Like, can you not just help a girl out? But obviously we didn't go all that way for nothing, so I told him to . . ."

The sound of Annalisa's voice trails off as Aiden very casually leads her into the main part of the apartment as she tells her story, away from me and the cursed file.

As soon as she's far enough away, I quickly shove the file into my bag.

I find my keys and hastily detach my house key from my car keys, throwing my car keys back in my bag and making sure it's completely closed so the file isn't visible. I try to school my expression to look somewhat normal and walk out of the room.

"Found it." I hold up the key in what I hope is a nonchalant manner, but Annalisa barely glances at me, still deep in her story.

"So, after we bought a bunch of garbage that he said wasn't selling, tried to bribe him, and got Char to fake cry in an actually very convincing performance, he finally let us check the cameras."

I throw my key on the coffee table and sit down beside her on the couch, catching Aiden's eye and giving him a small nod to let him know I took care of the file.

"Luke was there, and he was *very* drunk. It was actually really sad and kind of embarrassing. I recorded it on my phone."

She shows us the video, and she's right. It *is* kind of sad. He can barely stand straight and stumbles around. He throws some money on the counter, shoves the receipt and change into his pocket with most of the change dropping on the floor, and somehow makes it outside without tripping. The camera view switches to outside the store, where Luke promptly leans over and throws up. He then stumbles out of view of the camera and the video stops.

"The time stamp when he walks off camera is 5:25. So I thought this would be good proof, you know, the guy is too drunk to even stand, let alone kill a guy. But stupid Julian had to be practical and remind me that it could technically be argued that he still had time to get to Aiden's house and it doesn't prove where he was *at* the actual time, so we still have some work to do."

Annalisa looked so hopeful for a second. I can only imagine what was going through her mind when she thought this was the proof she needed to clear Luke's name.

"Did you send it to Luke's lawyer anyway?" Aiden asks.

"Of course I did, but we're still going to figure out where he went after that."

I glance at my bag, an action that doesn't go unnoticed by Aiden.

He gives me a look, one that says he knows what I'm up to, that he knows I took the file. Of course I'm taking it this time. No way am I leaving it here where someone else can stumble upon it.

I don't know what's going on, and I don't need Annalisa poking around it and asking questions. Plus, I need answers, and there's only one guy who can give them to me.

11

When I get home, I park in the garage and open the door, only to be met with loud, Spanish music coming from upstairs. *Annoying.* It only means one thing: Mom's upstairs with Mason's dad.

I slam the door and chuck my shoes across the foyer, where they hit the front door and land with a thud. I march through the house into the kitchen, slamming doors and cupboards and trying to be loud in general.

The music turns off, and I throw the metal knife I was using to make my Nutella sandwich into the sink, where it bounces around with loud, satisfying clinks. They know I'm home now. I just ruined their *date*.

Ugh. Gross.

I sit at the table, making sure to scrape the chair loudly across the floor as I pull it out, and calmly eat my sandwich.

Mom's bedroom door creaks open, and soon she's standing in the kitchen.

"Oh, what are you doing home?" she asks, trying to fix her still messy hair. At least she's fully dressed.

I put down the rest of my sandwich and stare at her with incredulity. "Are you serious? It's 6 p.m. School ended hours ago. Technically I'm *late*."

She tilts her head as she considers my words. "Huh. I guess we lost track of time."

I scoff. Unbelievable. Who's the adult here?

She walks back to the hallway and stands at the base of the stairs.

"Brian, it's just Amelia!" she calls up to him.

I join my mom in the hallway and lean on the door frame, crossing my arms as Brian comes into view.

"Where were you this whole time? Why were you late?" Mom asks me and I openly stare at her.

"Does it matter? You didn't even know I was gone."

Brian meets us at the bottom of the stairs. "Oh, hi, Amelia. We need to stop meeting like this."

His attempt at a joke is lame and doesn't work. I grind my molars together. "Can't you guys at least *try* to be discreet? It's like you're begging to get caught. What if I brought my friends over after school?"

Brian shrugs his jacket on. "I did park around the corner, but you're right, we should be more careful."

"What you *should* do is put an end to this and tell your family what a piece of shit you're being right now."

"Amelia!" Mom immediately scolds me. "Respect your elders."

"I'll respect my elders when Brian respects his vows."

She's about to snap, but I'm not afraid. We've been at odds

ever since we moved here. First she tried to get me to stay away from Aiden, and now it's only gotten worse since she decided we should move. I thought we were on the right track when she let me go to the beach house with everyone, but now that this thing with Brian is out in the open, we've been going back and forth arguing with each other more than we get along.

Brian puts his hand on my mom's arm. "It's all right, Caroline. I should get going anyway."

She frowns but kisses him, and I audibly gag. They pull apart and Mom glares at me as she hands Brian his keys.

"We really do appreciate your discretion about this whole situation, Amelia. Aiden's as well. I'm still trying to figure out the best way to handle this. I don't want to hurt Mason, but I can't stop seeing your mother. It's not just an affair . . ."

I don't care for his excuses and I don't want his words to sink in. He cares about Mom? It's more than an affair? What is he saying? That they're in *love*? I can't even think about that right now. All I can think about is Mason's face—how disappointed he'll be when he finds out, how he'll hate that I knew before him and didn't say anything.

Instead of replying, I open the door and gesture outside, effectively kicking him out.

"Until next time." He steps out the door and onto the porch.

"There shouldn't be a next tim—"

Annalisa is walking up the driveway and I snap my mouth shut. Mom spots her too. Her eyes widen, and she quickly turns to run up the stairs.

Brian notices Annalisa when it's too late. There's a hitch in his step but he recovers quickly, continuing his walk and pretending that this is all normal. Like, *Just another normal day. Totally not cheating on my unsuspecting wife and fooling my son. Yup, just a normal day. I'm not a complete douche bag. No ma'am, not me.*

"Hi, Anna." He greets her as they pass each other, then continues down the street.

She looks at him with her eyebrows drawn, confused, then back at me as she walks up the porch steps.

I practically hold my breath when she stops and meets me on the porch. She holds up a key. "You forgot your house key again. I brought it since I figured you'd be locked out of your house, but I guess you got in okay."

I stare at it like I've never seen it before in my life. I must've been so focused on getting out of there with the file that I forgot it on the coffee table.

"Oh. Yeah, I came in through the garage. Thanks."

She drops her arm and looks back at where Brian disappeared into the distance. "Mason told me his dad left on a business trip this morning. Why would he—"

Blood rushes in my ears. I say nothing as she connects the dots in her mind. I know the second the realization hits her because her bright blue eyes widen.

"*Holy shit!* Your mom and his dad? No way! Mason's gonna flip his shit when he finds out!"

I shush her and pull her closer to the door and away from the nosy neighbors.

"No, Anna, we can't tell him. At least not yet." I need to convince her to stay quiet about it. I'm trying to get my life back to some semblance of normal. Telling Mason about our parents is the complete *opposite* of what I need right now, of what *he* needs right now.

She stands her ground. "What? Why not? He should know.

His *mom* should know. Oh my God, poor Natalia. Have you ever met a nicer woman than her? She's going to be crushed."

"Anna, I know. But please. This isn't what he needs right now."

"Wait, how long have you known about this?"

I rub my temples, feeling a headache coming on. This is getting a lot more complicated. "A while, I guess."

"Amelia! How can you not tell him?"

"I know, I know, I'm a terrible person. I just can't do that to him right now. I'll tell him, I swear, just not right now. Plus, I told Brian that he needs to tell Mason. I shouldn't have to be the one to hurt him. If Brian doesn't tell him, *then* I'll say something."

One thing at a time. Get Luke out of jail. Take down Aiden's dad. Get Ryan and Kaitlyn off my back. Stay hidden from Tony and off that stupid S-Live Time app. Break Mason's heart.

Then I'll be back to normal.

Annalisa crosses her arms. "Does Aiden know?"

I nod solemnly.

She exhales with defeat and runs a hand through her hair. "Wow. And he didn't tell him?"

I wrap my arms around myself and hesitate before I answer. "I convinced him not to." I sound selfish even to myself. "I'll tell Mason, just not yet. I can't keep being the reason he's unhappy."

She stares at me for a while, not saying anything. I shift from foot to foot under the scrutiny of her gaze.

Finally, she sighs. "I won't say anything. But we're going to have to tell him. For real, Amelia."

"If Brian doesn't, we will. I promise."

I hope it doesn't come to that. Maybe I'll be long gone by the time Brian tells Mason and his wife. Maybe I'll get to keep being a coward and not have to deal with it at all, even if that's not what

I want or what Mason deserves. And then there's the whole "It's not just an affair" thing Brian threw at me. Is this a real thing? Are they going to keep seeing each other when we move? Are they going to be together when this is over? I just want everything to be normal, but it's all spiraling, and normalcy is slipping right through my fingers, and I can do nothing but stand here and helplessly watch it happen.

12

The days of the week fly by quickly and insignificantly. Mason doesn't seem any different, so I guess that means Annalisa kept her promise to stay quiet about the affair. But that also means Brian hasn't said anything to him either.

I'm getting ready for school Thursday morning when I get a text from Aiden.

I'm picking you up this morning. Be there in 10.

A giddy feeling rises within my chest. A morning with Aiden? Fine by me.

Since Monday's encounter with Ryan I've been wearing long sleeves that are tight around the wrists so that they won't accidentally ride up and reveal the bruise on my wrist, and Kaitlyn's been doing the same. Not that we talked about it. She's doing her damn best to avoid me, while still managing to be a bitch. How? I have no idea. It must be her special talent. Some people can juggle bowling pins while riding a unicycle; Kaitlyn can be a bitch while not even in the same room as you.

I study the ugly bluish-yellow bruise in the shape of a large handprint wrapped around my wrist and scowl. At least it's fading.

A loud car pulls up in my driveway and I peer out the window. It's a black Challenger. I practically squeal out loud.

Grabbing my bag and jacket, I run down the stairs and out the door, locking it behind me. Aiden's standing in front of the car, a grin on his face. It softens all his expressions and makes him look younger than he normally presents himself. He looks his age.

"You have a Challenger again!" I call out to him and open the passenger-side door, peeking inside to see if anything's different.

He sits in the driver's seat, his excitement almost palpable. "It's the newest model too. Even faster than my old one."

Once I'm seated, I throw my bag in the backseat and put my seat belt on.

"It's pretty, but I'm going to miss the minivan," I joke.

"I am *not*." He groans. "I'm especially not going to miss all the stupid jokes. If Noah called me a soccer mom one more time I was going to lose it."

He pulls out of my driveway and drives down the street, and it's painfully obvious that he's trying his hardest to do the speed limit and not test out the car's engine.

"You're still coming with me tonight to the interview, right?" he asks as he takes a turn unnecessarily fast.

Another news station has asked to interview him about his relationship with Andrew Kessler, and basically remind everyone that Andrew is a shitty human being who doesn't deserve life outside of prison, never mind be the governor of an entire state. Aiden hasn't done any interviews since leaving

Torywood Springs after everything blew up, but he accepted this request, and asked me to join him for the first time.

"As long as I don't have to be on screen."

"Yeah, you'll just sit on the sidelines and cheer me on. You can even scroll my social media for a bit while they set up."

Since I don't have social media, sometimes Aiden indulges me and lets me browse through his to see what's going on out there. It's fun, pretending to be normal. Even if his is currently littered with a mix of moral support and death threats. I usually block those people for him before he sees what they're saying.

"Then you got a deal," I reply, spying my favorite button on the car's console.

"Oh look! The butt warmer!" I reach to press the button when Aiden suddenly brakes a bit too hard.

"What is that?" His tone serious, harsh.

"The butt warmer? You know, you press it and it warms up your seat?"

He safely pulls over on the side of the road, grabs my hand, and shoves up my sleeve. The one that's covering my bruise.

"No. I meant this."

I automatically yank my hand out of his grasp. "It's nothing. You're overreacting."

Aiden narrows his eyes at me. He's deathly calm, his gray eyes cutting right through me.

"It's not nothing. That was the shape of a hand—finger imprints."

I cradle my arm defensively as my pulse speeds up, wondering if he can hear how loudly my heart is racing. "You didn't even get a good look at it. You can't possibly tell what it looks like. And that's because it looks like *nothing*. It's just a bruise, I'm clumsy.

You know this." My words come out shaky. I'm doing a very poor job making this lie believable, and he knows it too.

He takes a deep breath, trying to steady himself. His jaw clenches. I can tell he's trying his hardest to stay calm and not erupt in anger.

"When were you alone with Ryan?"

I'm taken aback. I try to read the expression on his face but he's put his guard back up. My heartbeat is the only noise in the small space. "How did you know it was Ryan?"

He studies me, his hands clench into fists. "You do remember that I'm actually very smart, right? Plus, you just confirmed it."

Damn it! I can't believe I just fell for the oldest trick in the book.

This is the last thing we need right now. I can't have Aiden defending me by picking a fight like when he found the bruise Dave left on my stomach after that time at the Tracks. I need to defuse this situation before he does something stupid. "Aiden really, it's not that bad."

"*It's not that bad?* Jesus, Thea! There's a literal handprint on your wrist from where he grabbed you!" He pauses as his eyes widen. "Where else did he hurt you? Let me see. I swear to God if he—"

He moves to, I don't know, take off my sweater to check for more bruises, but I push him off of me. "I'm fine, Aiden. Really. You're overreacting."

He studies me with an expression I don't like seeing on him. His eyes are alight, and there's a fire in them that promises pain.

"What happened?"

"He was being rough with Kaitlyn and I intervened. It's fine, I'm fine."

His eyes narrow. "You *swear* to me he didn't do anything else to you?"

"I swear. It's fine, Aiden."

Suddenly, he puts the car in gear and roughly pulls back onto the road. "I've said it before and I'll say it again. *No one* hurts *my girl* and walks away without paying for it."

He's not doing the speed limit this time. Not even trying.

"Aiden! Stop!"

He says nothing as his knuckles turn white from gripping the steering wheel, only relaxing his grip when he needs to shift gears.

"Aiden we're almost in a school zone and you're in fifth gear! Slow down!" I'm not scared of Aiden, but I am scared *for* Aiden. What is he planning on doing?

He doesn't say anything and the determined look on his face doesn't falter, but he does slow down to the speed limit. Unfortunately, he still makes a scene with his loud car as he screeches into the parking lot haphazardly and turns the engine off. He gets out, his back rigid and his muscles taut as he scans the parking lot.

"Aiden, seriously, listen to me. You need to calm down."

I've caught up to him now by the driver's side of the car, but it's too late. He's already zeroed on the target. Ryan's just pulled into the parking lot some distance away to drop off Kaitlyn. Noah, Mason, and Annalisa come up to us.

Noah looks between me and Aiden. "Hey, what's with the I'll slit your throat for breathing in my direction look on his face?"

Aiden ignores him, ignores all of us, and steps around me, calmly walking toward Ryan. But I know better. This will be anything *but* calm. I run in front of him and put my hands on his chest, trying to stop him.

"Aiden, stop. We're in a school parking lot. You'll get expelled."

His calculating eyes meet mine, the thinly veiled fury in them meeting me with full force. He glances at my hands on his chest, at my bruised wrist since my sleeve rolled down again.

Shit. Stupid mistake.

A muscle in his jaw ticks. He puts his hands on my hips and gently moves me out of the way, then continues walking toward Ryan.

I run around him again, shoving my sleeve down this time and stopping in front of him.

"Stop! Please. We all know you can beat him up without breaking a sweat. He knows what you can do. But I don't want you to do that for me. I'm *begging* you. Just leave it."

Something I say must reach him, but the anger is still there. "I can't just let him get away with doing that to you."

"We won't. But this won't solve anything. You'll get expelled, and then what? He still wins." I lower my voice. "We don't know how much time I'll have left with you. I don't want to waste it on Ryan. Or us not being able to be together in school."

I sense an opening. He's still pissed, but he's listening. I grab his hand and lead him in the opposite direction, toward the school, and away from Ryan and the impending fight.

Aiden lets me guide him to the school, but his attention is still locked on Ryan's car until he pulls out of the parking lot and speeds away into the distance, unaware of just how close he came to swallowing all his teeth.

13

Aiden was tense for the rest of the day. It was obvious to everyone who crossed his path. I know he's upset and it means a lot because I know he cares about me, but I'm glad that situation didn't escalate to a point where Aiden got expelled because of me. Aiden's smart; he can get scholarships without a problem, and I can't screw that up for him by letting him start a fight over me. His future is more important.

We didn't get to talk about it all day, so when he drives me home after school, I tell him the whole story, about Ryan grabbing Kaitlyn and everything.

He doesn't really say much, except to swear under his breath.

He mumbles something about hoping Ryan doesn't turn out like his father, a statement that punches me right in the gut. It's easy to forget that Aiden had to live with Ryan's abusive dad as a kid.

Aiden drops me off and promises to be back soon to go to the interview he has scheduled today to talk about his father. I grab something to eat and get changed while Aiden picks up his brothers and takes them to Mason's house, where Aiden tells me Natalia happily dotes on them, pestering them to fill their plates with her homemade tamales. He comes back to get me a bit later, with a tamalé that I eat with a guilty conscience, and soon we're at the news station.

We haven't heard from Kessler since his birthday card threat, but Aiden hasn't let that stop him. If news stations request interviews from him, he's happy to give them. The more people who learn about what a shitty person Kessler is, the better.

Once inside, they whisk Aiden away to the interview, and I stand off to the side behind the cameras while the news team sets Aiden up with a mic and gets him into position. He looks at ease, confident as always, like he knows exactly what he needs to say and isn't afraid to say it.

I take a seat in a chair off to the side and unlock Aiden's phone. I don't snoop through it—I don't need to. If anyone was hiding things in this relationship, it was me. But not anymore.

I open S-Live Time as they prep Aiden for the interview, start their sound checks, and do all that other stuff they need to prepare. It's a local station, but people from the whole state tune into this show. Scrolling through S-Live Time, I laugh at the stupid pictures and videos. It would be so cool to just be able to have social media. To post pictures with my friends and not worry about giving my location away to a murderer. I could theoretically have an anonymous account, but then I'd just get sad looking at everyone posting while I couldn't share selfies or pictures of my friends.

I stop scrolling when I come across a video. It looks familiar, so I put the phone on mute and press Play. My heart drops. This is not happening to me. This can't be a coincidence. First the file and now this? People are talking around me but I can't make out the words. It's all just mumbled-together sounds.

The chair I was sitting on tips over as I stand, and I think I get yelled at for making noise while they're live on air, but I don't care. I need air.

Somehow, I get through the building without actually seeing anything I'm looking at or processing the signs. Once outside, I lean against the sturdy brick wall and take a few big, deep breaths. I hold out the phone in front of me, turn the sound on, and press Play.

It's a video shot inside a high school, *my* high school, of Kaitlyn and me going at it in our first big fight. My face is clearly visible. My voice is clear as water. There's the GO LIONS! mural in the background, even if it's just in the corner of the frame.

It's me. Online. The very place I've been trying so hard to avoid.

I think back to when this video was taken. I went to Ethan Moore and tried to get him to take it down. He refused. I had to trick him into a locked closet and steal his phone and laptop, only to be told by Aiden that he'd already taken care of it.

Aiden said he'd taken care of it.

Then why is it still here? Why is my face still on the internet?! Has it been here the whole time? Has Tony already found it? Is he on his way here? The door opens, and Aiden steps outside. He looks around then spots me leaning against the wall.

"Hey, are you okay? You ran out of there."

"Have you been lying to me this entire time?" I ask.

"What are you talking about?"

I wave his phone erratically in front of his face, my heartbeat loud in my ears. "Have. You. Been. Lying. To. Me?"

Aiden's expression gives nothing away, his voice annoyingly calm despite my outburst. "I heard what you said. Would you care to elaborate?"

My throat closes. How can I elaborate? There's a video of my face and location on the internet! All I can do is shake the phone in front of him. He reaches out to gently stop my flailing hand and takes the phone from it. He unlocks it and watches the video that's already on his screen.

I find my voice. "You said it was deleted!"

I can't believe this. How long do I have until Tony finds me? Does he already know?

Aiden's face turns hard. "I did delete it. Ethan didn't post this."

"Then why is my face still online?!"

My head pounds. I have so much to lose. After all I've been through, *this* is what's going to take me down? Kaitlyn's going to win after all.

Aiden clicks around on his phone for a bit, then asks, "Thea, did you even look at who the original poster was?"

That takes the angry wind out of my sails. "No. Who?"

"It's one of those cat-fight accounts. They find videos of girls fighting and post them on their own account. This was posted a while ago. They must've seen the video when it was originally posted and saved it before we deleted it."

I drag my hands across my face and slide down the wall to sit on the ground. I guess this is me learning the hard way that once something is on the internet, it stays on the internet.

"I'm going to have to move sooner rather than later, Aiden. I can't push it back now. Can we even still keep in touch? What if he keeps tabs on you? What if he figures out what you mean to me? Oh God, my mom's going to flip."

I don't want to leave a second earlier than I need to. I shouldn't have to. All I wanted was to be *normal* for two damn minutes before I never see my friends again, before I won't feel Aiden's hand in mine again, or his lips against mine. Why is my life so messed up that I'm going to be torn away from my friends and people I love?

The gravel crunches as Aiden kneels beside me. "No, you're not. I just convinced you to stay. You're not going anywhere until the last possible second."

Tears escape, and I can't help it. I'm being dramatic since I need to leave anyway, but now I won't accomplish anything I wanted to do. I promised I'd help my friends—that I'd set everything right before I disappeared, leave them with a positive memory of me. But now I'm going to leave before I can fulfill any of my promises. Luke's still in jail. Charlotte's still confused about Noah and Chase. Chase himself is still heartbroken. Mason still doesn't know about his dad, and Aiden's dad is still an asshole out to hurt him. My heart cracks.

"I have to tell Agent Dylan, Aiden." He's the guy in charge of my case. He's going to need to know something like this.

Aiden gently takes my face between his hands and forces me to look up at him. His thumbs brush the tears off my cheeks, and his eyes soften, a stark contrast to how they've looked all day.

"Thea," he almost whispers. "You know I love you. You know I'm not just going to let you go that easy."

This isn't the first time he's told me that, but every time feels like the first time.

"But—"

"No buts," he interrupts. "Do you want to leave?"

I give him an incredulous look and move my face out of his grasp. "Of course not. You know that."

"Then don't. We can work around this. We can make the most of the little time you have." He sounds hopeful, almost desperate. He's trying to find a simple solution to a very big problem. "There's nothing about the location in this video. Do you know how many high schools in America have lions as their mascot? Tons. The chances of Tony finding the video is already small, then he'd have to recognize you, and then figure out where it was taken."

"You think I'm overreacting?" I ask him, not accusingly, but genuinely wanting to hear the answer.

He brushes the hair out of my face. "I think you're already leaving anyway, so there's no point in leaving before it's time."

"There's always a chance, Aiden. And I'm sorry for accusing you. I know you'd never let me down. You're the only person I can truly trust, I mean it. That was all the panic talking."

He brushes off my apology, wrapping his solid arms around me as I rest my head against his muscled chest, and his chin rests on top of my head. I instantly feel better now that I'm cocooned in his arms.

"If it makes you feel better, call Agent Dylan. Tell him about it. Your safety comes first and foremost."

I think about Aiden and my friends. Is it selfish of me to not say something about this because I want to spend more time with them? Mom's face pops up in my mind. No matter how at odds we are with each other right now, I don't want her to get hurt because of me. I know what she'd want me to do. I know what I *should* do.

"I'm going to call him and let him know." The words come out strong even though I feel anything but.

"That's a good idea. You can also find out exactly how much time we have left together. I hate waking up and not knowing if it's the last day I have with you."

The sincerity and vulnerability in his voice bring tears to my eyes. "Me too," I whisper. I pull back to look at him. "Did you just run out of a live interview?"

He shrugs, a sheepish smile tugging at his lips. "Maybe. But you scared me."

I pull him back to me and laugh into his chest, my own full of love for him, and so grateful to have him.

"Worst case, he comes here looking for a girl with long, strawberry-blond hair."

I look up at him. "It can't be as simple as just dying my hair."

"Of course not. But at least it'll throw him off if—and that's a very big if—he does come here."

I don't want to leave. And Aiden's right. What are the chances that Tony even *finds* the video *and* figures out where it was taken?

Aiden picks up a strand of my hair and lets it drop. "It'd have to be something drastic."

Platinum blond, here I come.

14

The morning after Aiden's interview is Friday, and I waste no time calling Agent Dylan as soon as I wake up. I pace my room as the phone rings, nerves making me jittery. What if he's mad at me? He puts so much effort into keeping me safe, and here I am, getting on video within a few weeks of moving here. Plus, there's the whole I hid the video from him when it was first posted before the break thing. Maybe I won't tell him that part. I have no idea what time zone he's in, but he picks up on the fourth ring.

"Amelia? Is everything all right?" His voice is deep and oddly comforting even though I really only talk to him when bad things happen.

"No, not really." My voice sounds small, and he waits for me to continue. "There's a video of me online. It was taken a few weeks after I arrived here in King City. I'm not sure how long it's been up, but our school mural is in the background. It doesn't say the name of the school in it though, just Go Lions in the corner."

He's silent for a moment, and I shift my weight from one foot to another.

"Hmm." Is what he finally settles on.

Hmm? What's "*Hmm*"?

"So . . ." I hesitate. "What now?'

"Well, we're already in the process of relocating you anyway. Just sit tight."

The wind is knocked out of my sails. I feel empty, and stumped. That's all? Sit tight? I had a whole fit of terror and yelled at Aiden for "*Hmm. Sit tight,*"?

I sit on my bed and stare at myself in the mirror. My face is blank, my hair in a messy bun on top of my head. "Okay. Do you have a date for when I'm officially leaving?"

I hear papers shuffle from his side of the phone. "Not yet. We're still finalizing everything, sorting out the paperwork, that sort of stuff. Can you send me the video so I can assess the situation better?"

"Oh, okay." That doesn't really answer my question. How long do I have left with Aiden? With my friends? I put him on speaker and text the video to him.

"Maybe two weeks? Or three?" I push on for answers.

"Probably," he replies. I'm silent as the video plays in the background. I hear my voice, then Kaitlyn's. More paper sounds in the background. "We're doing everything we can to find him, Amelia. This isn't the end of the world. Focus on your schoolwork. Try not to get caught on camera again, okay? We're keeping your mom updated with anything pertaining to your relocation."

His lack of concern confuses me. I guess everything is fine and I overreacted? If anything, I feel like he's *under*reacting.

"All right, then." What else is there to say?

"Thank you for telling me about the video," he says, almost as an afterthought. "Is there anything else you need from me, Amelia?"

For a second, I consider telling him about the file I found in Luke's apartment, the one with information about Tony in it, but for some reason I hesitate. I'm not sure why, but something in the vagueness of his responses today has me holding back.

"Nope," I say. "Have a great day."

"You too. Call me if you need anything."

The phone call ends, leaving me staring at myself in the mirror, the phone still pressed against my ear. That whole conversation left a funny taste in my mouth, but I'm not even sure why.

>> <<

I'm still replaying my conversation with Agent Dylan in my head at school when Aiden appears beside my locker, making me jump.

"Didn't mean to scare you," Aiden says as I finish packing my books into my bag. "How did the call go?"

Weird is what I want to say, but instead I reply, "Okay, I guess. He wasn't specific about when I'm leaving. I think two or three weeks."

Aiden purses his lips thoughtfully. "I can work with that."

I can't. I need more time. I'll always need more time, but it'll have to do. I close my locker and fully face Aiden.

"Tomorrow's Saturday," he says as we walk through the hall. "Are you still okay with going to visit Luke and getting to the bottom of the file he had?"

I want to know why Luke had information about Tony in his house, but I also don't want to know. I have suspicions, but

I don't want to be right. Or what if it's actually worse than I originally thought.

"Yeah. Let's not tell anyone what we're doing, though."

The warning bell rings, and we approach my homeroom class.

"Right," he says. "We'll talk later. Don't stress out about it too much."

He gives me a quick kiss on the lips and disappears down the hall to his own class. Try not to stress? I've been nothing *but* stress.

I make it to history before Charlotte, Mason, or Noah, so I sit in my normal spot, trying not to think about Luke, Tony, or Agent Dylan.

"Hey, k-bear," Mason says, sliding into the seat beside mine.

My heart twinges at the nickname. "Hey." We're still in the don't talk about the beach house phase of our relationship, and that's fine with me.

"I feel like we haven't seen much of each other this week," he continues, and I can't deny the truth behind his statement. After Aiden's birthday party last Friday, then the visit to the jail on Saturday, and Luke's apartment visit Sunday, I had to use the rest of the week to catch up on homework, so I haven't had time to hang out with everyone after school. Aiden's interview last night was the first time I went out after school, which sucks because I really should be making the most of my time here while I still can.

"I know, I'm sorry. Maybe we'll do something this weekend," I tell him, ignoring the way his brown eyes shine because it's like a punch in the gut.

"Our parents are involved! It might be more than just an affair!" I want to shout, but instead I just bite my lip and nod at him as he continues talking.

"I'm helping my mom with some stuff tonight, but we should hang out tomorrow," he says, "Let's go play mini-golf. See if anyone else wants to come too."

I've distanced myself from Mason ever since I found out about our parents because I can't stand the pit that forms in my stomach when I see him, but then again, I also hate that we haven't hung out that much and I'm going to leave soon. Who knows when I'm going to see him again? When I'll be able to enjoy his stupid jokes and cocky grin and easygoing attitude.

I'm about to say yes, but then I remember what I'm doing with Aiden tomorrow.

"Sorry, Mason, I'm busy tomorrow, I'm hanging out with Aiden. Maybe after?" I can barely meet his eyes.

"Oh, yeah." He visibly deflates. "No problem."

Charlotte enters the classroom just as the final bell rings, and Noah a few moments later. Mason stands from the seat beside me as Charlotte approaches so she can sit.

"We'll talk later," he says with a tight smile and moves to the seat behind us that he shares with Noah, who immediately launches into a story about his morning donuts.

"What was that about?" Charlotte asks as she slides into the seat beside me.

"Nothing," I lie, grabbing my books from my bag and ignoring the tightening in my chest. He doesn't have the problem; I'm the one with the problem. Mason thinks I'm avoiding him, and even though I am kind of, I hate it.

15

Saturday couldn't come soon enough.

I spent *hours* last night at the salon trying to get my hair the right color. It's *hard* to get red toned hair to platinum blond without either frying your hair or having it turn orange. Luckily, my hair is neither fried nor orange. It's platinum blond, cut to just above my shoulder, and is slightly waved.

I haven't decided how I feel about it. I've really grown accustomed to the long, reddish hair I've had since becoming Amelia.

When Aiden came to pick me up this morning, he looked at my hair for a while. He said it suited me, but I think he misses my old hair too.

Oh well. It's just hair. And neither of them is my real hair color, so what does it matter?

We leave early in the morning to make the drive to visit Luke. We have to get there during visiting hours, and now that Aiden's in his car and a little heavy footed on the gas, we make it in no time.

I have to get to the bottom of this whole file thing. It's been eating me up inside and I can't wait until visiting hours so I can grill Luke about why he would even have the information in the first place.

We didn't tell anyone we were coming here. My mom doesn't know anything about the Luke situation—unless Brian told her, but that's unlikely since she hasn't said anything to me. In any case, she doesn't know that I'm visiting a jail to talk to Luke, and she especially doesn't need to know *why*. The rest of our friends just think we're having some couple time or whatever. Technically they're not wrong, but it sucks that the only us time Aiden and I seem to have these days is when we're running around either fixing problems or starting them.

Once we're in the jail, they make us sign in and go through the security checks like last time. I'm not allowed to bring my bag in, so I leave it in the car and just bring in the file I stole from Luke's apartment, holding it close to my chest as if guarding it from peering eyes. I'm lucky they let me bring it in, but they take all the staples and paper clips out.

A guard leads me and Aiden to a metal table—a different one from the first time I was here with Annalisa—and we sit down. I place the file in my lap and try not to look around at the other inmates talking quietly with their loved ones. Like last time, there's a woman sobbing, and the sound makes my skin crawl.

I hate this place.

Luke's on the other side of the door, the guard stopping him to remove his handcuffs, then leading him over to our table. He looks a bit better than the last time we saw him, but still tired looking and older than his twenty years. He has rough stubble along his jaw and dark circles beneath his eyes.

"Where's Anna?" He looks back and forth between me and Aiden.

"She couldn't make it today," Aiden answers in his smooth voice.

"What's up? Why are you here? Any news about where I was that night?"

Even though I don't completely trust him since finding that file, I figure we might as well tell him what we've found.

"We got a video of you puking your brains outside Howard's Convenience, but you walk off camera at 5:25. Still plenty of time to murder Greg."

Did my voice come out accusatory? It sounded harsher than I meant it.

"I guess you don't know where I went after that?" he asks, dejected.

"Do you?" Aiden asks.

"Your guess is as good as mine." Luke sighs.

I feel like I'm glaring at Luke. Am I? I just can't look at him the same.

"Are you all right?" Luke asks, leaning in to analyze me.

Was I staring at him without blinking?

"We were searching your apartment for clues, and we found something . . . interesting," Aiden answers for me, drawing Luke's attention.

I pull the file from my lap and place it on the table. "Do you want to tell me why you have this?"

He takes the file and opens it, skimming through the contents quickly.

He looks up somberly. "Did you tell anyone about this?"

"Only we know," Aiden answers, folding his arms across his muscled chest.

Luke sighs and turns the file toward us. "I started doing some research when I ran into you guys at the Tracks, when Anna made it very clear that she wanted nothing to do with me."

I tense. I knew it.

He continues, "I wanted to do something for her, to get back on her good side. It's always just been me, Anna, and our mom our whole life. My dad was barely there for me, and obviously he wanted nothing to do with Anna, she's not even biologically his. I figured maybe she'd want to know who her biological father was."

This is not going where I expected it to.

Oh no.

Aiden starts to interject but Luke cuts him off. "Yes, I know that her biological dad raped our mom at a party and that's how she got pregnant. But I don't know . . . at least I could give her the *choice* to know him or not."

Oh no. No. No. No. No. I want to unhear this entire conversation.

"There's three men in this file, but as you can tell, most of it is about this guy." He points to the picture I'd know anywhere. "I'm about ninety-five percent sure this one, Anthony DeRosso, is the one who raped our mom at that party. I wasn't able to do too much digging into him before I got arrested, but I know he's a real lowlife, that's why I haven't told Anna about it."

The room spins. My life is a soap opera. Annalisa is my best friend. My best friend is Anthony DeRosso's biological daughter.

Anthony DeRosso. Known to me as Tony Derando. The man ruining my life.

Aiden senses that I'm too shocked to speak even though he's staring Luke down with an intensity that radiates throughout his whole body.

"Have you contacted him, this Anthony DeRosso?" Aiden almost spits the name out, as if it pains him to say it.

"Um, no. Why?" Luke hesitates at the noticeable shift in Aiden's demeanor.

"Are you sure?"

"Yes, I'm sure," Luke says defensively. "I haven't figured out how yet. Is it that terrible of an idea to contact him? I know he's not a good person, but I think Anna should know."

It's a terrible, horrible, horrendous idea.

"Anna wants nothing to do with her biological father," Aiden states with authority. I can't seem to find my voice. "*If* this man is her biological father—"

"I'm pretty sure he is," Luke interjects. "I was digging through our mom's old stuff. He's mentioned a couple times. There's a picture of them together at a party too. I just wish I knew where Anna's birth certificate was. I'm sure Mom would've listed the biological dad, even if he was, you know—"

"*If* he is Anna's biological father," Aiden continues, "contacting him will only make things worse. For everyone."

Especially me. Especially my friends. They have no idea the pain and danger they'd be inviting into their lives by contacting Tony—Anthony DeRosso. How would he act at finding out he has another daughter? The whole reason he snapped is because his daughter, Sabrina, died in a car accident my father caused.

Luke leans back in his seat and purses his lips in thought. "I just want what's best for Annalisa."

"Getting involved with this guy is the *worst thing* you could possibly ever do for Anna! He's a psychopath!"

Luke's eyebrows draw together at my outburst, and I feel Aiden's reassuring hand on my leg under the table.

Calm down, Amelia. You're acting all suspicious.

"A psychopath? You know him?"

I clear my thoughts and try to think of something that sounds logical.

"I only know what Anna's told me," I say. "This man brought her into the world by raping her mother. I'm assuming he's committed more crimes since then." *I know he has.* "A man like this would bring nothing of value into Anna's life."

Aiden's eyes narrow. I have no idea how he's managing to be articulate and thoughtful. I feel like the room's spinning; I can barely process my own thoughts.

"So to clarify, you don't have a way of contacting him?" Aiden asks.

Luke shakes his head. "Getting the information I have was hard enough."

For the first time since we started this conversation, I feel like I can breathe a bit. Luke doesn't have any contact information. He couldn't contact Tony even if he wanted to. All he's got are some pictures and a name Tony doesn't even go by anymore. I take a calming breath without trying to make it obvious. My life isn't going to crash down around me.

"But I'm going to find it," Luke adds confidently.

What?

"What?" Aiden echoes my thought out loud.

"Anna should be given the choice if she wants to know him or not. She deserves a shot at a real family. Maybe he's changed his ways and isn't a terrible person. I've changed."

Tony hasn't changed! He's a terrible person!

My head whips over to Aiden, my eyes wide, practically pleading for him to do something—to fix it.

"Have you not been listening to anything we've been saying?" Aiden's tone is low and cutting. "*We're* her family. She doesn't need a criminal to add to her problems."

Luke crosses his arms and leans back in his seat. "I'm a criminal. You're visiting me in *jail*, and she still wants me in her life. Give her some credit, maybe she'll want to get to know her biological father if she's given the chance."

"Luk—"

Luke cuts Aiden off. "My mind is made up. When you guys prove my innocence and get me out, I'm going to do everything I can to track him down. Anna deserves the choice."

No! The last thing Annalisa deserves is to have Tony in her life. Do I tell him? Do I tell him who Tony is, what he's done? He'd listen then, right? He'd have to see that it's a mistake inviting him into Annalisa's life if he knows everything Tony's done, everything he's capable of. I gnaw on my lip as I consider it.

A guard announces that our time is up and to say our good-byes, and I feel like I'm drowning. Walls are crumbling down around me and there's nothing I can do about it. Everything's imploding.

"I'm telling you, finding that man will be the worst mistake you've ever made." Aiden tries to convince Luke in a last-ditch effort.

But Luke's mind is made up; he's set on finding Anthony. "I get that you guys are her found family, but I'm blood, and so is he. Our mom's dead, and if I get the chance to reunite Anna with another blood relative, then I think she deserves the opportunity to get to know him. If I get out, all my time will be devoted to finding him. For Anna."

A guard comes over to our table and hauls Luke up. "I'd appreciate it if you guys didn't tell Anna anything. I don't want to give her any false hope before I can actually find him."

I'd appreciate it if you didn't tell Anna, I scream at him in my head, but he's already gone, pulled back through the door and handcuffed, leaving Aiden and me sitting on the metal bench, too stunned to realize just how royally screwed I am.

≫ ≪

The ride home is tense to say the least.

If Luke gets out, he's going to hand deliver me to the guy devoting himself to hunting me down. All of this will have been for nothing. I'll be served up on a platter for Tony to devour at his leisure.

Aiden's jaw is clenched and his knuckles are white from gripping the steering wheel.

I can't believe everything I've been working to protect is all about to be torn away from me. I don't want to leave, but at this point, it won't even matter if I do. I'm leaving to keep my friends safe from Tony, but if we set Luke free, he's going to personally invite Tony into their lives.

"What are you thinking about?" I ask Aiden once I can't take the silence anymore.

He takes a moment before he answers. "A lot of stuff."

"Me too." My mind is all over the place.

"Don't you think," he starts, choosing his words carefully, "that it's odd you ended up here?"

I don't follow his question. "In the car?"

"No. Here. In King City. With Anna."

It *is* a huge coincidence.

He continues. "Out of all places you could've been relocated to, they put you here, in King, where the man you're running from's *daughter* happens to be? Everything started because he was obsessed with the death of his daughter, and here you are, best friends with his other daughter? It's all just a little *convenient* if you ask me."

I connect the dots he's laying out. "You think they put me here on purpose?"

Aiden's jaw ticks. "It's just way too coincidental."

After everything I've gone through, would Agent Dylan actually do that to me? Put me somewhere Tony has a vested interest in? The wheels in my mind spin.

"You know," I start, "when I called Agent Dylan yesterday morning, something felt off. He was being really vague. I couldn't figure out why I felt so weird about that whole phone call, but if what you're saying is true . . ." My thoughts drift off. Are they actually planning on relocating me? He didn't seem all that worried by the video, and relocating me didn't seem like it was too urgent. "It felt like he was stalling."

Aiden's grip tightens on the steering wheel before he moves a hand to shift gears.

"Maybe they're stalling because they want him to find you." He scowls. "I did some searching on Tony, you know, and there's public outcry for him to be found. He shot at the cops. He killed a security guard at the mall. People are mad he hasn't been found yet, and every time something new about his past comes to light, it puts more pressure on them to catch him. Maybe they can't offer you up to him as bait legally, but why not plant you somewhere in case he happens to find out about Anna and comes to check her out?"

My stomach sinks and I slump back in the seat. The trees blurring by my window become even more unfocused. Would they really do that to me? Dangle me in shark-infested water as bait? Sure, they didn't handcuff me to a giant neon sign with arrows that says "Hey! Remember me, Tony? I'm right here!" but they left a trail of bread crumbs to that sign.

"You sound like a conspiracy theorist," I say without much conviction.

Aiden glances at me. "Our government's done worse things."

If that's true, is there really anyone I can trust? If they *want* Tony to find me here, isn't my presence here even more risky? I'm putting everyone in danger. No matter what I do, I keep grasping for a lifeline that's just out of reach. How can I take control of this situation? Should I tell Luke the truth? Or leave before Luke gets a chance to contact Tony? At least if I'm not here, Tony won't know I'm friends with everyone and won't hurt anyone? Is that grasping at straws? I need to do *something*.

"I know what you're thinking, and I don't like it," Aiden says, his muscles rigid.

"I don't know what you're talking about," I reply innocently, unable to look at him.

Aiden takes his eyes off the road for a few seconds to scan my face. "You're thinking that you're putting us all in danger and we'd be better off if you left."

Is he reading my mind? How does he always do that?

He answers my thoughts again. "I know you, Thea, and it's written all over your face."

"Can you blame me, Aiden? Luke might as well just kill me himself if he invites Tony here. Plus you guys will be in the cross fire and I couldn't stand it if—"

My body jerks as Aiden suddenly pulls over on the deserted road and hits the brakes, then shifts the car into Park. He turns in his seat to face me, the emotion and intensity in his eyes hitting me at full force and stealing the air from my lungs.

"You are not going anywhere before you need to. I literally just talked you off the ledge the other day. Let's talk this through and not do anything rash."

"But him seeing me in a video is way less risky than him actually *coming* here! And now that risk is double because of Anna! Why are you so adamant about putting yourself in danger? Just associating with me is a huge risk."

Aiden's voice is determined when he says, "Listen to me, Thea. You almost *died* because of me. My father basically ordered a hit on you." He looks away from me for a second, as if collecting his thoughts. Tenderness and vulnerability are in his voice and written all over his face when he speaks next.

"Thinking that I almost lost you, that you were in danger because of me, is probably the worst I've ever felt in my whole life."

My heart is breaking. Aiden is always so strong and confident and larger than life that it's easy to forget that he can be vulnerable too. I want to hug him and kiss him and reassure him, but I need to stay strong to get my point across.

"So you know exactly what I'm going through!"

Aiden doesn't hesitate. "I'd rather be in your life knowing there's a risk of danger than lose you completely."

I've died and gone to heaven and have been reborn as someone lucky enough to have Aiden Parker look at me the way he is right now.

"Aiden . . ."

"You could've left me," he continues. "You could've left me right then and there and no one would've blamed you. You know all the death threats I get every single day. You know my father's still out there, smiling for the cameras. You know he still hates me, and you know he could still hurt you to get to me. Hell, he even sent me a threat on my birthday saying exactly that. But you still stuck around. Not only do you have Tony to worry about, but now Andrew too. And you never even considered leaving because of me."

"The thought never even crossed my mind," I confess softly.

"I could tell you to leave to get away from Andrew, but honestly, when do you ever listen to me anyway?"

He chuckles at the last part and a small smile tugs at my lips. He brushes my hair behind my ear and rests his hand on my cheek.

"You're putting yourself at risk to be here for me. Let me do the same for you. I *can't* lose you, Thea."

It's the break in his voice that gets to me, almost tears me in two. I kiss him, wishing I was able to scramble over the center console, desperate to be near him, to get closer.

"You're not going anywhere," he says against my lips, his grip tightening on my waist. "And nothing is going to happen to you. If you're really in danger and need to leave, I'll be the first damn person packing your bags and shipping you off, but Luke can't do anything from where he is, and Agent Dylan knows about the video. Let's just slow down. We'll figure it out. Together."

I don't know how, but the conviction in his voice is sure and strong and reassuring. This is *Aiden*. He can do anything. I nod, words escaping me as my mind is consumed with all things Aiden.

"I love you," I tell him between kisses, feeling it with all of my soul.

My universe is whole when he whispers against my lips, "I love you, too, Thea."

16

The sun is setting as Aiden crosses into King City, right as Charlotte calls. I put her on speaker and mute the car's music so we can both hear her.

"Hey, Char, you're on speaker. Aiden's here."

"Thank God! I've been texting but you haven't answered." Her voice comes out in a rush. "Where are you? Are you home?"

"No, we'll be home in about . . ." I look at the clock, then at Aiden, who shrugs and fills in the blank for me. "About twenty minutes."

"Good," comes her relieved voice. "My parents are out of town for the night and Jake's throwing a party. You need to come."

Aiden and I exchange a glance. We were supposed to talk out what to do about this whole Luke situation. I'm still feeling frazzled about it. Can I really just go to a party and pretend Annalisa's *not* the daughter of my mortal enemy?

"Amelia?" Charlotte prompts. "Come on. It's going to be a bunch of Jake's friends and they're all college kids and I don't want to be outnumbered in my own house. Anna and Julian already bailed; I need at least one of my girlfriends here. Mason, Noah, and Chase are coming, but you know how they are at parties, I probably won't even see them the whole time."

I try to gauge Aiden's opinion, but he just downshifts and says, "Up to you."

"If it makes you feel better," Charlotte continues, a hopeful note in her voice, "no one will crash since it's a college party, so no Ryan."

I can't bail on Charlotte. House parties are part of feeling normal, and I'm trying to feel normal despite everything spinning out of my control. "Sure, we'll be there."

A high-pitched squeal emits from the phone and I hold it away from our ears. "Yes! Awesome! Look hot—well, you always do— but still! See you soon!" She ends the call before I can say anything.

"Guess we're going to a party," Aiden says.

We pull into Mason's driveway in no time. Natalia offered to watch Aiden's brothers while we went out today. We're picking them up so they can get ready for a birthday sleepover they were invited to, then we'll get changed and go to Charlotte's house.

I'm tempted to sit and wait in the car so I don't have to face Natalia, Mason, *or* Brian, but that feels rude, so I walk up to the door with Aiden and he rings the doorbell. Natalia opens the door, a wide smile on her face as she takes in Aiden and me.

"Amelia! So nice to see you again! Come in, come in." She ushers us in and closes the door behind us. I glance around, waiting for Brian to pop up.

"It's good to see you too." My face heats but I do my best to ignore it and try to plaster a look on my face that doesn't scream her husband is cheating on her. I hope it's not a grimace.

She gestures down the hallway and into the kitchen. "I just made enchiladas, Mason's favorite, so the boys are eating. There's plenty for everyone, come, grab a plate."

It *does* smell delicious, but I feel like throwing up. I try to hide the deer-in-the-headlights look on my face behind my hair. Where is Brian? The sick feeling in my stomach doubles over on itself at the thought that he might be with my mom *right now*.

"We ate already, but thank you, Natalia," Aiden answers since I apparently swallowed my tongue. We did pick up some fast food, and I'm grateful for it, because every second I stand here talking to Natalia is like a punch to the gut. She's such a kind, sweet woman.

"Are you sure? Do you want to take some home for lunch tomorrow?"

I force myself to stop eyeing the stairs in anticipation of Brian.

"We're okay, really, Natalia, thank you." Aiden smiles in his disarming way, and she concedes.

"All right, well, let me grab the boys." She walks away and then pauses and turns back. She lowers her voice. "Also, Aiden, between you and me, I think something's up with the boys. Maybe they should cut down on the violent video games, it might be affecting them more than you think. They're arguing and yelling at the TV . . . well, more than normal."

Aiden's eyebrows draw together. "Really? Thanks for telling me. I'll talk to them."

"And Aiden, as I keep offering, you boys are more than welcome to stay here. Sell your house. You don't need to move out; I love having a full house."

Aiden shakes his head. "Your help with the custody and mortgage paperwork is more than enough, thank you, Natalia."

She gives Aiden a small frown and mutters something about stubborn teenagers, but heads down the hallway, calling for Jason and Jackson. I think about what she said about the video games. Is Greg's death affecting the twins more than we were led to believe? Are they bothered about Andrew? Aiden's been sheltering them from the truth about the death threats, both from their biological dad and from strangers online.

"Hey," Mason greets us, appearing from the kitchen. He's wearing a gray crew neck sweater that accentuates his broad shoulders and jeans.

"Where's your dad?" I blurt and internally curse myself. Even Aiden shoots me a what the hell–play it cool look.

If Mason thinks it's weird, he doesn't let on. "He had to go into work today. You're coming to Char's right? You haven't been answering in the group chat."

Is being at work code for being with my mom? I clear my throat. "Yeah, sorry, we've been busy today and didn't check our phones. We're coming."

Mason leans against the wall beside us. "Cool. Fun date?"

No. "Absolutely."

"Oh, also, dude." Mason straightens up and lowers his voice like Natalia did. "Something's up with the twins. We were playing *Return of the Zombie Aliens* and they were yelling about killing and calling each other liars and they started pushing each other. Like, it was worse than any time we played at the beach house."

Before Aiden can say anything, the twins appear.

"Hey, guys." Aiden greets them as they throw on their jackets and shoes.

"Hi," they say in unison.

"We'll see you soon," Aiden says to Mason. Natalia's reappeared with two Tupperware containers of what I'm assuming are her enchiladas. She shoves one into Aiden's hand and one into mine.

"I really made too much. Take it for lunch tomorrow."

I might actually puke.

"Thanks," Aiden says for the both of us since my throat is dry. "And thanks for watching the twins for me today."

"Anytime," she says, her warm smile so like the one I'm used to seeing on Mason. "You really should ask for help more often. I'm happy to do it. And really, Aiden"—she puts a hand on his shoulder and gazes deeply into his eyes—"Stop being so stubborn. You're welcome to move back in any time you want."

I can't take it anymore. "Thanks for the food!" I blurt, running out of the house before anyone can comment on my odd behavior. I had to get out of there before I erupted from her genuine kindness. Aiden and his brothers follow a moment later, and soon we're all buckled up in the car.

Once we're on the road, Aiden's the first to break the silence. "So, boys, how was Mason's house?"

"Fine," they say together. They're sitting in the back, looking out the small windows on opposite sides of the car.

Aiden keeps his tone neutral. "So, is there anything you want to tell me?"

Jason and Jackson look at each other. It's almost creepy how in unison they are with their twin abilities. They're making faces at each other.

"Maybe you should wait until I'm not around," I tell Aiden. Whatever is going on with them might be something they don't want to admit in front of me.

"I want to tell you something, but Jason says we shouldn't," Jackson blurts, earning him an incredulous "*Jackson!*" from his twin.

They start arguing with each other about telling versus not telling, and Aiden pulls the car over on the shoulder of the road. He engages the parking brake and twists in his seat to look at his brothers.

"Hey!" he calls with authority, and even I stop whatever I was going to say. The twins stop arguing immediately. "Someone tell me what's going on right now."

Jason and Jackson glance at each other.

"Boys . . ." Aiden's looking at them in a way that scares even grown adults.

Jackson opens his mouth but Jason beats him to it. "I'm getting bullied in school!"

"*What?*" Aiden and Jackson exclaim at the same time, although Jackson's is more with shock, and Aiden's with rage.

"Who's bullying you? What are they saying? When did this start happening? Are they hitting you? Jackson, are you getting bullied too? Why didn't you want to tell me, Jason?" Aiden fires off question after question, the expression on his face one of barely restrained rage, not at his brothers, but at the bullies.

Have the kids at school found out about Greg? About the twins' biological father, Andrew? About what people are saying about Aiden online? Children are ruthless and it breaks my heart to run through the possible scenarios of the bullying they're facing.

Jason's face pales. "Not long. And no, no one's hitting me."

"They hit you, you hit them back harder, got it?" Aiden demands, and Jason's and Jackson's heads bob up and down.

I don't think that's the same advice a responsible adult would tell them, but I don't disagree with Aiden, and we would be huge hypocrites if we told them not to fight back.

"What are they saying?" Aiden continues, then looks at Jackson. "Why aren't you standing up for your brother? What are their names? I'm going to chat with them on Monday. Every one of those kids are already terrified of me, and that was before they pissed me off."

Jackson's face lights up bright red, and his twin seems equally flustered.

I put a hand on Aiden's arm. "You're scaring them."

Aiden's jaw ticks. He forces himself to take a breath. "Sorry. I'm sorry." His tone is much softer than before. "Why didn't you want to tell me, Jason?"

Jason finds his words. "Because . . ." He pauses for a beat, two, looks at his twin, who just glares at him, for help. Jason gestures at Aiden and waves his arms in his generic direction. "All this. You marching in is going to make it worse. Yeah, that's why I didn't say anything . . . about being bullied."

Jackson groans and looks out the window again.

Aiden's eyes narrow at the two of them. "You're being bullied and expect me not to do anything about it?"

Jason shifts in his seat. "Yes?" He sends me pleading eyes.

"Hey, Aiden, I know it's not my place, but I think Jason didn't want to tell you because he wants to sort it out himself. It might make it worse if you storm in and threaten a bunch of kids. Plus, that's kind of illegal." It's definitely illegal.

Jason sits up straighter and nods in agreement, and Jackson continues looking out the window at nothing, probably wishing to be anywhere but here.

Aiden scowls. "I wouldn't *threaten* them."

"Let me handle it, please?" Jason pleads.

Aiden's jaw works as he thinks it over. After what feels like forever, he exhales. "Fine. But if it gets worse, you tell me. Got it?"

Jason's head bounces up and down so fast I get dizzy. "Can we just drop it? And we're going to be late for Franco's birthday, so . . ." He points to the road a couple of times.

"Are the bullies going to be at the party?"

"No."

Aiden gives Jason and his brother one last serious look for good measure, then finally turns around and puts the car in gear. His hand is clenched around the stick shift, but he doesn't say anything else, not even when Jason tries to discreetly shove Jackson, probably as retribution for admitting they were hiding something from Aiden. I don't blame them; Aiden can be scary. But I'd rather they tell him so we can help if we can. I just hope it gets better before Aiden really decides to do something about it.

>> <<

Aiden doesn't say anything else to the twins about what happened in the car, even though I know it's bothering him. They grab their stuff for Franco's birthday sleepover while Aiden gets changed for Charlotte's house, then Aiden drops them off at the party, and we finally arrive at my house.

Mom's not home, and I can't help but wonder if she's with Brian. I send her a text to let her know I'm home but going out again, and store Natalia's enchiladas in the fridge. I wonder if Brian will come over and recognize the Tupperware and the food inside.

Since Mom's not here, she can't say anything about me bringing Aiden up to my room. He's sitting on my bed, pretending to look interested when I hold up different outfit options. The folder sits on the edge of the bed near him, taunting me. Every once in a while he picks it up to scan it, as if new information will appear, and I figure he's trying to distract himself from thinking about his brothers. He told me he didn't want to talk about it when we dropped the twins off, so I let it go. For now.

"Which one, Aiden?' I ask, ignoring the stupid folder that's making me feel like everything I've ever known was a lie. Does Agent Dylan even care about my safety? Did he even care if I post stuff online? It's been a year since this all started—are they tired and just want to use me as bait so it's over with?

"The first dress you showed me." Aiden gestures noncommittally, then moves the folder out of my view. "Stop thinking about it, at least for tonight. Don't worry about Luke. What information can he realistically find out from jail?"

I throw the dresses I was holding onto the bed and plop down beside them.

"But what if he *does* find a way to contact Tony?" I frown, and Aiden puts his hands on my waist and pulls me closer to him.

"He can't do any research in jail, Thea. And even if he *does* contact Tony, what are the odds that Tony even wants anything to do with Anna? Isn't he devoted to hunting you down? You think he's going to drop all that to reconnect with a kid he didn't even know he had and probably wants nothing to do with?"

My frown deepens as I study my hands. "I don't know? Maybe he'd think of Anna as, like, his replacement for Sabrina?"

Aiden's thumbs move in small circles on my waist. "Okay, how about Anna? I'm almost one hundred percent positive she'd want nothing to do with her biological father if Luke went to her with contact information."

"I guess. But what if Luke thinks he knows what's best for her and contacts him anyway?"

Aiden sighs, and it must be a testament to his patience that he doesn't get frustrated with me being so exasperating.

"And like I said, he's in jail."

Realistically, he's right. But there are way too many possibilities—way too many risks and variables that could go wrong, and I'm not willing to risk it.

"Or," Aiden continues, "you can always just tell Anna."

My head snaps up and I all but shove him away from me. "Are you serious?"

He holds up his hands in defense. "Hey, just thinking of all angles. If you tell Anna about Tony she'll tell Luke to stop looking."

"I cannot just go around telling everyone about my secret identity!" I throw a pillow at him. "It's supposed to be a *secret*, remember?" Even if Agent Dylan apparently wants it *not* to be.

He catches the pillow as it harmlessly hits his chest and sets it down. "I know. It was just a suggestion. We should consider all options."

"I can't tell her that her biological dad's a psychopath."

"Why not? My dad's a psychopath and I'm nothing like him."

"I know that, and I know she's nothing like Tony. But her brother's in jail for murder. If we tell her about how her biological father actually has killed people and is hunting me down, she's really going to start believing the gossip at school and think that she's from a . . ."

I drift off, knowing that Aiden knows I mean a "family of killers," like everyone's saying.

"So." I stand up. "That brings us back to the whole what are we going to do about Luke situation."

Aiden studies me seriously. "Like I said, he can't do anything from jail."

"And we're working to prove that he's innocent. If we're successful, he won't be there for long."

"But what if he's not innocent?"

"Are you saying that we should stop looking?" Annalisa's destroyed over this, and she's put all her trust in me to help her out. We really couldn't do that to her.

Aiden shrugs a single shoulder. "He probably did it, anyway."

"But we promised Anna we'd help free him." *I* promised Annalisa we'd help free him.

Aiden gets off the bed to stand in front of me, his full height forcing me to look up at him. "If they have no intention of relocating you to keep you close to Anna, then the answer seems clear to me. Keep Luke in jail, keep Tony away from you, and keep you here, with me. I don't care what happens or what promises we have to break, as long as you're always still here, with me."

Those words erupt like millions of butterflies in my chest. Is he right about them wanting me to be here because of Annalisa? Can we really be that selfish? Can I really just live happily ever after with Aiden, everyone else be damned?

Annalisa's broken face pops into my mind. She's always so strong and fierce and has always had my back, no matter what threats I've faced. Can I really sabotage her only chance to reunite with her brother?

"Do you have a better solution than to just let the legal system find him guilty and keep him in there?" Aiden asks, sensing my hesitance.

"I don't know. What if he *is* innocent and we could've done something about it, like we promised Anna."

"How about this. We still help look. For all we know, Luke really did it. All the evidence points to him, anyway. But because

Brent Library Service

Customer ID: ********4670

Items that you have borrowed

Title: Still with me
ID: 91120000530072
Due: 09 October 2023

Title: Why is nobody laughing?
ID: 91120000527776
Due: 09 October 2023

Total items: 2
Account balance: £0.00
Borrowed: 2
Overdue: 0
Hold requests: 0
Ready for collection: 0
18/09/2023 14:30

we care about Anna and want to help her, we can keep looking. If we find evidence that he really didn't do it, then we'll figure out what to do when we get there. You might not even be here by then. But if we happen to find something before everyone else, then we can decide what we want to do."

I don't answer Aiden right away because I can't even begin to consider not helping my friend, but what he's saying holds some weight.

"I'm not saying we condemn an innocent man," he continues. "I'm saying let's find out everything we can and take it from there."

He's putting a lot of faith in Luke being guilty and us not finding anything to free him. But if we *do* find something, could we really not tell our friends? Could we really put my fear of Tony and need to stay with Aiden over everything else?

"Did you forget everything I said to you earlier? I am *not* going to lose you. I watched one man almost shoot you. I'm not going to stand around and let Luke invite another man to come and do the same. Understand?" Aiden wraps his arms around me and pulls me into his strong embrace, and I'm lost for words. We're technically not doing anything wrong. We might not even find anything. And if we do, we'll do the right thing.

Probably.

Wrapped in the safety of Aiden's embrace, I let my mind drift to all the things I need to do before I can live a normal, boring life: find evidence of Luke's innocence before everyone else, keep Luke from contacting Tony, tell Mason about his dad's affair with my mom, take down Aiden's dad, get Kaitlyn and Ryan off my back, and pass calculus.

Simple.

17

By the time we get to Charlotte's house, it's pitch-black outside and the party is in full swing. The music is loud and plays throughout the house, and various Solo cups and empty beer bottles cover every table in sight. A couple of people are playing beer pong on a gray folding table in the hallway, with others around them cheering them on. There are a bunch of people I've never seen before all over the place, and I decide I don't mind. As far as I can tell, any fights or drama happening tonight will not involve me or my friends.

Following Aiden through the house, I greet random people as we pass. Everyone seems friendly, and older, since Jake is in college.

"Aiden! We were wondering when you were going to get here!" Charlotte exclaims. "Where's Amelia?"

I step around Aiden and watch Charlotte do a double take. "Ohmygod."

She gets unnecessarily close to me, picks up a strand of my

hair, and holds it an inch away from her face. "Your hair! It's so pretty."

I shift my head and my hair slides out of her hands. "Are you drunk?"

"No. But my friends took so long to get here, and I was all awkward and alone. So I joined in on some drinking games."

"Where's everyone else?" I ask her, looking around the crowd for our friends.

She waves her hand noncommittally. "Here somewhere. They said something about hot college girls and took off."

A group of guys walk by us, the one in the lead winking at Charlotte as he passes, leaving her blushing and biting back a smile. When he's out of sight, she turns back to me and exclaims, "*Oh my god,* did you see that?"

"The one who *totally* just checked you out? Yes!" I exclaim.

This is what I've been missing. Just being at a party, having fun, talking about boys with one of my best friends.

Aiden dips his head near ours. "I'm going to find the guys. Don't get into too much trouble." He drops a kiss on my head and turns to get lost in the crowd.

"Okay, so that guy is one of Jake's best friends." She grabs my arm and leads me to the living room slash dance floor.

We spot him near the wall at the far end of the room, talking to some other people.

"His name is Marcus," she continues. "Isn't he *so hot*? Jake gets mad at me when I say it, but it's not my fault he's friends with hot guys."

Marcus *is* a good-looking guy, with broad shoulders, dark skin, stubble covering his jaw, and what seems like an outgoing confidence and an easy smile.

"Why don't you go over there and talk to him?" I ask as Aiden comes back to us. "Did you find them?"

"Yeah, they were . . . preoccupied."

I fake gag and laugh with him, not asking for any more details since I can already guess what's keeping the guys "preoccupied."

Charlotte looks at us, then at Marcus, then down at the drink in her hand. "You know what, I think I will."

She downs the rest of her drink and hands me the empty cup before making her way through the dancing bodies and over to the group of people Marcus is talking to.

A Siren of the Heart song comes on that I like, and I automatically move my hips a little to the rhythm.

Aiden notices. "Dance with me."

I'm taken aback a bit. For some reason I can't picture Aiden dancing.

"Really? You want to dance?"

He grins, and I set Charlotte's empty cup on a table as he pulls me onto the makeshift dance floor. He tugs me closer to him, and together we move to the music, laughing and singing along to the songs that come on. My heart soars. I'm having so much fun that I forget I'm not Amelia. It's just me and Aiden having fun at a party like anyone else our age.

Aiden dips his head and his lips graze mine before he's yanked away from me and we're ripped apart. Confused, Aiden turns to see who pulled him from me, and we find a very angry-looking Noah, yelling something about "How could you cheat on Amelia?" over the music.

Cheat on Amelia? Did I hear him right?

I can't hear what Aiden's saying, but Noah looks over at me for the first time and stills.

"Amelia?" Noah asks.

"Yeah?" I reply.

Noah's eyebrows draw together in confusion for a second, then he bursts out laughing.

"Oh my God, dude, you scared me," he says to Aiden. "Sorry, but I thought." He pauses and scans me. "From behind and in this lighting, I thought you were Kaitlyn, you know, 'cuz of the hair."

The blood drains from my face. Oh no. Everyone's going to think I changed my hair because I wanted to look like Kaitlyn. Maybe I should've gone darker instead of lighter.

Noah notices my uneasiness. "No, don't get me wrong, you look great! Superhot, like always."

I laugh when Aiden shoves him, and Noah turns to apologize to the guy he bumped into. He tells him it's not a problem, then notices Aiden.

"Hey, Aiden Parker, right?"

"Yeah, do I know you?"

"Oh no," the guy says. "But I've seen you all over the news. Sorry about your shitty father. But hey, recent polls have said his popularity is decreasing, so congrats."

"Yeah, thanks," Aiden replies before the guy is off talking to other people.

Noah continues talking to me, but Aiden retreats into his own mind. That's not the first time someone has said something like that to him, but that's probably the first one who's actually old enough to vote *and* knows what's going on in the polls.

"There you guys are!" Mason comes up to us. "We've got a problem."

A problem? Really? A problem?! Can't we just go to one damn party without someone telling us there's a problem?

Automatically, I scan the place for Ryan, but stop when Mason adds, "It's Chase."

"Is he okay?" I ask.

"No—I don't know. We were just drinking and having a good time when he checked his phone and saw that Charlotte uploaded a video to her S-Live Time profile, and he started freaking out."

Aiden, Noah, and I exchange confused glances as our minds race. What could she have posted that would make Chase react like that?

Mason holds out his phone and opens the app. "He said something like 'Really, a fucking college guy?' and started swearing and broke a lamp and then I lost him."

We crowd around Mason's phone and he clicks Play on Charlotte's latest video. It's posted to her story profile, so it goes away in twenty-four hours. It's her and Marcus. She's sitting on his lap and they're singing along with the song to the camera. She looks like she's having fun.

Good for her. I'm glad that she's getting out there and having fun. Then Marcus grabs her face, turns her to face him, and kisses her. The camera cuts out. *Oh*. I'm still proud of her, but that explains why Chase flipped. The video jumps to them singing again, but Marcus is behind her, and it looks like they're walking up the stairs?

Aiden and I lock eyes immediately.

"You don't think . . ." he starts.

"He wouldn't . . ." Noah adds, all our minds jumping to the beach house when he and Chase had a fistfight.

Oh no. Oh, no, no, no. Chase *cannot* do this to her.

Not again.

We take off toward the hallway where the stairs are. There were a bunch of chairs stacked up at the base of the stairs to discourage partygoers from going upstairs, but the chair barrier was destroyed, as if someone ripped it open in a hurry.

This is not good.

We file in through the opening and run up the stairs where the music isn't as loud, and right away we hear yelling coming from Charlotte's room. When we get there, the door is wide open. Charlotte and Chase are squared off in a yelling match, and Marcus is standing off to the side looking confused and a little concerned.

"You can't keep barging in on me whenever you feel like it! The door was closed for a reason!" She looks incredibly mad, not even caring that she's standing there in her bra and jeans.

"The first time was an accident!" Chase defends his actions.

"And this time wasn't! You need to mind your own damn business and not care about who I hook up with in my own room!"

This is a different side of Charlotte. I don't know if it's because she's been drinking or has just had enough of the double standards, but I don't think I've ever really seen her mad, never mind actually yelling at someone. The last time this happened, she was more timid and let Noah deal with it, but it looks like she's not backing down this time.

"I can't do that when you're prancing around posting videos of you making out with strangers for the whole damn world to see!"

Charlotte scoffs. "Stranger? Marcus is one of Jake's best friends! And it was just a kiss! Barely even three seconds!"

Marcus shifts his weight from foot to foot. His shirt is on inside out and he's looking back and forth at the two of them like he can't decide if he should jump in and defend Charlotte or get the hell out of here.

"Still!" Chase huffs. "You shouldn't be posting videos like that and you shouldn't be in your room with this guy! You look like a—"

"Like a what, Chase? Say it," she challenges, her eyes narrowed in deadly slits.

"Like a slut! You're acting like a slut!" he fills in, and my jaw drops open.

He. Did. Not.

"*Oh, really?*" she shouts. "*I'm* the slut?! Were you not just in the bathroom with Olivia, like, ten minutes ago?"

I look over at Mason, who nods in confirmation.

"That's different!" Chase defends himself, but Charlotte isn't having it.

"You're right. You're worse. You're a hypocrite. You hook up with girls left, right, and center. Why is it okay if you do it but if a girl does, she's a slut? You have no right to say anything. Do you even remember half of their names? I kiss a boy I actually *like* and *I'm* the slut?"

"That's not what you look like to everyone els—"

"Honestly, Chase, fuck off. Fuck *right* off. I'm not going to stand here in my own house and have you call me a slut."

Who *is she*? The girl in front of us right now isn't the timid and nonconfrontational Charlotte we know. She's *better*.

Maybe hanging around me and Annalisa is starting to rub off on Charlotte because she is not taking anyone's shit and standing up for herself, and I'm living for it. Or maybe she was just tired of not speaking up. If Annalisa had come tonight, she'd be behind Charlotte with pom-poms cheering her on.

Chase looks just as shocked as the rest of us. Charlotte's never sworn at him before. He doesn't let that take any of the wind out of his sails, however, and recovers quickly.

"I'm just looking out for you! You're drunk! You're not seeing clearly!"

"I'm seeing more clearly than I have in a long time." Her voice is steady, and I notice for the first time that she isn't slurring like she was when we got to the party. "Get out of my house."

"Not until you delete that video. Give me your phone." He spots her phone resting on her dresser.

"What? *No!*" she yells, racing him to the dresser.

"What's with all the yelling?" Charlotte's brother Jake asks, walking into her room and freezing as he takes in the scene in front of him.

Chase and Charlotte don't even glance at him. Chase gets to the dresser first, turning his back to Charlotte and punching in the code to unlock her phone.

"You have *no right*," she yells, trying to reach around him.

"I'm looking out for you!" he argues, twisting and turning so that his large back is always facing her, preventing her from grabbing her phone.

"You're being an *asshole!*"

Charlotte uses Chase's shoulders for leverage and jumps onto his back like he's giving her a piggyback, wrapping her legs around his waist and reaching over his shoulder for her phone.

Aiden puts his arm out in front of me and pushes me back a couple of steps. Everyone else steps back a bit, too, giving them space as they grapple around the room.

Chase turns to his side and throws himself onto Charlotte's bed, taking her down with him. Charlotte's small and quick, so she manages to scramble over him, yank her phone out of his hand, and jump off of the bed.

Chase gets up as well and is advancing toward her when suddenly Charlotte winds her arm back and whips her phone as hard as she can onto the floor. The action takes everyone but

Charlotte by surprise as the phone shatters, and we all stare at it with wide eyes.

"*There*," she yells. "Now get the *fuck* out of my house!"

Whoa. I did *not* see any of this coming when I got here a couple of hours ago.

Chase gives her an incredulous look, as if *she's* the one who just barged into his room while he was hooking up with someone, called him a slut, and tried to invade his privacy.

Jake's look travels from me, Aiden, Mason, and Noah beside him near the door, to his disheveled friend Marcus across the room, to a shirtless Charlotte, and finally to a pissed off Chase. The story clicks together in his head.

"I think it's time for you to call a cab, Chase." Jake gestures to the door with his head.

"Fine." Chase storms past us and out the door, not sparing any of us a second glance. I think we're all too shocked to say anything to him anyway.

Marcus walks up to Jake. "Dude, I know she's your little sister and I'm sorry I just—"

Jake holds up a hand without looking at him. "Stop. Just don't."

Marcus sighs, then sends Charlotte a look that I'm assuming is a silent apology, and walks out of her room.

"Are you okay?" Jake asks his sister.

"Peachy," she replies, picking up her shirt and slipping it on.

He gestures at the shattered pieces of her phone. "That was a little dramatic, don't you think?"

She shrugs.

Jake picks up the bigger pieces of Charlotte's phone and brushes his finger across the hardwood. "Oh shit, you scratched the floor. Dad's gonna flip."

She sighs, the fight from earlier leaving her as her shoulders slump. "I'll deal with it later. Get a rug or something. Whatever."

He places the pieces on her dresser and leaves her room to get back to his party. The five of us remain as an awkward silence settles over us, all unsure what to say.

"Well, that's not fair," Noah breaks the silence. "Chase punched me last time, and Marcus walks on out of here without a single hair out of place."

All of us turn to look at Noah like Really?! and he holds up his hands in defense.

"What? Someone had to say it!"

18

When I show up at Charlotte's house Sunday morning, I'm met with a disaster. Apparently, Jake went to sleep without even attempting to clean up the mess from the night before. We would've volunteered to help clean up, since we were all here, and even Julian came by after helping his dad with work, but she told us not to worry about it.

"Don't mind the mess. Jake's so lazy he said he hired some people to come clean later today," she says, closing the door behind me.

We head upstairs, stepping over discarded Solo cups and dried up spills, and avoiding glass bottles. Charlotte closes the door to her room and we sit cross-legged on her bed.

"So." I don't even know how to start. "Do you remember anything from last night?"

"Oh, you mean the whole thing about my best friend since elementary school calling me a slut and trying to go through my phone and control my life? Yeah, I remember."

"I'm sorry that happened, Char. It was a shitty thing for him to do. We probably should've intervened but I'm glad you stood your ground."

"No, I'm glad no one stepped in. It was time for me to say something. He can't turn violent every time I'm with a boy and try to make my decisions for me. Just because I don't feel the same way as he does, it doesn't give him the right to control me."

I think that's the first time Charlotte's blatantly stated that she doesn't like Chase. She usually says she doesn't *think* she does, or she doesn't know how to feel. But this is signed and sealed. She does not like Chase as more than a friend, and I'm pretty sure after what he pulled last night, there's nothing he could do to change her mind.

"How do you feel about him as a friend?" I ask. They've been friends for ten years; it would suck if their friendship ended like that.

She hugs a pillow to her chest. "Until he realizes what he did and apologizes, I don't want anything to do with him. *No one* has the right to go through my social media and censor what I can and can't post. No one's taking my free will, even over something this stupid. It's the principle of it."

I understand what she means. I can't even have social media because of a man and it sucks. Charlotte's a free person and can do whatever she wants, and no one should be telling her what to do with her own life, especially not someone motivated by anger and jealousy.

My eyes zero in on the spot where she smashed her phone, and I feel a smile form as the memory shapes in my mind. "Was that really necessary, though? Now you don't have a phone."

"Yes. I made my point, didn't I?"

We look at each other and start laughing, replaying the incident over and over.

"I already miss my phone, though," she says eventually. "Do you mind if I use yours to look at the videos I posted last night? I want to see them again."

I hand her my phone and we download the S-Live Time app since I don't have it, and she logs into her account to watch the videos now saved to her profile.

"Wow, Marcus is so hot. I can't believe Chase screwed that up for me. I *never* cockblock him when he's with whatever girl he's with!"

"You're not madly in love with him," I state as she hands me my phone to watch the videos.

"If I was madly in love with someone, I wouldn't be hooking up with people left, right, and center like he does."

It's sad when you think about it. Chase never told Charlotte about his feelings because he didn't want to ruin their friendship, but in not telling her, he ended up ruining it anyway.

I watch the videos again, and they seem harmless enough. She's singing and laughing with Marcus and the kiss barely lasts one whole Mississippi. Chase's reaction was definitely not a reasonable response to the video she posted.

As we're analyzing the videos, my phone rings, and Chase's name pops up. We drop the phone on the bed and stare at it like it just came to life and is cussing us out.

"Should I . . . ?" I hesitate.

"I'm not here," she says, promptly answering and putting it on speaker, looking at me expectantly.

I clear my throat. "Hello?"

His voice is clear through the phone. "Hey, Amelia. Have you talked to Charlie since last night?"

Charlotte fake vomits at the use of his affectionate nickname for her, then shakes her head to tell me to say no.

"Um, not really?" I flinch since it came out like a question.

"Oh," he sounds sad, empty almost. "How mad do you think she is?"

"I don't need to talk to her to know that she's pissed, Chase."

Charlotte hums her approval.

"I know, I just—I don't know. I was drinking and saw her with that guy and lost it. That should be me. Not Noah or Marcus or whatever guy doesn't know her like I do. *Me*."

Charlotte's nostrils flare and her leg starts bouncing.

"You can't make that decision for her, Chase."

Charlotte writes something on a piece of paper.

"I wasn't thinking. I want her to know I love her and I was trying to look out for her."

She holds up the paper that she was writing on for me to see and shakes it to make her point. *He called me a slut!!!*

"You were trying to control her," I tell him, then add, "and you called her a slut."

Charlotte overexaggerates her nod to let me know she likes that I worked that in for her.

"Well, she was upstairs with a guy she just met . . ."

Charlotte and I are both wide eyed. Oh, I am *so ready* to fight.

"But," he continues, "I know I had no right to say that, especially not with how I act. I realize it makes me a hypocrite, but man, did seeing that piss me off."

Charlotte's furiously scribbling on the paper and I read her main points as she writes.

"Marcus wasn't random, he's friends with Jake and she's known him for years. And even if he wasn't, that's none of your business.

Plus, whatever she did or didn't do with him isn't any of our business. And you're right. You were literally with a girl *you* barely knew that same night and no one called you a slut."

Charlotte all but throws the pen down. This would be so much easier if she would just talk to him instead of pretending I'm not with her right now.

"I know, I know. I just wish I could talk to her and tell her—"

"Hey, Char! Your brother let me in." Annalisa's voice is loud and crystal clear as she walks into the room. "What the hell happened with Chase last night?!"

"Gottagobye!" I yell into the phone in a single breath and end the call as quickly as possible.

Charlotte and I shoot Annalisa a pointed look and she pauses. "What?"

For some reason I feel like laughing. This is what normal teenage girls do, right? Worry about boy drama and help their friends through it? Out of all my problems—Luke, Andrew Kessler, my mom's affair, Tony—this one's the one that doesn't even affect me directly, but it's the one I'm most glad to help out with. If only mediating phone calls between fighting friends was my biggest problem. But then I stare at Annalisa, really stare at her, and it all comes back to me. She's Tony's daughter. She doesn't look like him, does she?

Charlotte fills Annalisa in on the events of last night, but the whole time I'm just struck by the thought that this is the first time I'm seeing Annalisa since the revelation of who her father is. It was just yesterday that Luke spun my whole world around with this information, and I haven't really had time to process how I feel about it. Annalisa is my friend; she's nothing like the man who has kidnapped me, stabbed me, thrown me down the stairs, and killed the people around me.

But she *is* his daughter. Could she really be like him?

I look at Annalisa like I've been given a new pair of glasses and now have a different view of the world. Sure, she's more aggressive than me or Charlotte, but she's not violent, and she's definitely not a psychopath.

"Earth to Amelia?" Annalisa waves her hand back and forth in front of my face to get my attention.

I shake my head to clear my thoughts.

This is Annalisa we're talking about.

Annalisa.

She's been my friend practically since day one. She's always had my back and she's never done anything to hurt me. Aiden is right; he's nothing like his crazy dad and he actually grew up with him for some time. And after that, he was left with Greg as his guardian, and he's nothing like him either.

Annalisa has never even met her psychopathic father, Tony, so not only is she free from his corruption, but he was basically just her sperm donor. Annalisa is her own person and just because she might be biologically related to the man ruining my life, it doesn't mean she's anything like him. Annalisa has a good soul and she is a good person, and I know that no matter what, she'll have my back.

"Sorry, what were you saying?" I turn my attention back to Annalisa and try not to picture any resemblances she may have to Tony. As far as I can tell, she looks nothing like him, thank goodness.

"I was just saying how I talked to Luke yesterday."

That *really* gets my attention. Aiden and I were just with Luke yesterday. Did she see us? Did Luke tell her about our visit? Did he already tell her about Tony?

I try to school my expression to one of interest and not absolute panic. "Oh really? When did you go see him?"

"No, he called yesterday. We were trying to figure out a different angle of where he could have been that night. He suggested we try checking all the bars that he used to go to before he got sober. He thought that would be a good lead."

She's not looking at me with suspicion or asking why I went to see her brother without her. Either Luke didn't mention our visit, which I hope is what happened since he didn't want her to know about her father yet, or she's just a very good liar. I remember what Aiden said, about us trying to find information on our own to protect me, and feel guilty.

"Do you want us to come with you to check them out?"

She waves me off. "No, I already went to some last night and didn't find anything."

Charlotte wraps her arms around Annalisa reassuringly. "We'll find something, Anna. You'll get him back in your life."

And if she does, she might get another man in her life as well. One that she's completely better off without.

19

The next day at school is business as usual; or at least it is before Kaitlyn shows up. Annalisa is at my locker before school starts when Kaitlyn walks by.

"Oh my God, what happened?" I ask Kaitlyn, genuinely concerned.

She looks *terrible*. She has an angry black eye that's tinged with purples and greens, there's a small cut in her eyebrow and her lip, and her arm is in a sling.

Even though I don't like the girl, I've been there, and I know it *sucks*. She looks from me to Annalisa, and back at me with narrowed eyes.

"Like you don't know," she answers coolly before walking down the hallway.

Okay, that was weirder than usual.

"What was that about?" I ask Annalisa, who just shrugs.

We barely make it ten steps down the hall before two school officers stop us, Principal Anderson between them. I've only met

Kaitlyn's mom once when I first transferred to King City High. She's a petite woman with pale skin and has the same intense eyes as Kaitlyn.

"Ms. White. Come with us."

Annalisa and I look at each other, confused.

"Why?" she asks, eying the two school officers.

Other kids start to notice and are pausing to whisper to each other. I hear mumbles of "Wacko Anna White" and clench my fists to remind myself not to make a scene.

"Just come along. Let's not make this harder than it has to be, Annalisa."

Annalisa's eyebrows are drawn together when she looks back at me, but she steps toward Principal Anderson anyway, and they make their way down the hall.

I'm left standing there confused. Why would the principal need to talk to Anna? And why would she need *two* officers to do it? That fact doesn't go unnoticed as Annalisa walks down the hall with her head held high. "Wacko Anna White" is being mumbled by almost every student she passes. With nothing else to do, I send a quick text in the group chat and go to first period before the bell.

I sit with Charlotte in class, Mason and Noah in the desk behind us, and none of us can figure out what happened. It isn't until the end of class when we're walking to our next class that we find out. I meet Aiden at my locker as usual to get my books for calculus when Annalisa comes up to us, fuming mad, the two officers still trailing her.

"*They expelled me!*" she yells, the anger and irritation rolling off of her in waves as she marches toward us.

"What? Why?" I ask.

"They said I beat up Kaitlyn! *Me!* I didn't touch that stupid bitch."

Aiden's confused. He hasn't seen Kaitlyn yet, so I quickly tell him how we saw her this morning.

"Why did they say you did that?" he asks, eyeing the officers behind her.

"Kaitlyn sat there crying to her mother about how I ran into her Saturday night and 'decided to attack her and beat her up for no reason other than being crazy.' Can you believe that?! As if I wouldn't have a reason."

Saturday night we were all at Charlotte's party. Well, all of us except Annalisa. She said she was checking Luke's old bars. Did she lie to us?

"Ms. White, you need to be off school property," one of the guards reminds her.

"*I'm going!*" she snaps at him, then turns back to look at us. "I'm going to have to go to Commack now. I'm going to be a Silver! This is fucked up on so many levels!"

She hits a locker beside me out of frustration and I automatically flinch. I feel Aiden's reassuring hand rest on my waist.

"Ms. White," one of the guards warns, and she focuses her deadly gaze on him. She's about to unleash her wrath when Principal Anderson appears.

"You are no longer allowed on school property, Annalisa. Collect your things and leave immediately."

Annalisa's eye twitches. "I didn't hit your *fucking delusional daughter*, and if I did, I'd own up to it because she would've deserved it!"

I've seen Annalisa mad before, but this is probably the angriest she's ever been. Now that I know who she's related to, it's hard not to get flashbacks and make connections. Will she snap, like *he* did? Is she really capable of flipping a switch and attacking someone out of nowhere?

I shake my head. Annalisa is *nothing* like Tony. Just because she shares his DNA, it doesn't mean she's like him.

At her outburst, Principal Anderson takes a few steps back from Annalisa, and of course, all the students walking by are paying attention. This isn't helping the rumors going around about Annalisa at all.

"We've been over this. It's your word against hers. And given the fact that it's no secret you're prone to outbursts, especially toward my daughter, as attested to by multiple students, it's obvious that you're lying. You're lucky we're not pressing charges. Now, please collect your things and remove yourself from school property."

Attested to by multiple students?

The rumors.

Aliyah was saying how everyone was talking about how Anna snapped at Kaitlyn for no reason the other day. The rumor mill works fast, and in this case, against us.

Annalisa's nostrils flare, and her eyes are doing nothing to hide her outrage. "*I am not lying! You and your daughter are both giant fucking cu—*"

"Anna!" I interrupt, stepping forward to grab her arm. "We'll fix this, don't make it worse," I whisper to her.

How? I don't know. But I'm pretty sure calling the principal and her daughter the C-word isn't going to make anything better.

"Fine," she says, straightening her black sweater and composing herself. "I'm going. Can you guys get my stuff in my locker for me?"

Aiden and I tell her we will.

"Great. I'll see you guys after." She turns to Principal Anderson and shoots her a sinister smile. "I don't need the escort off of school property, I'm leaving. Fuck you, and have a nice day."

With that, she pivots on her heel and struts down the hall, the officers following her anyway, her head held high despite the stares and murmurs about her following in her brother's footsteps.

Aiden and I stand there staring after her, trying to process everything we've just learned.

Principal Anderson tugs on the sleeves of her blazer. "Get to class, Mr. Parker," she directs at both of us, I'm assuming leaving me out since she probably doesn't remember my name, and then she turns to leave.

>> <<

News about Annalisa's expulsion spreads fast. Aiden and I barely get to calculus before we get texts from our friends about what happened. Some people are even brave enough to come right up to Aiden and ask him before scurrying away in fear from the warning look he shoots them.

By the time lunch period rolls around, it's all anyone is talking about. The usually calm and levelheaded Julian had to walk out of school in the middle of third period to stop himself from punching a kid in the face.

I haven't seen Kaitlyn yet, but I'm sure she's lapping up the attention. No one's stopped to wonder whether Kaitlyn is full of shit or not. Hell, even *I* thought Annalisa did it for a second there. It's only when I'm walking to class after lunch that I run into Kaitlyn. I skip all the preamble and jump right to the point.

"Anna didn't touch you. Why in the world would you say she did?"

I'm almost tempted to pull a She's Faking It! and rip the sling off her arm and wipe the FX bruising makeup off of her face. I wouldn't put it past her to make this up just to screw with us. But I've been injured enough to know that her face really *is* bruised, and her lip really *is* split.

She studies me with her piercing eyes, the bruise doing nothing to hide the animosity within them.

"What are you talking about?"

The arm in the sling isn't in a cast, and I can see the very faintest reminiscence of a bruise in the shape of finger imprints, identical to the one currently on my wrist, even though they're both almost completely gone.

How did I not make the connection sooner?

"Kaitlyn." I move closer to her and lower my voice. "You and I both know Ryan's the one who did this to you." I gesture to my wrist to make a point. "You need to tell someon—"

She steps away from me like I threw ice water all over her.

"I have no idea what you're talking about," she insists, her voice hard and final.

But I hear it. The very slight waver in her voice that tells me I'm right. Even though we're enemies and she just got my best friend expelled, I feel for her.

"You don't need to go through this alone," I persist. "Ryan can't keep hurting you—"

"You have no idea what you're saying." She cuts me off, then projects her voice so the people walking around us can hear. "Annalisa White did this to me! She's psychotic. You can spin whatever lies you want but the truth is she attacked me out of nowhere and was rightly expelled for it."

"Kaitlyn—"

"You and your friends need to leave me alone," she sneers, leaning in threateningly toward me. "And don't think I haven't noticed your hair. You're trying so hard to be me it's pathetic."

And with that, she spins on her heel and struts down the hallway, leaving me no room to protest.

How do you help someone who doesn't want to be helped? Especially when that person hates you with a burning passion.

20

Since all our friends still have no idea what's going on, and Annalisa wants to talk about what happened, we get together after school. Aiden's house is the most logical spot to meet since he has a free house and doesn't have babysitting for his brothers.

Charlotte and I volunteer to stay back and grab all of Annalisa's stuff from her locker, so by the time I get to Aiden's, everyone else has already taken up the parking spots in his driveway. Apparently, someone else on his street doesn't care it's a Monday night and is throwing a party, because there are cars everywhere. I have to park down the block, but I don't mind, since it's a pretty nice day out.

"So, have you and Chase still not talked?" I ask Charlotte as we walk to Aiden's house.

Third period chemistry, the class I share with Chase and Charlotte, was awkward to say the least. She's still mad at him for the way he acted at her brother's house party, and I think Chase just doesn't know what to say to make it right. The only reason lunch wasn't an awkward disaster was because we were all wrapped up in what had just happened with Annalisa.

"Nope. And I don't plan on talking to him unless he makes the effort to come up to me first," she says with a stubborn set to her jaw.

I can't really blame her. I'm sure if my best friend of ten years acted like that toward me, I'd be much pettier than her right now.

When we get into Aiden's house, Charlotte makes sure she sits on the complete opposite side of the room from where Chase is, squeezing in between Julian and Noah, who are talking to Jason and Jackson.

"Did you see our new video game? Bet we can beat you this time!" Jason holds up the box with a mischievous grin. "It's a continuation of *Return of the Zombie Aliens Part Three and a Half!*"

The box he holds up is similar to the one they were obsessed with at the beach house, and I'm assuming it's the one they were playing at Mason's house. I guess since we got to the bottom of their behavior, they've been okay with playing normally.

"*Psh*, I doubt it, even *Charlotte* beat you last time," Julian teases, making the twins' faces turn red.

"That doesn't count! Noah was distracting us last time!" They defend themselves, earning laughs from Noah and Charlotte.

"Hey, don't hate the player, hate the game," Noah says.

They argue back and forth about whether throwing chocolate chip cookie pieces is considered cheating, while Annalisa fidgets in her seat, clearly about to burst from holding in her anger all day.

As always, Aiden notices. "Hey, boys, why don't you go upstairs and practice playing, and Noah and Julian will come up and kick your butts later?"

"They will not!" Jason and Jackson huff at the same time, but head to the stairs anyway, strategizing between themselves about how they can win and what snacks they need to hide from Noah.

As soon as they're out of earshot, Annalisa asks, "Who punched Kaitlyn in the face for me after I left?"

Oh boy. We all look around at each other.

"Anna, you know we can't just do that," Julian reminds her.

"Okay, you guys no." Her sharp eyes land on me and Charlotte. "But Amelia? Charlotte?"

I make eye contact with Charlotte's wide ones. Even with Charlotte's newfound confidence, I can't see her punching someone. And I'm trying to get through senior year as normally as possible. Punching the already bruised daughter of the principal doesn't really fit into that plan.

"Anna . . ." I start.

She crosses her arms in a huff of annoyance. "Fine. Still would've been nice. I just wish if I was going to go down for it, I would've at least *done it*."

"Who do you think did?" Noah asks her.

"This is a calculated move orchestrated by her and Ryan. They're trying to get back at me for what they think my brother did to Ryan's dad. All that Wacko Anna White bullshit? They planned this. Are you sure it's not just makeup?"

I mean, she's not wrong. It is convenient that Kaitlyn spent all that time making sure everyone knew Annalisa was threatening her "for no reason," but I know it's not makeup. Would Kaitlyn allow herself to get beaten up just to get Annalisa expelled? Especially when she doesn't really have a direct problem with Annalisa? She only hates her because one, she hates everyone.

And two, her boyfriend hates Annalisa. But is that enough reason to subject herself to a black eye and everything else?

"It's not makeup," I reassure everyone. "I talked to her earlier today to ask why she would lie and could tell her injuries were real."

"Sure, Kaitlyn's crazy, but I don't think she's crazy enough to throw herself down a set of stairs just to get you expelled." Mason voices exactly what I was thinking.

Annalisa gets defensive. "What? You think I'm lying? If I hit her, I'd tell you I hit her."

"I'm not saying you're lying," Mason says, trying to think out his next words carefully. "I'm saying I don't think her intention was to get beaten up just to blame you."

"I agree with Mason," I jump in, ignoring the cut eyes Annalisa's sending me. "She probably came home like that and when her mom asked her who did it, she blamed the person who made the most sense to her. Maybe Ryan even told her to blame you."

Mason smiles at me. It's warm but makes me feel so far away from him. It's a smile that I can't return since I'm a terrible person who still hasn't told him about his dad, because I just can't bear to keep breaking his heart.

"I can't believe you of all people are picking her over me!" Annalisa exclaims.

She's angry. She's not willing to listen to anything other than "Let's go kick Kaitlyn's ass!" But still, I try to reason with her.

"I'm not picking her over you. But if those bruises and her arm being in a sling weren't caused by you, the next probable suspect is Ryan, and that means she's probably being abused," I say.

Beside me, Aiden's jaw clenches. He knows all too well what it's like to be abused, especially at the hands of a Simms. He of all people knows what kind of violence Ryan witnessed as a kid, and what he's probably replicating.

"I can't believe you." Her leg bounces like she's about to jump out of her seat. "I've always had your back when she pulled her shit on you at school!"

"I *still* have your back," I insist. "I'm not saying any of this is your fault. But there's a difference between her trying to embarrass me with stupid and cruel pranks and her coming to school with a black eye and a sprained wrist. You've always had my back and I love you, but intimate partner violence is serious, and she needs help. If we help her, she might even clear your name and admit who really did that to her."

Annalisa leans back farther into her seat with angry resignation. "If you think she'd ever help us, you're delusional."

"The only way you'll be allowed to come back to school is if she tells her mom you didn't touch her." Aiden backs me up.

"Guess I'm going to have to get used to the fact that I'm going to graduate as a Silver, alone," she huffs, then continues when Julian is about to say something. "And no, I don't want any of you to transfer." She gives Julian a pointed look and his shoulders slump, as they've had this conversation already.

I'm about to tell her that she'll never be alone when her phone rings and she answers it. The conversation continues around us, and I decide to go to the kitchen to get some water.

"Anyone else want something from the kitch—"

"*You weren't supposed to kill him! It's game over now!*" Shouting from upstairs interrupts me.

"Hey! Boys!" Aiden calls up to the twins, but the arguing continues. Aiden leaves the room and runs up the stairs, and the shouting stops when I assume Aiden arrives.

I leave the room to grab a glass of water, still thinking about Annalisa. I'm not taking Kaitlyn's side in this. Of course not. Annalisa didn't deserve to get expelled, but no one should feel scared or trapped in their relationship. I know what it's like to wake up terrified of someone hurting you every day, and I wouldn't wish that feeling on anyone. There has to be a way to help Annalisa *and* Kaitlyn.

"Hey, k-bear, wait up," Mason calls to me, and he emerges from the hallway into the kitchen.

My heart warms at his affectionate nickname. There's a cool breeze coming in from the open sliding door and his hair ruffles a bit, giving him that messy-on-purpose hairstyle.

"Hey, want something to drink?" I open the fridge, grab a sparkling water, and hand it to him.

"Yeah, thanks. Actually, I know this probably isn't the best time to ask with all of this going on, but we haven't hung out in a while. You wanna do something this weekend?"

Do I want to do something with Mason? Of course I do, but I've been avoiding him ever since I found out about our parents. But now, looking into his chocolate-colored eyes, I know I can't keep avoiding him. I miss my friend, and I want our relationship to go back to normal.

"Yes! Let's do something this weekend. I'll even let you challenge me to a mini-golf rematch since I always kick your butt."

"Did you kick my butt? Or did I let you win since the winner treated the loser to ice cream?"

"You did not!" I love how easy it is to fall back into our normal, bantering friendship. "Next time the loser's going to treat the winner to ice cream, and we'll see if you really 'lose on purpose.'"

He laughs with me, but before he can reply Annalisa pops her head in the kitchen. "Hey, that was Ray, he works at the bar my brother used to hang out at. I asked him to check the cameras that night for clues about Luke and he found something. Julian and I are going to go check it out. I'll message the group with what I find."

Before either one of us can reply, she's out the door, rushing to find out what she can to free her brother.

Mason and I return to the living room, where everyone else still sits minus Annalisa, Aiden, and Julian.

"Mason and I are going mini-golfing this weekend. Anyone in?"

"Amelia." Aiden reappears. He hovers at the threshold, close to the stairs. His face is unreadable. "Come here. Now, please."

What? Am I in trouble? Seriously?!

I follow him out of the room and down the hall to the front of the house. "You can't possibly be mad that I'm going out for mini-golf with Mason. It's not a date."

Aiden seems confused, then shakes his head. "I don't care about that. You need to hear this."

That gets my attention. He leads me up the stairs to his bedroom, where the twins are sitting together on his bed. Jason is hugging himself nervously and Jackson looks like he swallowed a bug.

"Tell her exactly what you told me," he instructs them.

"Are we in trouble?" Jackson sniffles.

"Jackson wanted to tell you before but I convinced him not to say anything," Jason jumps in.

Aiden's face softens, but I can still see the anger simmering underneath. "You're not in trouble. I promise. Just tell Amelia."

Jason bites his lip and hesitates for a second before he says, "We lied before. I'm not getting bullied. I just said that because Jackson was going to blab."

Jason looks for reassurance from Jackson, who nods.

"We know who killed Greg," Jason says, then takes a deep breath. "We did."

I'm so shocked all I can do is blink at them. They're *children*. How can children *kill* a person, especially a grown man like Greg? But Aiden's serious face tells me this isn't a joke. My heart pounds.

"What? How? You guys weren't even home."

Jason fidgets in his seat but Aiden says, "It's okay. Tell her what you told me."

"We were at Tyler's house, and we told him that Aiden got us the new *Return of the Zombie Aliens* video game. We wanted to play, so Jackson and I walked home to get it."

Aiden's jaw is clenched. He's heard this story and doesn't like it.

Jackson continues, "We know where Aiden keeps the key, so we just let ourselves in to get it."

I try to paint a picture in my head, and remember that Aiden keeps the key under a brick in the walkway near the door.

"We got the game and locked the door, but when we turned around, a bloody, angry man came up to us."

This can't be real. Two nine-year-olds did not overpower and kill a grown man. Aiden's staring straight ahead, but it's clear his mind is running a mile a minute. It looks like he's trying to take steadying breaths.

"What happened next?" I ask them, even though I feel like I'm holding my breath.

"We recognized him as Greg . . ."

Jackson picks up when Jason trails off. "We knew he used to hurt Aiden, and we were always scared of him."

Aiden's hand clenches and body stiffens. He thought he'd protected the twins from the truth. He thought they didn't know Greg abused him.

"He—he wasn't normal," Jason continues. "His eyes looked weird. And he was saying stuff about us belonging to him. Then he grabbed me. He was trying to pull me away from the house." Jason's crying now, and my heart breaks.

I sit beside him on the bed and he buries his head in my shoulder. Aiden walks out of the room and I hear something glass break. Someone calls up to ask if everything's all right, but I block out Aiden's reply to focus on the twins.

I feel like crying, but I hold it together so they don't see me scared. "It's okay, Jason. You're okay."

These poor kids have already been through so much: Greg, Andrew. It's a wonder that they're not terrified to leave their house. Aiden comes back in the room seemingly calmer, but then I realize it's not just anger in his eyes, in his rigid posture, in the set of his jaw. It's fear. Fear that he could've lost his brothers. And fear that they're going to be taken away now.

"Tell her what happened next," he prods them.

"I was trying to get him to let go of Jason, but he wouldn't," Jackson continues since Jason is still sniffling. "So I ran behind him to try to stop him from taking him, when Jason slipped out of his grip. We looked at each other and we . . . I mean, we do this all the time on friends and stuff and no one's ever died!"

"What did you do?" I ask him gently, imagining a bunch of different scenarios where the outcome is Greg's death.

"When Jason slipped out, I was already behind Greg. So I just . . . dropped down to my hands and knees behind him—"

Jason continues, sitting up from where he was leaning on me and dragging his sleeve over his nose. "And I shoved him while he was trying to grab me."

The scene unfolds in my head; I can picture it. Greg grabbing Jason, Jackson running around behind him. The two boys locking eyes, already coming up with an unspoken plan. Jackson dropping to all fours behind Greg, and Jason pushing him backward over his brother. Greg falling . . .

Jason hugs himself and looks down, the memory of that day filling his mind. "He fell and . . . we hadn't put the brick back in the walkway from when we got the key. It was out, and when he fell . . . his head . . ."

"It exploded on the brick," Jackson states bluntly.

My mouth drops open. Jason and Jackson literally killed Greg *by accident*? They start speaking practically at once.

"We didn't know what to do! We put the brick back and ran to Tyler's house."

"Jason wanted to tell you but we didn't want to get in trouble. We were sure he was fine. I made him promise not to tell anyone."

"But we can't take it anymore. We keep arguing over if we should tell you or not," Jason says. "I promised Jackson we would tell you after the beach house because it was Christmas and we didn't want you to worry."

They're looking back and forth between me and Aiden, waiting for us to say something. Aiden's face is still a hardened mix of anger and careful calculation, and I'm too shocked to process.

Honestly, I was kind of convinced Luke did it.

I turn to the two scared boys. "Listen to me. It was an accident. It wasn't your fault. You didn't mean to hurt Greg. It's the very definition of an accident."

"You did a good thing telling us," Aiden says, putting his hand on Jason's shoulder. "I'm going to take care of everything, okay? You don't need to worry about a thing, you'll be just fine."

"Are we going to jail?" Jason whimpers.

Not on my watch.

"You guys know that your brother will do everything he can to protect you. You're not going to go to jail. We'll figure everything out."

Jason and Jackson say nothing, leaving me to stare at Aiden. What are we going to do?

"Let's keep this between us for now, okay, guys?" Aiden says, his voice softer than before. "Don't tell anyone else, got it?"

They nod, and Aiden continues. "Perfect. Why don't you guys go grab some snacks or something, okay?"

They take off out of Aiden's room, leaving Aiden and me to stare at each other. I don't know what to say, what to think, how to process this.

"Fuck." Aiden slumps onto the bed beside me. "We are so *fucked*."

"It was an accident," I start. "The police will understand." Right?

Aiden rubs his temples. "Yes, but a man is dead. They hid evidence, then ran away and kept quiet about it for a month after. I just started the process of filing for custody, and at a lucky minimum that'll be denied."

I try to think through our options but come up short. The one good thing to come out of this is that Luke really *is* innocent, which will make Annalisa extremely happy, but how do we tell our friends or the authorities without hurting the twins?

"We can't tell anyone, at least not yet," Aiden says, his spine rigid. "We have to think this through. I'm going to have to find a lawyer, someone who can handle this all quietly and discreetly. I know what it's like to get death threats and comments from strangers on the internet. Can you imagine what'll happen if the media finds out about this?"

I can imagine, and I don't like it. Aiden's already getting a bunch of media attention, and if it gets out that his brothers *killed* someone, even accidentally, it'll be a media frenzy. Not just for Aiden, because Aiden can handle it, but for the twins. What kind of reputation would follow them around? Kids really *are* ruthless sometimes, and what would happen if their classmates found out about it? They may not actually be getting bullied right now, but after this got out?

"What about Brian's friend? The lawyer who got you off Greg's murder charge in the first place. Alan. We can call him, get him to help."

Aiden suddenly looks tired, much more than he was moments ago. "That's probably a good idea. I'm going to look into it first, see the best possible way to handle this without jeopardizing custody or their futures."

"What do we do in the meantime?"

Aiden meets my eyes. "We act normal. Nothing's changed. We help Anna look for evidence to help Luke . . . *shit.*"

The realization hits me at the same time it must hit Aiden. If Luke really didn't kill Greg, then he's free, and if he's free, he can contact Tony, who will come here, and find me.

I feel even more defeated than possible. I really don't know what to do; all the cards are stacked against me. We need to help the twins, and we obviously can't let Luke go on trial for murder when he's innocent. But if he's out, he's going to look into Tony. If he doesn't find out the truth about Tony and expose me himself, then he's going to invite him here into Annalisa's life, and consequently into mine, which might possibly be what Agent Dylan wants. I don't want anyone to get hurt because of me, but I can't be so selfish as to keep Luke in jail so I can continue living peacefully in King City with my friends.

Aiden puts his arm around my shoulder and pulls me closer to him.

"I think we might need to tell Anna. About everything," I say, my voice coming out small. I don't want to tell her about me but it's not looking like I have any other choice. I don't see any other options.

Aiden pulls me closer to him. "Let's not do anything right now, okay? Let's take some time, think everything through, and do it properly. We don't have room for error here."

I rest my head against his shoulder. He's right. We should think everything through properly, then decide what to do.

"Hey!" Noah's voice calls up to us from the bottom of the stairs. "Are you guys done doing X-rated things and want to join us? We ordered pizza! It should be here soon."

"Why does he always think we're fooling around?" I ask Aiden, happy to let Noah distract me for the moment.

Aiden must appreciate the distraction, too, because he shrugs and helps me stand up. "Maybe he wants to watch?"

"Ew! Gross!"

"Let's go get ready for food. Try to act normal, for now at least."

Normal. I'm starting to despise that word. All I want to do is be normal, not *pretend* while dealing with a million things all designed to hurt me.

>> <<

Even though it's January, the weather's mild, so Aiden leaves the sliding door open to let in the fresh air as we sit around the table and stuff our faces. The kitchen quickly gets warm with all the bodies piled in eating pizza, so I even have to take off my sweater. The air is worth it since it helps me stay focused. *Act normal.*

After dinner, when the sun's starting to set, everyone starts to head out. Chase pulls an unexpected move and asks Charlotte if he can drive her home. She hesitates, but I think she realizes he's probably planning on making up with her about what happened at her party, so she accepts. I stay a bit later after Mason and Noah leave to help Aiden clean up and go over some calculus homework, but I can tell his mind is elsewhere, and I don't blame him, so I call it a night around nine.

"Let me walk you to your car," Aiden says as I'm pulling on my shoes.

"It's not that far, I'm fine. Talk to the twins, make sure they're really okay." They were quiet over dinner then went upstairs to watch television, but they weren't acting any different than before.

When I straighten from tying my shoes, Aiden's right there. He tugs me closer to him and rests his forehead against mine. "A lot went on today. Anna was expelled. We found out about the twins, but no matter what happens, we deal with it together." His voice is low and sweet. "Me and you. All in, remember?"

I can't take the distance between our lips anymore. My lips press against his. It's light at first, but then he deepens it, and I follow his lead. It's brief, but perfect, and still causes my heart to pound in my chest when I pull away.

"I love you," he says against my lips, and I feel like I'm soaring.

"I love you too," I reply, untangling myself from him. If I don't leave now, I'm going to be here all night. I open his door. "Text me later, okay?"

"Of course. Good night, Amelia."

He waits until I'm down the driveway and out of view before he closes the door, and I walk the block with a stupid smile on my face despite the shitstorm we're in. We'll figure out what to do, I'm certain of it.

Once I open my car door and the coolness of the temperature within it hits me, I remember that I left my sweater in Aiden's kitchen. Deciding it's better to stay warm on the drive home, I head back to Aiden's house, preferring to walk so I can use the time to think. Do I tell Annalisa? Is it that simple?

Once I turn the corner and have a straight view to Aiden's house, I spot two men in business suits, seeming completely out of place in Aiden's quiet neighborhood. A large black SUV sits parked on the road a few houses away from Aiden's in the opposite direction of me. My next step falters. Is that Aiden's *dad*?

My eyes go wide when I realize that it *is* Aiden's dad, and the man with him is Harvey Vedenin, the man who tried to *kill me* the last time I saw him. They're walking toward me.

What are they doing here? Do I run? Do I scream? They seem too calm to be coming here to kill me in the middle of a suburban street. How did they know I was here? Quickly, I duck behind a car parked in a driveway down the street from Aiden's house. Peeking around to track their progress, I don't think they see me as they casually glance around the neighborhood. My heart beats louder and louder in my chest as they stop their progress toward me and instead turn onto Aiden's driveway.

They haven't come for me, they're here for *Aiden*.

I ignore my racing pulse and pull out my phone, trying to dial Aiden's number as calmly as possibly. I watch as they frown at Aiden's Challenger in the driveway, my blood rushing in my ears. What's happening? This can't be just a friendly visit. I can't see them from where I'm standing anymore.

"Did you forget something? I hear you knocking, I'm coming," Aiden's teasing voice greets me through the phone.

"*No, don't!*" I can't rush the words out fast enough. "That's not me, Aide—"

There's a loud bang. I can hear it from where I'm standing on his neighbor's driveway.

"*Aiden?!*"

There's some rustling, some yelling, and I can't take it anymore. I take off at a sprint, thinking of nothing but Aiden and his brothers. *Aiden, Jason, Jackson. Aiden, Jason, Jackson,* runs through my mind with every furious heartbeat and every slap of my feet on the asphalt.

When I get to Aiden's house, his front door has been kicked in, and my mind registers that that's what the bang must've been.

Some part of my brain stops me just as I'm about to charge into his house. Somehow, through the fear and panic, something allows me to think logically. Some part of my brain is staying calm and telling me not to race in helplessly and be no help to Aiden or his brothers.

Seconds later, I'm racing around to the side of his house and hopping the fence into the backyard, scraping my knees in the process. I stalk through his backyard as quietly as possible, remembering that the sliding door is open and that they would hear me.

The sight punches me right in the stomach as I peer in a window at the side of the house. Aiden's there, in the kitchen, back rigid and shoulders squared, holding the twins behind him, his unwavering gaze fixed solely on Andrew and the gun in his hand.

I feel dizzy, like someone has their hand around my neck and is slowly squeezing.

Ducking down and out of sight, I dial 911 with shaking fingers. Every ring lasts an eternity.

"Nine-one-one," comes a woman's voice.

"Hi, my name is Amelia Collins and there's been a break-in. Three boys are being held at gunpoint." My words are rushed and low. I recite Aiden's address, grateful that I know it by heart.

"The police are on their way, Amelia. Where are you? Are you safe?" The operator's voice is calm, greatly juxtaposing how I feel right now.

I pop my head up to look in the house and suddenly her reassuring tone isn't good enough. They're talking, but it doesn't look calm, and there's still a gun pointed at the man I love.

What am I doing? Aiden would never sit around and watch as I was in trouble. I can't just sit here and do *nothing*.

The woman on the phone is saying something, but unless it's "The police are there," I'm not really interested. Instinct guides me as I hang up on the 911 operator, then slink over to the back door and crouch down. Their voices are audible through the mesh of the screen door, but now they can see me if they look down.

What do I do? What *can* I do? This isn't a movie. I can't just barge in there pulling some crazy, heroic shit and have everything come out my way, no matter how much I want to. I have to ignore every fiber in my being that's telling me to rip open the screen door and knock the gun out of Andrew's hand and be the hero of my own story. There's nothing I can do.

Like always, Aiden somehow notices me even though I'm basically holding my breath, and as if it's possible, his body goes even more rigid.

Andrew's going on and on about his political career, and Aiden's eyes flit back to him to not give me away. He slowly and subtlety starts taking steps to the side, forcing Andrew and Harvey to move too in order to stay directly in front of him. Because of Aiden, now Andrew and Harvey's backs are to me so they won't spot me.

I have to do *something*. I look around the backyard as if something will magically pop out that'll help me. *There's nothing I can do.* I've never felt as helpless and out of control as I am in this very moment. It sickens me; makes me want to punch a hole in the wall and scream and scream until my lungs have nothing left to give.

Aiden's eyes find me quickly, just for a barely there second, just long enough to give me a look; a look I know all too well.

Get the fuck out of here.

But he should know me better by now.

I check my phone to see how long it's been since I called 911, and then remember the new addition to my phone.

Nothing I can do? Fuck that.

Jason and Jackson are hiding behind Aiden's back.

Aiden's eyes dart back to me. He knows what I'm doing now. From behind Aiden, Jason peeks out, his face tear stained. He notices me and his jaw drops, but without turning around, Aiden pushes him back into place behind him.

"Why are you doing this, Kessler?" Aiden's voice is clear and steady, and he manages to sound like he's in control of the situation despite not being the one with the gun. "Why are you in my house pointing a gun at your sons?"

Andrew scoffs. "You saw this coming. You've been warned countless times. You're ruining my life. You know my wife, the one from the very, *very* rich family I married into? She's threatening to leave me if I don't get this shit under control. I signed a pre-nup, I'll get *nothing*. I'll be back to where I was when I was stuck here in this godforsaken dump. Plus, I made some deals with some people who don't like to get screwed over."

Harvey's taken a seat at the kitchen table, as if he's bored of this whole situation already, and Aiden's laser focused on Andrew now.

"You sent your henchman to kill me and my friend last time." Aiden tilts his head at Harvey without breaking eye contact with his father. "You're doing the dirty work yourself this time?"

"Since you've repeatedly refused to take back your statements and stop ruining my good name, I figured I'd have to end it myself this time. *For good.* I gave you countless chances, Aiden. We could've done this the easy way. You didn't want to reunite, you didn't want to play the part of the dutiful son, and you didn't want hush money. So, this is what it's come to."

Harvey reaches into his coat, and my heart stops beating at all. *This is it. It's all over.* I brace myself to barge in and I don't know, tackle him? But Harvey pulls out a little orange bottle, and sets it down on the table, making me pause.

"Here's what we're going to do," Andrew continues. "You're going to swallow this handful of painkillers. Your breathing's going to slow, dangerously so. You'll probably have a heart attack, and then the rest of your body will shut down. You'll forget how to breathe, and then you'll stop breathing at all. It won't be pretty." He swivels so that the gun is aimed at Jason, who is standing slightly behind Aiden but not fully covered by his large body because he keeps peeking out. "And if not, I'll shoot him.

And not to kill either. It'll be slow, and painful, and you'll have to stand there and watch."

Andrew says this all with a cool detachment, very businessman-like, as if it's a business transaction.

Aiden remains calm, his eyes calculating. "And after I'm dead? My brothers?"

Andrew takes a step closer to Aiden. "Maybe I let them go, or maybe I kill the boys and leave the gun with your prints on it. You had a mental breakdown; you couldn't take the responsibil-ity anymore. You killed your brothers but then the guilt was too much to handle and you took a handful of painkillers to end it all." He shrugs, like it doesn't matter one way or the other. "I guess it depends on how cooperative you are."

There's a flash of fury in Aiden's eyes, and you can tell it's tak-ing every ounce of self-control to hold back his rage. He doesn't like not being in control either. "You're sick. You'd do this to your own sons? Just for an election? You're not fit to be a father, never mind govern a whole state."

Andrew tenses and Harvey suddenly stands up from the table.

This is it; I feel it. I need to do *something*. Now.

I stand up from my crouching spot and whip open the screen door, taking everyone by surprise. Aiden uses the distraction to his advantage and shoves Jason and Jackson away, telling them to run in the opposite direction. He watches as they run down the hallway and out the front door in nothing but their pajamas and socks. I hope they keep running, far away from this house, until they get somewhere safe.

"Say hi for the world, Andrew Kessler!" I gesture to the phone in my hand. "Remember me? I've been recording this conversa-tion this whole time."

Andrew's calm face cracks for just a second before he collects himself. "You're always getting involved in stuff that doesn't pertain to you. You don't even *know* what's coming for you."

I ignore his threat and inch closer to Aiden. Andrew raises an eyebrow at the phone in my hand. "Dumb girl. I'll just kill you and delete the video."

He steps closer to me, gun raised, when I step back and yell "*It's live!*" I raise the phone higher, as if it's a shield between the two of us. Thank the powers that be that Charlotte downloaded S-Live Time on my phone the other day and that she's still logged in to her account. "You can't just kill me and delete the video. It's live, there's an audience, and once I stop recording, the live video is saved to my profile, where it can be watched over and over by whoever wants to see it. News channels, judges, juries. Anyone."

He pauses for a second and looks over at Harvey, as if they're trying to decide if I'm bluffing or not. That hesitation is all Aiden needs. As if he's been playing professional football his whole life, he tackles Andrew to the floor.

I don't see where the gun goes, but I hear sirens in the distance.

Harvey moves to grab Aiden off of his father, and I see red. I don't even know what I do with the phone in my hand, but as soon as I see Harvey moving in on Aiden, I literally jump onto Harvey's back and wrap my limbs around him like a koala bear.

He instantly straightens, and I focus all my energy on my arms, which are tightly wrapped around his neck, and try to squeeze tighter.

All those feelings of fear and helplessness come rushing back to me. This man aimed a gun at me. This man *shot* at me. I'd be dead if it wasn't for Aiden. And I'll be *damned* if I let this man keep fucking up my life.

Harvey's spinning around, trying to get me to let go of him, but I just cling to him even more. My rage and fear and hatred fuels me, driving my exhausted limbs to hold on, to win this fight. I am taking back control. We're in the living room now; somehow Harvey's walked us away from wherever Aiden and Andrew are. He grabs my arms, and in a sudden movement, runs backward into the wall, slamming me into it. All of the air is knocked out of my lungs and my head feels like it's been split open, but I tell my arms to squeeze tighter around Harvey's neck, tell my legs to keep hanging on, tell myself to just keep hanging on.

I've faced Tony and won. Twice. I *will* win this fight too. For Jason, for Jackson, for Aiden, and for *myself*.

A booming gunshot goes off, then another one, and panic sets in.

"*Aiden?!*" I'm screaming. I have no idea what's going on, where Aiden is, who shot that gun.

He has to be okay. He has to be okay.

Harvey uses that moment of sheer panic to slam me into the wall again, and there's a sting of fire in every single vertebra in my spine.

My grip loosens and Harvey throws me off of him. My head is pounding and my entire body hurts, but I look around for Aiden, barely registering Harvey behind me trying to catch his breath.

Where is he?!

That frantic feeling is clawing its way through me, choking me. I race into the hallway just as a sea of blue charges in.

The pounding in my head is just getting worse. My lungs aren't working properly. *Where is Aiden?!*

Then I see him. He and Andrew are both being forced roughly into handcuffs. Andrew's nose is crooked and there's blood all over his face and shirt. There's blood on Aiden but he looks okay. No bullet wounds.

I can barely take a second to allow myself to feel relieved because then I realize that they're *handcuffing Aiden.*

"No, not him!" I force out, ignoring the officers talking to me, focused just on the ones trying to arrest Aiden. My head is pounding and the adrenaline surging through my veins is the only thing keeping me standing.

"My name is Amelia Collins, I made the nine-one-one call. This is his house." I point at Aiden.

After some back and forth, Aiden is released, and I basically tackle him. His solid arms wrap around me and relief floods through me.

His hands tangle in my hair, and he pulls me close until our lips meet. It's quick and frantic, like it's our first and last kiss all wrapped up into one.

"Are you okay?" He pulls away so his eyes can roam my body.

"I'm fine, are you? The gunshots . . . ?"

"I'm fine. We were fighting over the gun, the shots went through the wall."

I'm so overcome with joy and relief that I don't know what to do with myself. All I can do is pull him back down to me and kiss him; kiss him with everything I have, because we came so close to losing it all.

He pulls away and leans his forehead against mine. "Why can't you just stay out of it when I tell you to? I couldn't have lived with myself if something happened to you because of me."

"I'll *always* be there for you. Nothing happened; we're all okay," I gently reassure him, and as if to emphasize my point, an officer leads Jason and Jackson back into the house.

They run up to us and wrap their arms around Aiden, and I'm surprised when they include me in the hug too. I didn't think I'd ever see Aiden close to tears, but here he is, hugging his little brothers just as fiercely and protectively as they're holding on to him.

"You guys are so brave," he says to them with force behind his words. "I'm so proud of you. Everything's all right."

"Amelia?" Jason tugs on my shirt, and in this moment, I'm reminded of just how young he is. He looks vulnerable and unsure of himself, but still has every bit of that mischievous Parker attitude. "You're the coolest badass ever."

Despite everything, I laugh. Aiden wraps an arm around me and kisses my head. "That's why I love her."

I feel like laughing or crying or holding on to him and never letting go. Aiden's okay. I'm okay. The twins are okay.

We're safe.

We're together.

We're happy.

21

It's a long night, but it's worth it to finally see Harvey and Andrew arrested.

We had to go to the police station and give our statements about what happened, then head to the hospital to get some stitches. No one gave me trouble about my name, my identity, nothing. It was weird.

I find my phone before we go to the police station, and the video I took had been automatically saved to Charlotte's S-Live Time profile. It had already reached thousands of views, and by the time the police made me take it down and give them a copy for evidence, it was at half a million views. Even though I took it down, I know copies are going to be passed around, just like the video of me and Kaitlyn, but this video is way bigger, way more important, and has a much bigger impact and scandal attached. I bet it'll make national news by breakfast.

I'm not supervisible in the video—I made sure to double-check when I rewatched the video in the police station. You don't really see me at all. You see a brief shot of me on Harvey's back from when I dropped my phone on the floor, but then it cuts out, and my face isn't visible. It's not ideal, but I could be anyone. Plus, it *is* on Charlotte's profile, so for all anyone would know, it's Charlotte in the video.

Since Brian is technically still Jason and Jackson's legal guardian, we call him on our way to the police station. None of us are in trouble, though, so it's really only a formality that he be there while Jason and Jackson are questioned. He comes right away, asking the police the proper questions and snapping into responsible dad mode. Even though the sight of him makes me nauseated, having an actual adult around makes me feel a bit better, a bit more in control. It pains me to admit it, but watching Brian run around making sure we're okay and demanding answers from the police makes me see why Mason loves his dad, and I realize he's not the worst person around, even if he is having an affair. It reminds me of when we were sitting in this very police station a few weeks ago when Aiden was arrested, and it was Brian who made sure everything was okay, who got Aiden a lawyer, who accepted custody of Aiden and his brothers, who made sure Aiden was okay. It makes me miss my mom even though things between us are a bit strained right now, but when I call her, I go straight to voice mail. Her phone is off, so she must have just gotten on her usual flight. I send her a text to let her know I'm all right, knowing she'll get it when she turns her phone back on.

When we're allowed to leave, we tell Brian we're okay to head home ourselves. He's reluctant and offers to have us to stay with him, but I think the twins and Aiden want their own beds. I wear Aiden's huge hoodie and keep my face shielded when we leave the police station, as there are media following us and taking pictures because of his dad, people yelling for Aiden to give a statement, to tell them what happened. He doesn't stop for anyone, though, instead leading me and the twins to his car, where I keep my hoodie up even though his windows are tinted.

I keep feeling like I should call Agent Dylan, because this is the kind of thing he should know about, right? But then I remember how he put me here on purpose, how he *wants* me to draw Tony out, and I drop any thought of calling him.

We're all okay, just bruised. Aiden got a couple of stitches under his jaw, but he keeps reassuring me that he's okay. I can't stop looking at him; the stitches make him look more dangerous and hot.

By the time we get back to Aiden's house, it's early in the morning. I move my car from down the block into his driveway, and we all head to bed. Crawling into Aiden's bed with him is the most comforting and surreal feeling. I can't help thinking *I could get used to this*, especially when he wraps his arm around me and I curl into his side.

We lie in his bed, facing each other, staring into each other's eyes and letting all the unspoken words pass between us. The early morning light streams in through the sides of his drawn curtains, giving the dark room a faint glow. Maybe it's the adrenaline. Maybe it's because we've come so close to death for the second time and could've lost it all. But I can't stop staring at Aiden.

Aiden gently rests his hand on my face and strokes my cheek with his thumb, his eyes reflecting my thoughts.

"You are so fucking beautiful."

That's all it takes.

Before I can even process what I'm doing, I'm on top of Aiden, chest to chest, my legs straddling his waist and my hands tangled in his hair. I kiss him with all I've got, putting all my emotions into it, letting him feel my fear, my happiness, my desire, my love. He kisses me back just as fiercely and desperately, pulling me closer to him, like he's scared I'll disappear. I can't get enough of him. My heart is going to explode from how much I love him, from how much I want him.

Aiden's hands tighten on my waist and he flips us over so that he's on top of me. He breaks our kiss, and I'm only disappointed for a second before his perfect lips find my neck, trailing down the side and finding that sensitive spot that he knows drives me crazy.

I can't claw his clothes off of him fast enough.

My life isn't perfect, and at this rate it may never be. But this moment here, with Aiden, is perfection.

>> <<

Waking up beside Aiden is just as good as I remember it being from the beach house. After collecting our clothes from the floor, we spend the day with Jason and Jackson, playing games, baking cookies, and reassuring them that they're safe and that they'll never be hurt. We don't talk about Andrew and Harvey, and we especially don't talk about Luke or Greg. I think we all just need a wind down to escape the chaotic mess of yesterday. We're all relieved Andrew and Harvey are finally out of our lives. For the time being we don't have to worry about Andrew or Harvey—at least, not until the court case brings it all back up again. For now, we have a sense of peace. In a way, I'm glad this all happened, because now it doesn't feel like something huge is looming over our heads, waiting for just the right time to crush us. At least it's one *less* thing to worry about. We don't have to hold our breath, waiting for the shoe to drop, and if Aiden's happy, I'm happy.

It's around two in the afternoon when we're making pasta for a late lunch that my phone vibrates, and I find a text from my mom. I was wondering when she would get around to checking in on me.

> Just landed in Dubai, can't call. Brian sent me the video & texted me what happened. Are u ok? Y didn't u tell me?

I send her a quick reply.

> U were in the air. We're ok. Talk when u get back

I miss the days when I would run to my mom when I scraped my knee and she'd kiss it better. But things are different now. *We're* different. And I've learned to not depend on anyone. I catch Aiden's eye from where he's stirring the sauce, and he winks at me, melting my heart.

Well, I guess there are some exceptions to that.

I'll always have Aiden.

>> <<

Our friends come over to see us after school, and we're greeted with lots of hugs, and Jason and Jackson even get some presents.

After talking through what happened and reassuring them that we're okay, they finally get their heads wrapped around the fact that Aiden's dad tried to kill his own sons. As Charlotte said, he truly doesn't have a heart.

Annalisa's sitting near me on the couch as the guys crowd around the television playing *Zombie Alien Vampires Part Fifteen and Three Quarters* or whatever video game it is that the twins are obsessed with.

Annalisa nudges me and gestures at the twins. "I guess they sorted everything out after last night?"

It's hard to remember that it was just yesterday that the twins were arguing over video games and came clean to us about what really happened with Greg. Now that it's at the forefront of my mind, and I'm staring Annalisa in the face and thinking about how she wants nothing more than to prove Luke is innocent, the blood drains from my face.

"Oh. Yeah. They made up." Technically not a lie.

"We can hear you," Jackson says, not looking away from the screen.

"Yeah, we hear everything," Jason adds. "Just like the time at the beach house when Noah blamed Mason and Chase for eating all of Anna's chips but it was really him."

Annalisa sends an accusing glare at Noah. "There were, like, ten bags!"

Noah ignores her. "Hey, guys. Are we having a slumber party gossip session or are we playing a serious game here?" Noah snaps his fingers at the twins to get their attention. "Because from where I'm sitting, it looks like you *want* Julian, Mason, and Aiden to win against us."

"We *are* winning," Mason taunts, and I hear a musical sound from the game that doesn't sound good for team Noah, Jackson, and Jason.

"Aw, man! You used a cheat code!" Noah accuses, and all six boys start arguing over it.

Laughing, I leave the room to grab a snack in the kitchen, and Annalisa follows me. Charlotte's already there, pouring herself a tea.

"I'm glad the twins made up," Annalisa says and drifts off, leaning against the counter awkwardly as if waiting for me to notice something different about her. Nothing comes to mind, so she fills in the blank for me. "Wanna know what Ray told me about Luke? Remember I got a call from him last night, that's why I left early? I didn't text you to update you because I saw the video and knew you had a lot going on."

"Right. Yes." It completely slipped my mind. Now that I actually *know* Luke is innocent, and after everything that went on last night, I forgot about asking Annalisa if she found anything.

"He said they checked the cameras and saw that he left the bar around 4 p.m. According to Luke, he left the bar to go looking for his old drug dealer, Greg. We asked Ray where he would've went to find him, and he sent us to another bar."

Maybe if we find evidence of Luke not being near the crime scene we can clear his name *and* keep the twins out of it. It still wouldn't help me with the whole Luke's trying to contact Tony thing, but it's a start. If Luke left the bar at four o'clock, he was on camera at Howard's convenience around 5:15, and walked off camera around 5:25. Where was he between those times? And where was he after, since the time of death was around six?

"Did you find anything at the other bar?" I ask her.

"We talked to a bunch of people who looked like regulars. Some of them said that Greg was there that night, but who knows. We were told that the manager would know, but he wasn't there when we went."

Okay, so we're still not really any closer to knowing anything.

"Has Luke's lawyer said anything?" I ask. "Have the cops found anything out?"

"No. And apparently no one is looking for evidence to prove Luke *didn't* do it. He had motive, his DNA was all over Greg, and he admits they got in a fight."

"But Luke looked absolutely plastered in the video from the convenience store, and that was before Greg died. How could he kill a guy in that state?" I already know how, but I ask anyway.

Annalisa rubs her eyes and her black eyeliner smudges. "There was heroin in Greg's system when he died. They said it wouldn't have been a hard fight."

Charlotte chimes in. "How do they know he didn't overdo—"

"He didn't overdose," Annalisa cuts her off, her tone agitated. "They know the signs of an overdose. Plus, they said the cause of death was blunt force trauma to his head, remember?"

Charlotte pouts, mumbling something about just trying to help.

Annalisa sighs. "I know, I know. I'm sorry. I'm just annoyed that my brother is going to rot in jail over killing *Greg*, the worst person on this planet."

"Luke isn't going to be found guilty, Anna," I tell her, trying to put as much conviction into my words as I can, because it really is the truth. Luke didn't do anything, and it's just a matter of figuring out what to do about the twins so that Annalisa can be reunited with her brother. What happens after that, I'm not sure, because I sure as hell can't let him contact Tony. But for now, it's one thing at a time.

22

Since our friends told us it was a zoo at school with people asking them about us, we decide to skip school Wednesday, and then the rest of the week. Hopefully, things will calm down a bit by the time we return. Aiden's already facing a media frenzy as it is, and I'm trying not to draw attention to myself.

Mom's home, and as soon as she got back she called Agent Dylan to tell him about everything that happened. Like the last video I told him about, he didn't seem too concerned that I was on camera, and convinced her that you couldn't even see me. Even though it's true I'm only in it for a couple seconds, and the part I'm in is shot from the *floor*, I'm still suspicious when the viral video doesn't bother Agent Dylan at all. Why bother not having social media or never taking pictures with my own camera if the people who told me the rules don't care about my following them? Mom was confused, too, but he reassured her, which I think calmed her down. After all, if the FBI agent isn't worried, why would she be? I didn't bother telling her mine and Aiden's theory—that Agent Dylan *wants* me here and found, because that wouldn't accomplish anything at all. It would just make her double down on not wanting me to hang out with my friends, and that's not something I can live with. Maybe he wants me here and has no intention of moving us because it's their best chance of catching Tony. But how is he going to keep me safe at the same time if things like this don't worry him?

Even though Aiden and I skipped school much of the week, our friends have been dropping off our homework so that we don't fall behind, or more specifically, I don't fall behind. Aiden could practically teach every class, but we all know I need that extra help in calculus or I'm not graduating.

Aiden agreed to come over Friday morning after dropping the twins off at school to help me catch up. He follows me up to my room where we can sit comfortably while being tortured with math, but pauses before we get there.

"I just have to go to the bathroom first."

"Yeah, sure. Use this one." I point to the rarely used bathroom in the hallway as we walk by it.

I continue into my room and am setting up our books when I hear the bathroom door swing open, followed by some quick, heavy footsteps, then Aiden charges in.

He's holding a little plastic stick. It looks like a thermometer. His face is an almost comical mix of fear and confusion. He holds the object out to me, and that's when I realize it's a *pregnancy test*.

I feel all the blood drain from my face.

He trips over his words. "But we . . . But that's . . . we used . . . you're *pregnant*?"

It's then that the situation actually clicks in my head.

"*What?*" All the blood rushes to my head and the room spins around me. Pregnant? It says pregnant? No, no, no, no, no, it cannot say pregnant. There's way too much going on right now to handle that too. I rush over and grab it from his hand, then let a sigh of relief immediately escape.

"It says not pregnant." I set it down on my dresser, my heart trying to calm itself as I glance back at Aiden. His eyes are wide, the frustration and disbelief not dissipating like mine did.

"You thought you were pregnant and weren't going to tell me?!"

"Wait, what?"

He looks like he wants to pull all his hair out. "Thea! Were you not here when I just handed you your *pregnancy test*? Why wouldn't you tell me? We could've gone through this together."

He thinks it's mine? For some reason I feel like laughing even though this isn't exactly the right situation to laugh at.

"Aiden, that's not my pregnancy test. I have my own bathroom. If it was mine, it would be in there."

The anger and frustration is replaced by confusion. "But if it's not yours—" I wait a second for him to connect the dots when his jaw drops. There it is.

"Oh no."

Oh no, indeed.

"This is not good." He voices the words I'm thinking.

"I know. What would've happened if *my mom* was *pregnant* with *Mason's dad's baby*?"

All the possible scenarios run through my head, none of which end with Mason and me still being friends.

"Brian needs to tell Mason, and soon, or else you're going to have to."

I rub my eyes and flop onto my bed. "I know, I know. I'm going out with him tomorrow and I think it's best I tell him."

Aiden sits down beside me and rubs my back. "It's for the best, Thea. He deserves to know."

Mason's going to hate me. For not telling him. For destroying his vision of his perfect father. For ruining his family life. For my mom being the other woman. For everything. "How pissed at me do you think he'll be?"

Aiden tilts my chin up to look at him. "He cares about you. I'm sure he'll be upset for a bit, but he'll get over it. He'd be much more upset finding out some other way, like your mom going to his house and announcing she's pregnant."

Could I even imagine that scenario? What would happen if my mom *was* pregnant? Would Mason's dad embrace it? Leave his family? Would he say it wasn't his? Would he want nothing to do with it?

Thank goodness we don't have to find out, but it could happen down the line. And Mason needs to know before it ever gets to that point. I just hope I don't lose one of my best friends.

>> <<

"This is going to be the easiest free ice cream I've ever gotten," Mason says as I miss the first shot at the third hole in mini-golf, again.

We're at the only mini-golf place in town for our rematch. It's glow in the dark and every couple of holes there's a room with a different theme. The theme of the room we're currently in is dinosaurs, and Mason's white shirt glows neon blue under the black light.

"Hey, don't get your hopes up yet," I say, getting the ball straight in on the second shot.

My mind is off today. I don't want to tell him right away—the plan is to have some fun with him first, then before we get out of the car to get our ice cream, I'll break the news to him as gently as possible in private.

"Yeah, yeah. I'm already beating you by two shots, so maybe you should just call it quits right now." He lines up his shot and misses.

"Looks like you're only beating me by one now," I tease, laughing even harder when he shoots me a face but misses his shot again.

We play a pretty evenly matched game, and by the time we're almost done, I'm leading by three shots. It's fun. We've been laughing nonstop, and I'm reminded how much fun Mason is to be around. I feel bad for avoiding him this whole time, and even worse that he might avoid *me* for a while after I tell him.

Mason pauses from taking his shot.

"Are you sure Aiden is okay with us hanging out alone together?"

"Why wouldn't he be?"

Mason rubs the back of his neck awkwardly. "This is the first time we've hung out alone together since, you know, my outburst about the two of you at the beach house."

He's referring to when he got really drunk and told Aiden that he doesn't know me and isn't good enough for me.

"Of course he is. Plus, you guys are cool. He knows you didn't mean it."

Mason pauses for a second, pouting as if thinking about it.

"Besides," I add, "I can do whatever I want. I don't need Aiden's permission to do things. He's my boyfriend, not my father."

"Yeah, I guess no one can tell you what to do, not even your dad." His eyes widen, realizing his mistake. "I mean . . . when he was alive . . ."

He trails off awkwardly. We don't really talk about my dad. Only Aiden knows the truth; everyone else just knows that he died.

"I think I started becoming more stubborn recently," I say, just to fill in the lingering awkward silence.

He puts his ball down at the start of the next hole. "How are you handling everything? I mean, like, the whole no dad thing?"

It's cute, really. He wants to talk to me about it but doesn't know how to approach the subject.

"I'm all right. I mean, with everything going on, I haven't really had a chance to think about him. But every once in a while, when I'm home alone with no distractions. . . . Sometimes it hits me that he's gone."

"Yeah, I guess with everything going on with Kaitlyn and Anna and Andrew and stuff, your mind stays pretty occupied."

I meant more of the Tony situation, but sure, that too.

"I can't even imagine what I'd do without my dad," Mason continues. "He's one of the only people I know will always be there for me; he'd never let me down."

Oh boy. Ohhhh boy.

The guilt is eating at me.

Should I just tell him now? I feel like this is my opening. Brian hasn't said anything. It's been almost three full weeks and he still hasn't spoken to Mason. I can't keep lying to him. No one else is in here right now; I can get it over with. Rip the Band-Aid off. He needs to know.

"Listen, Mason. There's something I need to tell you. I should've told you a long—"

"Well, well, well, if this isn't a coincidence."

We turn at the interruption and find Noah, who just walked in with Charlotte and Julian.

"It's not a coincidence. You knew we were going to be here," Mason says.

Noah feigns innocence. "Me? It's not like I knew mini-golf is your *thing* with Amelia, as well as calling her k-bear."

"I can't tell who you're jealous of here, Noah. Mason? Or me?" I laugh.

"Please. I don't care about finding a thing with *Mason*."

"I thought you gave up on trying to find our 'thing'? You haven't mentioned it in a while."

"I did forget, because, you know, we had a lot of shit going on. But I promise you, by the end of the month, we will have a thing!"

We do have a lot of stuff going on, but it feels good to fall back into old habits, old comforts. My friends and me playing mini-golf, Noah trying and failing to find a "thing" with me that's better than anyone else's connection with me, Charlotte trying and failing not to laugh at Mason's jokes, Julian's shy smile and natural ability to make people feel at ease, even if he's not the loudest person in the room. It's a comfort, and I fill my heart with the way I feel in the moment, trying to hold it close, memorize its warm caress, so that when I'm miles away, friendless and all alone, I can recall this moment with ease.

"Hey, are you guys going for ice cream later? We're coming, my treat!" Noah announces, setting his ball up at the starting point and lining up his shot.

I feel my eyes widen.

No. No, no, no.

As much as I love Noah, I need this time with Mason.

Alone.

Before I can object, Mason answers. "It was supposed to be just me and Amelia tonight, but if you're volunteering to pay, who am I to turn you down?"

I try not to let the frustration show on my face. I guess I can't tell Mason tonight. But I'm going to have to do it ASAP, before it's too late.

23

Today's Sunday. I asked Mason if he wanted to come over later so I can break the news in private, but he said he had plans with his dad today, which makes me cringe. Maybe today's the day Brian will tell Mason and that's why they have plans. I hope Brian's the one to tell him, that he does the right thing.

Instead, I call Charlotte. With everything that happened, I haven't had time to ask her about what happened between her and Chase when he drove her home from Aiden's last week, so she gives me the rundown.

Basically, he told her he was sorry for what he said, and he realizes that he can't tell her what to do and has to let her live her life. Charlotte forgave him and she says they've made up, but she feels like they'll never really be the same again because he'll never be completely okay with not being with her.

She said they were okay with each other at school in their shared classes and at lunch, too, acting normal and joking around like always, which she feels proves they've put the whole incident at the party behind them. But he's stopped calling her Charlie, and for some reason that hurts even me. It's like he knows that version of Charlotte will never be his again, and he realizes that he has to move on.

She feels bad, but she doesn't love him like that. She's just glad she doesn't have to lose one of her best friends. I'm not sure she'd know how to handle losing Chase entirely. Hopefully, one day a girl will come along who loves Chase just as fiercely as he loves her, and Charlotte will be so incredibly happy for him because he deserves it. I only hope I'll be around to see it.

After our call, I have nothing else to do all day, leaving my mind to wander, which doesn't do it any good. Instead of spinning the wheels of my brain, I hop in my car just before sundown and go to the gym since I haven't been in a while. Getting back to the gym will be good for me. It'll help me think. Do I tell Annalisa about my past and Tony? Do Aiden and I tell our friends about Jason and Jackson? Is Agent Dylan really hoping I draw Tony out? These are the things going through my mind as I drive, taking the back roads so I have extra time to think.

As I drive, I spot a familiar red Mustang ahead of me on the road. My chest tightens. I haven't seen Ryan since he left a bruise on my wrist.

It has to be him, right? What are the odds of that specific car with those modifications being on this road? As I'm staring at it, the car slows down and I make out a flash of blond, and watch, stunned, as the car drives away.

Did he just kick Kaitlyn out of his car?!

There's no way that just happened. It has to be a trick of the eyes. But as I slow down, the shape of a girl is illuminated by my headlights. She rises from the ground and dusts herself off, or as well as she can with one arm in a sling.

Holy shit. It really is Kaitlyn. He really did push her out of a moving vehicle.

I pull up beside her but before I can roll down my window, she glances at me and starts walking back to town.

Does she know it's me? Should I just keep going? I want to see if she's okay and needs a ride back, but as I'm about to roll down my window, I pause. After everything she's done to me, does she deserve kindness? What she's put me through flashes through my mind: the humiliation, the threats, the bullying. Would she do the same thing for me if the roles were reversed? I think it over for a couple seconds.

Screw it. She can walk back to town.

Without giving myself time to change my mind, I start to drive again, but there's a gnawing feeling in my stomach.

Don't look in the rearview mirror. Just keep driving, Amelia. Don't you do it.

I look in the rearview mirror.

It looks like she's limping but trying to keep her head held high as the sun sets around her.

"Damn it."

I make a U-turn and pull up beside her on the opposite side of the road. My car comes to a crawl, keeping pace with her as she heads back to town, but she refuses to look at me.

"Hey, do you need a ride?" I call from my open window.

She looks at me for the first time. The makeup streams down her cheeks, making her healing black eye look black again.

"Great. Of course it's you." She looks away from me and continues marching forward. "Go away."

The devil on my shoulder's talking to me now. *See? She doesn't want your help. Just leave her. It's karma.*

I shake the thoughts from my head and take in a steadying breath.

I'm better than this.

I pull over on the side of the road and turn off my car. Kaitlyn doesn't slow her pace, so I hop out and jog to catch up to her. "Wait up!"

She glances back at me then looks straight ahead again. "Do you not understand English? I said to leave me alone."

When I catch up to her my legs match her stride, but she still doesn't take her focus off the horizon in front of her. I say, "I understand English perfectly. I just have a history of not doing what I'm told."

"So if I told you *not* to jump off that bridge over there?"

"Ha-ha." I jog around to stand in front of her and force her to stop by blocking her path. "Are you okay?"

She rubs the back of her good hand over her eye, smudging her makeup even more in the process. "Do I look okay? Wow, how does Aiden have a conversation with you?"

She shoves me to the side and continues walking, and I stand there staring after her.

I get it. We're not friends and I'm probably the last person she wants to accept help from. But she's hurting and lashing out. Well, actually, who knows if this is her lashing out? So far it's been a pretty standard Kaitlyn interaction. But either way, I'm going to at least try to help.

"Okay, you don't need to talk to me. But I can at least drive you home." I chase after her again, matching her stride.

She scoffs. "I don't need your help."

I glance at the limp she's trying to hide. "You were literally just pushed out of a moving car."

She stops walking and turns to face me. The perfect version of herself she shows the world has cracked. I can tell she's trying really hard to hold it together and muster up as much bitchy energy as she can to intimidate me, but it's kind of hard when she's all scraped up and her makeup's running down her face.

"Why won't you just leave me alone?! Does this make you happy? Seeing me like this? Are you getting off on seeing mean old Kaitlyn all beaten up?"

"What? Am I here making fun of you? I'm trying to help."

"I don't need your help!" she practically yells in my face. She turns away from me, but the tears she's trying to hide are clear to me.

"Kaitlyn." I don't know where to start. "You don't have to go through this alone. You don't need to stay with Ryan."

"Ryan is my boyfriend." She sniffles, still not looking at me.

"And? He's hurting you! Just leave him. Tell someone. Anything is better than putting up with that."

She turns back to look at me now. Her eyes look tired. "I'm not going to leave him, okay? Drop it."

Frustration claws at my chest and I try not to shake her. Kaitlyn's not my friend, and probably never will be, but I will never ever be okay with standing by and letting someone get walked all over. I'm not wired that way.

"What the hell happened to you, Kaitlyn? You're not the fierce girl I met when I first transferred to this school. That Kaitlyn ran the school. That Kaitlyn started a war with me over bumping into the guy she liked. That Kaitlyn would destroy a boy for looking at her the wrong way. But now? Now you're letting a guy treat you like garbage. You're letting him put his hands on you and hurt you. You don't *have* to be with him, Kaitlyn. You deserve better than him and you know that."

"Just mind your own fucking business, Amelia. You don't know anything about my situation."

"I don't have to know anything about your situation other than the fact that he's *abusing* you and that you don't have to put up with it."

"Yes, I do," she quickly snaps back. The air around us grows colder with the setting sun, with the chill of her words.

"No, you don't!"

"Yes, I do!"

"No, you don't!"

"You don't get it!"

"What don't I get? I get it perfectl—"

"He's all I have!" she explodes, tears welling in her eyes as the anger turns to sadness. "Happy? He's all I have."

"What are you talking about?"

"Are you deaf? He's the only person I have; my only friend, really."

"But what about Makayla? And Krista and Alexa and Br—"

She waves me off. "They're all just yes-men. They just agree with whatever I say because they're scared of me. You don't think they don't turn around and talk shit about me the second I leave the room? I can guarantee they do. They don't care about me, they're just friends with me because I'm popular. Hell, even you, the girl I hate more than anyone, know what my boyfriend is doing and my 'best friends' have no clue."

I don't know how to reply to that. I can barely even process what she's saying. "If you know that your friends aren't real with you, why not just try to make more friends? Why just settle for fake friends?"

She runs her good hand through her hair as her shoulders slump. She seems completely and totally drained; no wonder she's telling me all this. "I liked the way things were. Everyone was scared of me, and I was fine with it because I got to run the school my way. I could do whatever I wanted, decide who was cool and who was invited to parties. Girls wanted to be my friend and I could have any pick of the guys. I was even finally getting attention from the one boy everyone else wanted. But then you came along. You stole the boy I liked without even trying, and you showed the whole school that they don't have to be afraid of me. I lost the guy, I lost my rule over the school, and I'm barely holding on to my popularity."

Whoa. I didn't think Kaitlyn was that deep. I thought she hated me, like, for fun.

"Does popularity really mean that much to you? Is it worth staying with a guy who abuses you?"

She looks away in the distance, unable to meet my eyes as she murmurs, "It's not just about that. Without Ryan I'm just . . . I'm just alone."

I actually feel my heart kind of break. I never thought I would *feel bad* for *Kaitlyn*. But here I am. Feeling bad for her and genuinely wanting to help her.

"Hey, listen to me. You are *Kaitlyn Anderson*. You're stronger than this. And you're not alone. You have friends and people who care about you. Leave Ryan and get your shit back together."

"Oh God. Please don't tell me you're about to say that *you* care about me and that *you* want to be my friend. Because I'll tell you right now that will never in a million years happen. Like, ever."

"Please. I'd have to get hit *really* hard on the head for that to happen. Come on, let's get back to my car. I'll give you a ride home."

Finally, she turns around and treks back to my car. It's a small victory, getting her to accept a ride, but I still feel like celebrating.

Before I can say anything else, she grows serious, her voice coming out small, which is such a contrast to her normal personality. "Even if I want to leave Ryan, I can't."

We stop in front of my car and I turn to face her. "Why the hell not?"

She sighs, and I see her mental debate over if she should tell me or not.

In the end, she decides to tell me. "He has . . . pictures . . . saved on his phone."

"Pictures? So what? Who cares if—ohhh." The meaning of her words sink in, and we're left staring at each other.

"Yeah," she says solemnly, then leans on the hood of my car and stares straight ahead as the sun sets around us. "If I leave him, he'll send them out."

I move beside her and lean on my car too. "I know it's not ideal, but would you really prefer to keep getting beaten up over him sending some pictures out?"

"Are you stupid? If those pictures get out, I'm done. Colleges actually screen their applicants, not to mention the social embarrassment. And my parents? Oh my Go—"

"Okay, okay, I get it." I cut her off. "But you can't just stay with him because of that. How old are you? Seventeen?"

"Yes, but I thought of that angle already. If I report him, there's a chance I'd get in trouble for distributing child pornography."

"What? But it's a picture of yourself?"

She rolls her eyes for what must be the millionth time tonight. "I know, it's stupid, but that's the fucking patriarchy for you."

What do we do in this situation? I can't just let her run back to Ryan and continue getting hurt. But she clearly has her heart set on staying with him, at least as long as he has pictures of her. We stand there, leaning against the hood of my car, staring at the sunset, two girls who consider themselves enemies, in a comfortable silence, each lost in her own thoughts.

"Are they only saved on his phone?" I ask. "Isn't there a way you can take his phone and delete them?"

She huffs and tucks her hair behind her ear. "He's really controlling about letting me see his phone, even though I saw his password and memorized it. It's not that hard when it's all zeros." She scoffs and shakes her head, as if amazed at Ryan's personal choices. "He'd have to be distracted so I can delete them, but I can't distract him *and* delete the pictures at the same time. They also save to his computer automatically when he plugs in his phone, so I can't possibly delete all his pictures without him noticing, because then how am I supposed to get to his computer? I've thought it all out before, Amelia."

Except the one aspect she hasn't planned on is having an accomplice.

"If there was a way to get to his phone and laptop, is anything backed up to the cloud?"

If his photos back up to his cloud account that would complicate stuff, because even if she did delete everything, he'd have another copy stored online.

She shakes her head and scowls at the leaf that falls out of her hair. "He doesn't trust the cloud. He said something about not wanting the government to spy on him, which is stupid because it's not like Ryan has anything they would want. News flash Ryan, you don't have launch codes or didn't invent the next billion-dollar company. He's not smart enough for that—he literally can't even remember his own passwords; he writes them all down in a book he keeps in his closet."

She scoffs then looks at me as if noticing me standing there for the first time. "Ew. Why are we standing here talking like people who can actually stand being in each other's vicinity for more than ten seconds? Are you driving me home or what?"

We *were* being civil and having an actual conversation, and it's not the worst thing ever. I shiver at the absurdity of it all. As she walks to the passenger-side door and stares at me with annoyance as she waits for me to unlock the door, a plan starts forming in my mind. One that's risky, but I technically pulled off another version of it with Ethan Moore a while ago.

She pulls at the handle but the door doesn't open. "I know I'm hot, but are you gonna unlock the door or stare at me all night?"

"What if I can help you delete the pictures from his phone and computer?"

She eyes me suspiciously and walks back to stand with me in front of the car. The chill in the air is still prevalent and only getting worse as the sun disappears behind the horizon, but I don't feel any of it when faced with the cutting heat of her intense stare. "You'd do that?"

"If you leave him, yes," I tell her, but then continue before she can say anything. "*And* if you tell your mom it was Ryan, not Anna, who beat you up, and let her come back to school."

She thinks it over for a second, then reluctantly says, "Fine. *If* we delete all the pictures, I'll get Anna to come back to King. But you can't tell *anyone* about our plan."

Get Kaitlyn out of her situation with Ryan *and* help my friend? It's an easy decision. "Deal. But given our history, I'm going to need some insurance."

She scoffs. "I won't go back on my word."

I pull out my phone and unlock it. "Perfect. That's why we'll call this insurance."

I point the phone camera at her. "I won't send this anywhere if you hold up your end of the deal and get Anna back into King. Now state your name and say that Anna's innocent."

Her eyes narrow at me. "You realize that people having recordings-slash-pictures of me is how I'm in this mess in the first place, right?"

I put the phone down and give her a "duh" look. "The difference is that I actually keep my word. I'll delete this as soon as Anna's back at King."

"This is ridiculous. Fine. Start rolling."

I aim the phone at her and press Record.

"Hi. I'm Kaitlyn Anderson and I'm a big fat liar. Wacko Anna White may be wacko, but she didn't injure me. Ryan Simms did. She should be unexpelled and allowed to come back to King City High." She looks at me behind the camera. "Happy?"

"Are you saying all this of your own free will?"

"Oh, screw you." She flips me the bird and walks to the passenger side of the car.

I bite back a grin and end the recording. I guess that's as good a confession from Kaitlyn as I'll get, even if she does insult Annalisa in it.

"You know this doesn't mean we're friends, right?" she states as she clicks her seat belt into place.

Despite everything, I laugh. "I'm completely fine with the fact that we'll never be friends."

I'm not going to post her confession anywhere. I realize that I can just plaster this video all over the place and call it a day. But

I'm not going to do that. I genuinely want to help Kaitlyn. Would she do the same thing for me if the roles were reversed? Probably not. She's been a terrible person to me, sure, but can I just stand around knowing this information and do nothing?

Definitely not.

I follow Kaitlyn's instructions and soon I'm pulling into a quiet neighborhood with sprawling green lawns and large houses surrounded by even larger trees that must be hundreds of years old. Almost all of the properties are fenced in and have electric gates, and as we drive through the neighborhood, each house looks more impressive than the last, as if the neighbors are trying to outdo each other with their landscaping, with their immaculate lawns, with the grandiosity and importance of the house itself. None are as grand as Andrew's house, which I visited during his campaign gala, but I'd still classify these as mansions, making me see Kaitlyn in a new light. The wealthy display doesn't seem to affect her like it does me; she's not subtlety trying to crane her neck to gawk at the architecture like I am, and either doesn't notice my wonder or just doesn't care. She must be desensitized to it from years of this being her normal.

She directs me to a house, and I pull up in front of the gate, lowering my window to punch in the code she recites with clear boredom. The black iron gates slide open, and I creep up the driveway that's illuminated by lights and lined by large trees. The drive circles around a landscaped patch of greenery, so I steer around it and stop in front of her front door.

Her house is average size for the neighborhood, which is at least five times the size of mine. The outside lights are on but the inside looks still and quiet, not a single light on. I wonder how many rooms there are, how big Kaitlyn's room is, how many people live here, how alone she feels in the grandness of the house.

She's about to open her door but then pauses, her hand resting delicately on the handle. "We'll fine-tune our plan tomorrow after school. Right now I just want a bath and bed."

The silence of the car and darkness of the night suddenly feels heavy with all the words left unsaid, with this newfound, fragile truce we hold between us. "Are you sure you don't want to get yourself checked?" I eye her injuries.

"I'm fine." She pulls the handle and even though she must be sore, gets out of the car more gracefully than even I can sometimes manage.

She pauses before closing the door, ducking down to peer at me, but doesn't quite look *at* me. "Um . . ." Her jaw works for a moment as she thinks through whatever's on her mind. She meets my eyes, and whatever softness was on her face has disappeared. "Don't drive to school tomorrow. And for God's sake, don't get dirty tomorrow or you're not sitting in my car."

Without so much as a good-bye, she closes my door with something slightly gentler than a slam, and marches up her front steps, opens the huge front door, and disappears into the house without a backward glance.

I sit there staring after her for only a few beats before I shake off whatever misplaced shock I'm feeling and drive away. I might have been delusional in thinking that she was going to thank me. That's not the kind of relationship we have, and I can't expect it to change over the span of a car ride. But even so, I can't stop the tug of a smirk at my lips, or the bubbling excitement in my chest.

24

Aiden and I haven't been at school since the video of his father trying to kill him went viral, so we had no idea how the students were going to react when we stepped into school Monday morning.

A lot of kids are scared of Aiden, but he's friends with a lot of people, so he gets stopped almost every couple of seconds by people coming up to ask him about what happened. He barely deigns to give more than a few words answer before extracting himself from the conversation and doing his regular, brooding routine, with his hand wrapped securely around mine.

At the end of the day as I'm walking out of school with Aiden, I spot Annalisa standing where the boys usually park. Commack Silver High gets out before King does, so she would've had plenty of time to get here.

"Hey, what are you doing here?" I ask her as we approach. She's standing with Julian and Mason, near their cars.

"Haven't you checked the group chat?"

I haven't checked the group chat. I rarely do since the boys always talk about so many random things. "No, why?"

Annalisa brushes her hair out of her face as the wind picks up. "We're going to that bar Greg was seen at to ask the manager about Luke. He's there today and said he'd meet with us."

Aiden and I glance at each other in a totally inconspicuous way. At least, he was inconspicuous. I'm sure I look like my eye-balls popped out of my head.

"To find out about Luke?" Which we already know because the twins confessed, and we haven't figured out what to do yet? Aiden subtly elbows me. I clear my throat and try to stop acting so guilty. "Do we have to go, like, right now?" I ask her, looking around for Kaitlyn.

"Yeah. He says he has other meetings and if we want answers, we gotta get them tonight." There's a hopeful energy about her, as if she's sure *this* is the lead we've been waiting for, that this is what she needs to prove Luke's innocence. Even Mason and Julian seem more excited than usual.

Aiden pulls me closer. "What's wrong?"

He can read me like a book. I should've told him about what I'm doing with Kaitlyn, but then he'd get all protective and try to stop me because he doesn't want me near Ryan. He hasn't seen Ryan since he almost broke his face for grabbing my wrist, and I really don't want a replay of that situation; Aiden has enough going on as it is.

"Nothing." It takes every muscle in my body to pull away from him. "I just have something else I have to do. I can't get out of it."

Annalisa's face falls, that hopeful energy dissipating. "Oh, okay. I guess it's important if—"

A car comes speeding through the parking lot and screeches to a stop right beside us. It's Kaitlyn, in the very same shiny Porsche

I glitter bombed all those weeks ago. It's very easy to picture this car right at home in the house I got a glimpse of last night.

She rolls down the window. "Get in. We have to go."

Annalisa, Aiden, Mason, and Julian all glance around with perplexed expressions on their faces, as if looking for who Kaitlyn's talking to.

"Yeah, I'm coming," I answer.

My friends don't even try to hide the looks of shock and confusion on their faces.

Aiden tugs my arm and speaks in a hushed tone. "What's going on? Are you okay? Is she blackmailing you?"

I laugh at his cute, concerned face. "I'm fine. Everything's fine, I promise. I'm just helping her with something, I'll tell you about it after."

I give him a quick kiss and adjust my shoulder bag.

"Wait, wait, wait. You're *actually* going to go somewhere with her? To *help* her? Are you on drugs?" Annalisa exclaims before I can walk to Kaitlyn's car.

"It's a long story, Anna—"

"I've only been a Silver for, like, a week, and you're already best friends with the bitch who got me expelled?"

She's mad. Even the wind picks up, as if angry with me as well. It doesn't help that the last time we argued about Kaitlyn, Annalisa thought I was choosing Kaitlyn over her, which is kind of what this situation looks like.

"And did you say you're helping her!? *Kaitlyn*? Evil incarnate? The girl whose life goal is to make you miserable? The girl who lied and got me *expelled*? You're choosing to hang out with her and *help* her over me?"

"Anna, it's not like that and you know it—"

"What the hell are you *thinking*, Amelia? She's just going to screw you over and you know it. Do you ever think before you do shit or do you just rely on Aiden to clean up your messes? That's basically all he does."

"Hey." She gets a warning from Aiden and Mason at the same time.

That was undeserved and she knows it. Before I can think, I snap back, "Well, all Julian does is chase after you when you run out of a room after a dramatic outburst!"

I don't care how upset she is, that was uncalled for. I get that she hates Kaitlyn; she has a reason to. But that doesn't mean she can jump down my throat and not let me get a word in to explain myself. The wind whips my hair around my face, and beside us, Julian, Aiden, and Mason are silenced by shock. The normal sounds of kids laughing and talking as they emerge from school and get into cars is nothing but distant background now. The tension is louder.

I take a calming breath. I know she didn't mean it. "I'm sorry, I'm sorry. I didn't mean that."

"I did," she bites back.

Throughout all of this, Kaitlyn's been relatively calm. She hasn't even started honking impatiently or anything. Now, she leans out the window again. "Are you coming? Gas isn't cheap, you know."

"Give me a second," I tell her, then turn to look at Annalisa. "I know you're pissed, Anna, but attacking me isn't going to fix anything. I'll explain everything after, and when I do, you'll feel bad about saying that."

I turn back to Aiden and give him a reassuring kiss.

"Everything's okay. I love you," I murmur against his lips before pulling away.

He seems confused but doesn't stop me. "I love you too," he says possessively as I walk away.

"*Gag*, you guys are so gross," Kaitlyn tells me as I get in her car. Her arm's finally out of the sling, and she fixes her lip gloss in the mirror. I hate to admit it, but it's really nice inside this car; the leather feels smooth and expensive.

As I close the door, I try to ignore all the eyes following me. The confused ones from Mason and Julian, the accusing ones from Annalisa, and the intense ones from Aiden. But this is bigger than they know, and they don't need all of us to go to a bar and ask some questions. I'm doing this for Kaitlyn, I'm doing this for Annalisa, and I'm doing this for myself. I can't sit aside and be okay with a man thinking he can control a girl. Not now, and not ever.

Everything will make sense to them in less than twenty-four hours. I know it looks bad and confusing right now, but once I can explain everything, they'll understand.

>> <<

After we fine-tune our plan, Kaitlyn drops me off at home to get my car, and I follow her to Ryan's house. For the first part of the plan, Kaitlyn is going to show up at his house, where she assured me he'd be home alone. She's going to gather all her "old Kaitlyn energy" aka *demanding scary bitch energy*, and accuse him of forgetting some anniversary and demand that he take her out.

I park my car down the street and turn it off, ducking down in my seat so that I'm not visible. Ryan's neighborhood isn't bad. It's nothing like Kaitlyn's with the circular driveway and punch-code gate to get in, but it's not sketchy like Luke's apartment.

Kaitlyn pulls into his driveway, gets out of her car, and bangs her hand against the door. A few moments later, Ryan answers. His hair's messy and he's wearing jeans with a Commack Silver High hoodie. They talk for a bit at the front door, then Kaitlyn gets visibly offended. She's very expressive with her hands, her arms flailing out every which way. I can just imagine what she's saying.

What? You're telling me you didn't plan anything for today? How dare you forget that today is the two month anniversary of the first time you held my hand?! or some other absurd thing.

Every time he tries to speak, she nags over him. Eventually, Ryan pinches the bridge of his nose in exhaustion and Kaitlyn perks up, then he disappears into the house.

I guess he gave in. *Fine, Kaitlyn. Whatever. Happy three month anniversary of the first time I looked at you for longer than ten seconds. Let's go.*

I laugh at my own improv and duck down farther when Ryan emerges from the house with a jacket and his car keys.

Kaitlyn stops him and says something. She's telling him she needs to use the bathroom but wants her seat warmer already going when she comes back. They argue for a couple of seconds out on the driveway, then Ryan, apparently too tired from their first argument, rolls his eyes, thrusts his house keys at her, and turns to walk to his car.

Kaitlyn practically prances up his steps and unlocks his front door, disappearing into the house. Not even two seconds later, Ryan starts honking.

I was a bit worried at this part of the plan, since it relies so heavily on Kaitlyn antagonizing the boy who already isn't afraid of harming her, but she promised me that he wouldn't hurt her today. She said he has to be in a "certain mood," whatever that means. I guess she'd know and tone it down, but she seems right so far since he hasn't lashed out. Still, this isn't my favorite position to put her in.

Ryan gets out of the car and is about to walk back to the house when Kaitlyn emerges, closing the door behind her but conveniently "forgetting" to lock it.

They get into the car and I scooch lower in my seat as they drive off, even though they drive in the opposite direction.

My phone vibrates; it's a text from Kaitlyn.

> Left his laptop out on his bed. Second room on the left. The password book is somewhere in his closet but I didn't have enough time to find it

Why he doesn't just use the same three passwords like every other person, I'll never know, but in this case his paranoia works in our favor.

On it. Heading in now I text back, getting out of my car and casually walking down the street to Ryan's house.

As much as I hate drama and stuff, I think I secretly love this secret agent covert stuff. As stressful as it is, it gets the adrenaline going. It's fun screwing Ryan over, and even weirder, being on the same team as Kaitlyn. I have to give credit where credit's due—Kaitlyn was one hell of an actress. I'm almost scared of the power we'd have if we ever decided to be friends and team up for more schemes like this, but I know that'll never happen.

I walk right up Ryan's front steps and into his house, closing the door behind me. He lives with his mom, who isn't home, obviously. The house is small and slightly messy, but not dirty.

Without wasting time, I follow Kaitlyn's directions and head into Ryan's room. It's a simple room, with a bed in the corner, a bathroom off to the side, and another door to the closet. His bedsheets are a tangled mess at the bottom of his bed, and there are piles of clothes on the floor. He even has a couple of posters of naked girls up on his wall, which, I mean, *gross*.

His laptop is on his bed, and I head over to the closet for the password book. His closet isn't a walk-in, which I guess makes my life a bit easier, but it's not organized either.

A quick scan doesn't reveal any kind of book or notebook anywhere, so I roll up my sleeves and sort through the clutter on the floor. Should I be wearing gloves for this? Who knows what's in here? I pinch a pair of his underwear between two fingers and practically gag as I move it to the other end of the closet. Maybe I *should've* worn gloves.

There are a couple of textbooks but no notebook. There's a shelf at the top of his closet, so I say a silent prayer that my hand doesn't land on anything gross and blindly feel around for it.

My hand touches a couple of things that don't feel like notebooks, and I don't ever want to know what they are, before finally landing on a notebook. I pull it out and shake my hand out as if that will somehow help stop the spread of germs.

As I skim through the book, there are passwords written in his sloppy writing, but none of them are labeled, so I head over to the laptop and try a bunch of them. The laptop finally opens with "ilovehotchicks," which is real mature of him, and I start searching his photo albums.

This part of the plan I'm not too keen on either. I'm literally supposed to actively look for pictures of Kaitlyn naked. I almost throw up in my mouth just thinking of it. But, hey, she needed to distract him so we had no other choice. She's not too happy about it, either, but I'm just trying to get in, delete the pictures, and get out, not analyze each one.

The folders are organized by month, so I start from a couple months before I know they started dating just in case, and quickly click through each picture. He doesn't have a lot of pictures, which is good since it makes clicking through them and deleting any naked ones easier.

Kaitlyn said her face isn't in all of them, so I just go through and delete anything that looks like a naked girl. I don't even know if they're all Kaitlyn, to be honest, but if it's naked, it's deleted.

I finish and double-check the folders in case I missed any, then make sure to empty his recycle bin just in case. Hopefully I got everything, but I mean, that's the best I can do. He might not even notice that they're missing. The way the folders are set up makes it look like it's just an automatic backup from when he plugs his phone in.

I close his laptop and put it back where I found it, and do the same with the notebook. I eye the bathroom door, and just can't resist going to wash my hands. I feel like laughing and jumping up and down clapping. We're really going to get away with this. It can't really be this easy, can it?

A pounding on Ryan's front door answers my thoughts, making me freeze as I exit his room. No one knows I'm in here, right? Did a neighbor see me walk in? Is Ryan back? The pounding continues.

"Ryan?" It's a girl's voice, one I've never heard before.

Is his mom home? No, his mom wouldn't be knocking on the front door. I eye the doorknob helplessly as it jiggles. *Oh no*. Did I lock the door when I came in?

The door swings open and a girl around my age waltzes in. I'm frozen, staring at the door like a deer in headlights.

"Ryan? You were supposed to pick me up an hour ag—oh." She pauses when she sees me, tilting her head to the side. "Who are you and why are you in Ryan's house?"

Why *would* a random girl be standing in Ryan's house?

She's looking at me, waiting for me to answer her question.

"I'm, uh . . . Kaitlyn." I mean, we practically have the same hair, might as well use it. My spine straightens and I try to emulate Kaitlyn's attitude as best I can. "I'm his girlfriend. Who are *you*?"

She stares at me in disbelief. "I'm Cece. *I'm* Ryan's girlfriend."

Ryan's girlfriend?!

That was the last thing I was expecting her to say. Clearly Ryan's got a type, because she's giving me all the Kaitlyn vibes right now.

Shit. How do I get out of this now? *Think, Amelia!*

I fake outrage. "Ryan has another girlfriend?! That two-timing asshole! I'm going to go find him right now!"

I dodge her as I storm out and speed walk as quickly as I can to my car. I can feel her staring holes into my back all the way down the street. I hop in my car and book it out of there as quickly as I can.

Ryan has another girlfriend? I wonder if Kaitlyn knows. Did Cece just derail our whole plan? She's definitely going to call him and tell him about a girl named Kaitlyn standing in his house claiming to be his girlfriend, which will screw us up because he's currently *with* his girlfriend Kaitlyn. Ryan *can't* be stupid enough to answer his girlfriend's phone call while he's *with his other* girlfriend, right? But that's probably why she came over, since he's not answering her calls.

I shoot Kaitlyn a text and tell her I got everything from his computer and that I'm on my way to the next location, to which she replies *k*

I don't want to tell her about Cece in case she goes crazy and derails our whole plan. She's already planning on leaving him, so she can go crazy on him *after* we get the pictures off his phone.

The next part of the plan is getting his cell phone and deleting the pictures from there. He and Kaitlyn went to dinner, and now they're going to Sweetie's for dessert. I park in the arcade lot across the street and sit and watch for Ryan's car.

I put on a baseball cap and oversized sunglasses, even though the sun is setting, and shrug on a puffy jacket. Ryan hasn't seen me with my new hair, so I'm hoping that he won't recognize me with just a quick glance.

As I wait, I check my phone for messages from Aiden, who wants to know if everything's okay. I assure him everything's fine, then see Ryan's car pull into Sweetie's parking lot.

Putting away my phone, I let the adrenaline fuel me as I hop out of my car and quickly jog across the street. Ryan and Kaitlyn are in line inside, waiting to place their order, and Kaitlyn catches my eye. She gives me a quick nod, then turns to Ryan, who's looking at the menu on the board behind the counter. I spy an empty plastic ice-cream cup sitting on a table and pick it up.

"*Ow! Ryan!*" Kaitlyn shrieks. "Why would you shove me like that?! That hurt!"

I can't see his face, but I'm sure he's confused. "What are you talking about? I didn—"

"How would you like it if I shoved you?"

I'm standing directly behind him when she shoves him. We bump into each other and I pretend to fumble around a bit, before straightening up and grunting a quick "Watch it," over my shoulder as I walk to the front door. I throw the empty ice-cream cup in the garbage placed beside the door to make it look like I was on my way out anyway.

I don't know what happens next, but I'm hoping Kaitlyn is arguing with Ryan to distract him from the fact that I lifted his phone out of his back pocket during our "fumble."

My heart beats loudly in my ears as I move over to a quiet side of the parking lot and unlock his phone. His passcode really is just 000000, which, considering he has two girlfriends and is trying to hide them from one another, isn't very smart. Since I don't have much time, I open his photos and click Select All, then hit Delete. I click on his Recently Deleted folder and do the same thing.

This is almost too easy, I feel like he's going to jump out and catch me in the act, but a quick glance around tells me I've still got time. Though the parking lot is filled with cars, no one else is there except a few teenagers, huddling beside a car on the other side of the lot from me.

A notification pops up: *Are you sure you want to delete all photos? These cannot be recovered.*

Perfect, exactly what I want. And if he has anything important, he can back it up from his computer.

Confident I'm not going to get caught, I hit Yes, and breathe out a sigh of relief when the pictures disappear.

I look into the window where Kaitlyn is looking out for me to give her a signal, and send her a thumbs-up, waving Ryan's now pictureless phone in the air.

She smiles, the maliciousness and hostility that's been lacking from her eyes lately flooding back into them tenfold. It's like she grows triple her size and manages to loom over Ryan even though he's taller than her—the confidence in her shoulders and her posture that of a woman on a mission, of a person freed from the chains holding them back, and who's savoring their vengeance. It's a transformation as she turns from the tired, shadow version of herself into Kaitlyn *fucking* Anderson.

She says something to him, and everyone in Sweetie's attention is now on the two of them. She's shouting now, and even though I'm outside, I can tell she's cursing his name up and down. She marches outside to me and Ryan follows.

"You can't leave me, you stupid bitch!" He slams the door open after her. "Did you forget? I have all your pictures! I'll send them out, you know I will. Get a billboard and everything."

"Are you sure you have them?" I casually ask and hold up his phone so he notices me for the first time.

He pats his pockets, no doubt looking for the phone in my hands, and then takes a step closer to me, but I match his step with a backward one of my own.

"You're disgusting," I tell him. "If I somehow missed any pictures and you send them to *anyone*, I'll have you arrested for distributing child pornography. That's right, it's a thing. Kaitlyn's seventeen and will always be seventeen in those pictures. If you do anything other than delete them, you *will* be charged."

He doesn't need to know that there's a chance Kaitlyn would be charged, too, but I'm sure I got them all anyway. He stares at me with disbelief as I toss him his phone and he catches it.

"Oh, by the way, your other girlfriend, Cece, knows about Kaitlyn," I add.

Kaitlyn gasps. "I *knew* you were cheating on me!" She faces me. "I accused him of it in the car the other day and that fight is why he kicked me out!"

"I kicked you out because you're a stupid bitch!" Ryan explodes, then turns to me. "And of course Parker's bitch is involved in this. Does he not teach you how to behave?"

The people from inside are now all outside, watching the fight unfold, mumbling to themselves. Some parents cover their children's ears and steer them away.

Before I can say anything, Kaitlyn beats me to it. Apparently, she's been saving all the aggression I knew she was capable of for when he couldn't blackmail her anymore.

"*I'm* a stupid bitch? You're the asshole who's probably going to have to repeat senior year! But good luck doing that when they expel you for domestic assault! That's right, everyone! Ryan did all this to me and I'm not embarrassed to say it if it means fucking him over." She gets into his space, not scared in the slightest. "You come near me again and I'll shove your dick so far down your throat you'll taste it until the day you die. Now stay the hell away from me."

She marches off, then turns to look at me. "Are you going to drive me to my car or what?!"

I ignore the hostility directed at me, and instead lean toward Ryan. "If you come near me or Aiden or my friends again, I will destroy you."

Before he can say anything, I turn away from him and follow Kaitlyn to my car.

As I drive away, she laughs. It's not a maniacal or malicious laugh either like I'm used to. It's a laugh I've never heard from her before. A laugh of genuine relief and excitement.

"I feel *so good* right now! I can't wait until I file a police report and charge him for assaulting me. Do you think he'll cry? I think he'll cry."

I toss my hat and sunglasses into the backseat, the adrenaline from what we just pulled not wearing off. The energy between us makes me feel alive, excited for what's to come. "That was awesome. You were great!"

"Well, duh. I'm great at everything." She laughs, then pauses for a second. "This still doesn't mean we're friends. We're not. I literally never want to see your face again after today."

I'm so hopped up on adrenaline her harsh words can't even ruin my mood. Besides, her tone wasn't that of malevolence, one that she's used on me countless times before. While still firm and unwavering, it lacked that special punch that Kaitlyn packs into all her insults.

"After you clear Anna's name and get her to come back to King, I'm fine with never seeing you again too."

There are some people in life who will just never like you, and that's okay. You can't be everyone's best friend, and Kaitlyn and I will never be friends. But I'm okay knowing that Kaitlyn is out there, disliking me but not my complete enemy anymore.

25

After I drop Kaitlyn off at her car, I call Aiden on Bluetooth.

Since Kaitlyn announced it herself to all of Sweetie's, I was given permission to tell my friends about what we were up to. I would've told them some version of the story anyway, but at least now I won't feel bad withholding the whole truth from them, even though I really don't owe Kaitlyn my loyalty, no matter how much we bonded today.

Aiden picks up right away, and his deep voice fills the car, the mere sound of it adding to the joviality in the air. I briefly explain to him what I was up to after school, and he sighs. "I'm proud of you, but I wish you would've told me. I could've helped. What if something went wrong?"

"Would you have let me go alone if I told you?"

He pauses. "Fine. I'm just glad it all worked out. You love scheming, huh? You're good at it."

He laughs, and I join him. "I would think I was a secret agent in a past life or something, but I'm a terrible improv actor."

There's noise of people talking in the background, and it gets quieter as I assume Aiden leaves the room. "We're all at my house right now since we wanted dinner after the bar. Want to come and tell them the good news yourself? We could use some."

Checking my rearview mirror, I change direction on the road and head for Aiden's house instead of home. "Why, what happened at Greg's bar?"

He tells me that the manager confirmed Luke was there that night. He also said that Luke showed up and started a fight with Greg and they had to be pulled apart. He said they were both kicked out around 4:20, and told Annalisa that he had already submitted this evidence to the police. All it proves is that Luke was the one in the fight with Greg, which doesn't help his case at all. It could be argued that Luke went back to finish the fight. But we still don't know where Luke was at the time of death, and the others don't know how Greg ended up dying at Aiden's house.

I don't point out that we know what actually happened to Greg in case one of our friends overhears. "He was at Howard's Convenience alone at five-ish though? Where was Greg?"

"I don't know. But on the way home I drove past Howard's on purpose. There's a gas station down the street with cameras that point out. I know a guy who works there, his name is Ben. He makes a lot of money off of me from the Tracks, so I called him and asked for a favor."

A shiver runs down my spine and I check my rearview mirror again. Is someone following me? Is Ryan coming back for revenge? I didn't really give him a chance to say his piece. I check my mirrors, and no one is even remotely near me, so it must be the adrenaline.

I shake it off and focus on what Aiden's saying. If those cameras caught anything, that could help us figure out where Luke went next, and clear Luke's name without having to bring attention to Jason and Jackson. "Did the guy at the gas station find anything?"

"He said he doubted it, since the gas station is a bit down the way from Howard's, but he told me he'd take a look and get back to me."

"Have you told anyone?" I ask him as I turn onto his street.

"No. Let's just keep this between us for now until we hear back from him."

We can just add it to this list of things I'm keeping from my friends. By this point I'm pulling up in front of his house, so we hang up and he opens his front door for me.

He hugs me so tightly my feet lift off the ground, and I giggle.

"I'm so happy you're okay," he says, his breath tickling my ear.

He kisses me and finally sets me down.

"I'm fine," I reassure him. "And now Kaitlyn isn't being hurt anymore, either, and Anna can graduate with—"

I pause for a second and listen. "Is Anna crying?"

Aiden closes the front door once I walk in. Everyone is in the kitchen, but I can still hear her sobs from the front door.

Aiden runs a tired hand through his hair. "Yeah, she's saying Luke's going to rot in jail. It hasn't been a good day for her."

I lower my voice to a whisper. "Should we tell her about the twins?" It'll help ease her mind knowing that Luke's innocent and won't be in jail forever.

Aiden shakes his head once. "Anna's all wired up. She's going to jump the gun before we can get it all sorted out, and I'm not going into it without a solid plan. I've been calling the lawyer,

Alan, but only getting his voice mail, and I'm not leaving a voice mail about what I need help with. So we can't say anything yet, not until I figure out the best thing for the twins."

I take off my shoes and follow him through the house. This one isn't my call to make, so if Aiden wants to hold off on saying anything, I'll support his decision.

"Where are the twins?" I ask him, and he gestures upstairs.

"They've been doing their homework, but they'll probably make an appearance soon since Mason and Noah promised to play video games with them," he says as we enter the kitchen.

Everyone is sitting at the table, empty pizza boxes scattered around them, and their eyes all turn to me as I enter. They say hi, but Annalisa looks at me with an expression that looks broken. Her makeup is smudged and her eyes are swollen.

"How was your date with Satan?" she sneers at me.

She's still upset, I get it. We didn't end things on the best foot when I left school today, and now she's feeling hopeless about her brother. Hopefully, telling her that she doesn't have to stay at Commack anymore will make her feel better.

"It wasn't a date. But it actually was amazing. I have good news. You don—"

"Save it," she interrupts me, and I shake my head in confusion. She continues, "I don't want to hear it."

"But yo—"

"I don't want to hear it!" she repeats, tears flowing freely again. "You should've been there with me today. You promised you'd do this with me."

I did promise I'd be there for her every step of the way. But helping Kaitlyn helped both of them. I don't move from where I stand with Aiden near the kitchen door.

"I'm sorry, Ann—"

"I don't want your apology! You're supposed to be my best friend, but you chose Kaitlyn over me *knowing* that she lied and got me expelled. It's like I don't even know you. All I want to do is prove Luke had nothing to do with Greg's death!"

I'm too stunned to say anything; my thoughts are all over the place. She's not letting me get a word in. How can I make her see I'm trying? That I may not be perfect, but all I want to do is help her.

Aiden's tone is calm. "Attacking Amelia isn't going to help, Anna."

Somewhere in the back of my mind I sense Jason and Jackson standing behind us in the door, but no one pays them any attention.

Julian puts a hand on Annalisa's arm. "We all know the truth behind Greg's death. We just need to prove it. It'll all work out."

"You told them?"

Aiden and I turn around to look Jason, who just spoke. He's in his pajamas and barefoot when he walks into the room, Jackson following him. "You told me not to say anything about how we killed Greg. Does this mean everyone knows it was an accident now?"

My jaw drops and Aiden's whole body tenses.

"Wait, what?" Annalisa stands so abruptly her chair is knocked back. "What is he talking about?"

Aiden rounds on his brothers. "Boys, go upstairs."

Jason and Jackson look at each other before scurrying upstairs.

Annalisa moves around the table. "Why did Jason just say they killed Greg? What does he mean?"

I'm standing like a deer in the headlights looking between Aiden and Annalisa. Our friends are frozen in place at the table. This is not how everything was supposed to happen.

I meet Aiden's eyes as we sort through the best thing to say.

"Oh my God." Annalisa steps back, like she's in shock. "You both knew. Jason and Jackson killed Greg? Are you serious? And you weren't going to tell us?"

That snaps Aiden out of it and he jumps into action.

"No, they didn't," he states with a final authority.

My heart pounds in my ears. The tension that was already so prominent in the room thickens.

Annalisa stands her ground. "He literally just said he killed him, and it was an accident. What did he mean?" She shakes her head. "You had me going on a wild goose chase trying to prove Luke didn't kill Greg and you knew this whole time it was the twins?"

"It was an accident," I say weakly, deciding honesty is the best policy right now. "We haven't known for long. We're just trying to figure out how best to proceed before doing anything."

"Are you serious right now? My brother *didn't* kill Greg? The twins did. He won't have to go to jail. Oh my God. This is great! We need to tell *everyone*!"

"Are you hearing yourself? You don't even know the whole story," Aiden snaps, standing in her way when she tries to run from the kitchen.

"I know we can get Luke out of jail right now!" She sidesteps him and jogs to the front door. Aiden charges after her, and I scurry after him. The scrape of chairs and footsteps behind me tell me that our friends follow us out of the kitchen as well, but I'm not focused on them right now, I'm too busy watching Annalisa and Aiden go back and forth, too busy trying to keep my pulse under control, trying to keep the world from imploding around me.

"And what about the twins?" Aiden asks, an edge in his voice. "It was an accident. They were scared, and they hid it. That's not going to look good, and I'm not going to let the media attack them like I was."

She pauses. "We'll figure that out later. I'm calling the cops."

"Were you not listening when I said it was an *accident*?" Aiden asks, his entire body rigid with fury. "We need some time to figure out what to do, how to inflict the least amount of damage on the twins as possible."

"I heard you. You can tell that to the cops when we set Luke free."

"We are *not* telling anyone! Not this second. Come on, Anna, the most logical thing to do is to have a plan on how best to protect them. Luke isn't going to prison."

Annalisa stands her ground against Aiden's stiffened form. "If it was an accident, they'll just get a slap on the wrist and be sent on their way!"

"You're delusional if you think they'll just get a slap on the wrist," Aiden fires back at her. "They killed a guy and hid the evidence. They could still be charged, I could lose my custody petition, and they'll be famous for the rest of their lives for killing someone. We need to handle this *properly*."

Annalisa looks around the room at our friends' shocked faces. "So you're saying you're just going to let Luke take the fall for it? Knowing full well he's innocent?"

I promised her Luke wouldn't go to prison, and I'm standing by that promise. It's important to me that she know that, even though she's pissed at me right now for numerous reasons. "Well, we know Luke didn't do it for sure now. Aiden's getting a lawyer for the twins. In the meantime, we can still protect the boys by just finding out where Luke was at the time of Greg's death like we've been doing. Let's just take a second to think things through."

Annalisa sets her piercing gaze on me. "Of course you're going to take his side. As if you're not done betraying me this week, you're fine with throwing my brother under the bus for Aiden's brothers."

My breath stills. That's not what's going on and she knows it.

"They're just scared kids, Anna." Mason comes to stand beside me, and I'm grounded by his steady, familiar presence. "Amelia and Aiden are right. We don't have to jump on anything right now, Luke's trial date hasn't even been set."

She turns her sights on Mason, and I don't like the hard set of her jaw paired with the fire in her eyes.

"Really, Mason? I know you're only taking her side because you're in love with her. But did you know your dad is fucking her mom on a regular basis? And Amelia has known this whole time and asked me not to tell you?"

My heart stops. All my limbs turn leaden, holding me in place as her words sink in around the room.

She did not just say that.

She did not just say that!

"Mason—"

I don't even know what to say. Brian was supposed to tell him, and if not, I was supposed to break it to him gently, in private. I would've done it at mini-golf, but we weren't alone. That was probably the worst way she could've broken the news to him. And now he thinks I went around telling everyone behind his back.

He looks at me with his sad, big, brown eyes. "Is that true? About our parents?"

"It—I—" Nothing I can say can make this right. Everything is going to shit and I'm losing control of everything. "Brian was supposed to tell you. I'm sorry, Mason . . ."

The look of extreme betrayal and hurt on his face makes me stop any other excuses I could've come up with. He's looking at me like he's never seen me before. Like he's disgusted by the person standing in front of him.

A quick glance at Annalisa tells me that she regrets letting that slip, but she gets over it quickly and squares her shoulders.

"How long have you known?" Mason asks, looking between me and Annalisa.

My voice comes out small. I feel like shrinking into myself. "I found out when we left for the beach house."

Mason looks stunned. "We lived together for two weeks, and you looked at me every day knowing the truth and still decided not to tell me? You've been lying to me for over a month."

"I didn't want to hurt you." I feel like I'm grasping at air, clawing at nothing and praying for a miracle.

"Yeah, well, you failed."

My heart shatters into a million pieces.

He shoves his feet into his boots and throws open the door, leaving before I have a chance to say anything else. I watch him go, and feel tears drip down my face. I didn't want this to happen, I *never* wanted this to happen. This is the whole reason I'd put off telling him, because I didn't want him to look at me with that heartbroken and betrayed face, didn't want him to hate me—though part of me knew it was inevitable, that I was putting off something that was destined to happen no matter how he found out.

"That was uncalled for, Anna." I hear Aiden chiding her. "Do you know how badly you just hurt him?"

"I probably shouldn't have said that, but he needed to know anyway. You've been lying about Mason's dad, and you've been lying about the twins. What else have you been lying about?"

I swipe the tears from my face and turn away from staring into the dark after Mason. I'm tempted to say "Everything," because I have been lying about everything. What would she say if she found out my name isn't even Amelia? Julian, Chase, Noah, and Charlotte are standing off to the side, frozen, not knowing what's going on. We've never had a fight before. Aiden moves to stand in front of me, as if physically blocking Annalisa from looking at me will help the shattering of my heart.

"I think you should leave, Anna." Aiden crosses his arms, leaving no room for argument.

Annalisa squares her shoulders. "Not until you promise to go to the cops and tell them that Jason and Jackson killed Greg."

Aiden would never do that; it's like she doesn't know him. He's going to protect his brothers at all costs or die trying.

"I promise you, Anna, I will not let Luke get sentenced for killing Greg. Just give us some time to figure out what to do. I'm not turning my brothers in."

There's a challenge in Annalisa's eyes when she says, "And what's stopping me from going to the police and telling them myself?"

I make eye contact with Noah, who mouths, "Oh shit."

If looks could kill, the unwavering gaze Aiden fixes on Annalisa would obliterate her. "The police have actual evidence that could prove Luke did it. You think they're going to believe you, Luke's sister, who has no evidence, when you say two nine-year-olds killed Greg? Yeah, good luck."

"What do you guys think?" Annalisa turns on our friends, who stare back at her with wide eyes.

Before they're forced to pick a side, which will inevitably result in another fight, I say, "Why don't we take some time to cool down and we can figure it out tomorrow? I think enough damage has been done for the night. Let's just act like everything's normal until we figure it out."

Annalisa's technically got a point. We should tell the police what really happened. But at the same time, Aiden would never let that happen because who knows what would happen to the twins? Nothing good, that's for sure. It's best to talk to Alan who can help Aiden figure out the best course of action to protect them.

"Unbelievable," Annalisa scoffs, shoving her shoes on and walking out the door that was left open after Mason left.

Julian looks at Aiden, then after Annalisa. He moves to the door and hastily throws his shoes on.

"Sorry, man," he says to Aiden. "You know I won't say anything to anyone about this. But I'm her ride."

Aiden nods, and Julian gives Aiden one of those clasped arms, bro hugs for support, slapping him on the back a couple times.

"It'll be all right," Julian tells him before leaving.

Then it's just me, Aiden, Noah, Charlotte, and Chase, staring at each other, standing in the hallway in the shattered remains of our friendships.

"So . . ." Noah starts. "Is your mom really banging Brian?"

I burst into tears.

"Really, Noah?" Aiden asks, pulling me against him.

I started this night with great news that I didn't even get to share, and I'm ending it with my friendships in disarray and the truth about Greg's murder looming over us all.

The odds of getting through senior year as normally as possible with all my friends is looking slim to none now, and whatever control I have over my life is barely holding on by a thread.

26

In the morning, I drive straight to Mason's house. I'm hoping he hasn't left for school yet and that I can get him alone so I can make things right. There's no way I can sit in class and pretend it's a normal Tuesday, and it doesn't help that I didn't get any sleep last night. I look like a zombie with dark spots under my eyes and my short hair curly and frizzy instead of styled.

Everything keeps spiraling and I have no idea what to do about it. Annalisa's rightfully pissed off, and Mason's whole world just imploded. When I first arrived in King, Mason was really my first friend; he was the first person who kept putting effort into getting to know me, who went out of his way to talk to me. Then came Noah, Charlotte, Chase, Annalisa, Julian, and of course, Aiden, but Mason has always been my friend first and foremost, and ever since I found out about our parents, I feel like I've been letting him down. I've been a shitty friend, and the need to make it right consumes my brain until it's all I can think about.

When I pull up to Mason's house, I see his car sitting untouched in the driveway, and I sigh in relief. Using the tiny mirror in my visor, I attempt to tame my hair somewhat so I look like less of a disaster. There's nothing I can do about my dull skin and dark circles, so I close the visor and steel all my courage as I walk up his driveway. I don't see any other cars unless they're in the garage. Is Brian home? Is Natalia? Has Mason confronted his dad? Does Natalia know? I left so fast this morning I didn't get a chance to see Mom, but I'm sure she would've said something if her secret had come out.

I don't bother texting Mason to let him know I'm here because I don't want to give him the chance to avoid me. Instead, I knock on his door with as much confidence as I can before I lose my nerve. If Agent Dylan actually *does* relocate me, Mason's last memory of me isn't going to be that I kept a huge secret from him. No. He's going to know that I was trying to do the right thing, and he's going to know how much he means to me. I'll be damned if I leave King with strained friendships all over the place, especially considering I love all my friends like I've never loved friends before.

The door opens to reveal Mason, who pauses when he sees me, a half-eaten Pop-Tart in his hand.

Before he can decide what to do, I blurt out, "I know I'm probably the last person you want to see but I'm here to say I'm really really sorry and I never meant to hurt you and I thought I was doing the right thing by not telling you, and please let me explain."

It comes out in one big breath and Mason cocks an eyebrow at me. He stuffs the Pop-Tart in his mouth to finish it off, chewing slowly as he studies me. The silence makes me squirm. Before I can continue blurting the first thing that comes to my mind, he opens the door wider for me, gesturing for me to come in. My breath comes easier. That's a good sign; that means he wants to talk.

He closes the door behind me, and the anxiety forces me not to wait, to get everything out before he has the chance to change his mind.

"I found out about our parents the day we left for the beach house. Remember when Aiden and I turned back? I forgot something at my house, and I walked in on our parents . . . you know . . ." His face scrunches up in disgust as he pictures what I'm hinting at. I continue, "Yeah. They didn't know I was there, and I battled with whether I should tell you or not. I didn't want to ruin the trip for you, and I didn't want you to hate me for knowing or for my mom's role in it, but I felt so guilty I could barely look at you, and it strained our friendship. I'm really sorry for that too."

Realization flashes across his face. "So that's why you were avoiding me." It's not a question.

"I didn't know how to break the news to you. And then when we got back, I caught our parents again, and I told Brian to make it right with you, to tell you because you deserved to know, or I would. He obviously never told you, and I didn't want Aiden to have to do it for me. Anna put the pieces together herself, and I asked her not to say anything either so that Brian had time to do it himself. I was going to tell you at mini-golf the other night since it's been weeks and your dad never told you, but then our friends showed up and I couldn't do it in front of them. I'm really sorry you had to find out this way, Mason, really." As the words escape my lips, the pressure sitting on my chest decreases, and the more I talk, the lighter I feel, even if Mason isn't saying anything, even if he is still mad at me. "And I'm sorry for hurting you."

He takes a breath. "I'm not mad at you."

"You're not?"

"No, it's not your fault. You're not the one cheating on your wife, you're just the one caught in the middle. If the roles were reversed, I don't know if I'd be able to tell you either."

His words are a breath of fresh air, and I step closer to him, filling the space between us that, until this conversation, has felt like miles, even if he was only a few feet away. "Mason, you're my best friend and I hate that this is happening. At the beginning I really hated your dad and my mom, but I think I'm starting to realize not everything is black and white. I thought our parents were terrible people, but Brian's still always been there for us. He stepped up and got Aiden out of jail when he was arrested, he took custody of the twins, and he was there for us when everything went down with Andrew and Harvey. You should've seen him barking orders at the officers that night." I lose my train of thought. "I don't know where I was going with this, I guess, just so you know your dad isn't the worst?"

Mason surprises me when he closes the gap between us completely and envelops me in a hug. It's warm and comforting and the last thing I expected him to do. I wrap my arms around his back and hold him to me, each of us seeking and giving our own comfort.

"I'm supposed to be the one comforting you," I mumble into his shoulder. His sweater smells like a mix of fresh detergent and something purely Mason, which floods my body with warmth. *I missed my friend.*

"We are comforting each other." He chuckles, and my arms drop to my sides as he releases me. He continues, "I had time to think it over and I get why you did it. I wish you felt like you could tell me, but I get that it should've been my dad. But Amelia? Know that you can tell me anything, okay? You'll still always be my best friend."

If I already didn't feel like crying, the feeling would've hit me tenfold. I never realized how much extra weight I was carrying by keeping things from my friends. Now that everything's out in the open with Mason, I feel like I can breathe easier, but there's still something wiggling in the back of my mind, something weighing me down, something blocking me from being truthful with Mason. I can't take the lying anymore. Telling the truth has opened a floodgate and I don't care to stop anymore.

"I'm in witness protection." The words spill out of my mouth of their own accord, and I do nothing to stop them. "There's a man trying to kill me, and he's found me twice before. The last time he found me and almost killed me I was relocated here to King City and became Amelia. Please don't hate me."

Mason stares at me, his mouth slightly agape as he processes my words. Before he can say anything, the door on my left, the one to the main-floor washroom, swings open. Noah's there, staring at me just like Mason is. I'm just as shocked as I'm sure Mason feels.

Noah clears his throat. "So, I've been standing here for, like, ten minutes, not wanting to interrupt you guys making up, but . . . what?! You're in witness protection? Are you, like, a spy? Or an assassin? Wow, this is so much." He shakes his head as if trying to wrap his mind around it and washes his hands, talking loudly over the running water. "First all the stuff about Luke and the twins, then Brian and your mom, and now this? Next you're going to tell me your name isn't Amelia."

Mason snaps out of whatever stupor he's in as his eyebrows draw together. He glances at me, then back at Noah. "Um, Noah? That's kind of the point of witness protection. Her name *isn't* Amelia."

Noah dries his hands and stares blankly at me for a few moments before his jaw drops again, as if he *just* connected the dots. "Holy shit! So, what *is* your name? The real one, not Amelia, because we know that's not your real name. Obviously."

Instead of answering Noah's rambling, I round on Mason. "You weren't going to tell me Noah was here the whole time?"

"Yeah, I was going to. He just happened to be in the washroom when I opened the door, and you kept talking and I got distracted with, you know, what you were saying," he admits sheepishly. "But in my defense, I didn't expect you to tell me you're in witness protection."

I glance between Mason and Noah. A part of me, the part that's spent over a year running and hiding, is panicking. More people who know my secret means more people who are exposed to harm. But the bigger part of me, the part that always feels out of control, is relieved. Two of my best friends finally *know*. I don't need to hide anymore, at least not from them. No matter what happens, if I stay here or leave, three of the people closest to me will *know* me, the *whole* me.

"What are you even doing here?" I ask Noah.

Mason answers for him. "Same reason you came; he was trying to convince me not to be mad at you."

My heart warms as I look at Noah in awe. "We were all fighting and everything was going to shit. I figured I'd catch him before school, same as you. My mom dropped me off. But, come on, tell us about the witness protection thing, Amelia . . . if that's even your real name."

Mason and I exchange a look before Noah adds, "Yes, I *know* that's not your real name. I just always wanted to say that in real life."

My emotions are all bunched up, but a laugh escapes me.

Leave it to Noah to make light of every situation, and right now, I'm extremely grateful for that.

"I guess we should sit down instead of standing in the hallway? It's a long story," I say, trying to sort through my emotions and thoughts. They clearly believe me, so that's a good thing, and so far they don't seem mad at me. They aren't accusing me of lying and they're not freaking out. If anything, they seem excited. I take it as a good sign as I follow Mason and Noah down the hall, all the while Noah's guessing names and Mason's occasionally throwing one in. They really *aren't* mad, and a weight lifts off my chest. Is it really this easy?

As Mason and Noah sit on the sofa, my phone rings. It's Aiden.

"Hey, where are you? Class is starting and you haven't answered my texts."

"I'm at Mason's house with Noah. I guess we aren't coming to school today?" I reply, and Noah gives me a big thumbs-up with a grin, apparently on board with that plan. I've missed so much school since winter break ended that at this point I feel like it hardly matters, though I really should be getting back on track if I want to graduate.

"Is everything okay?" Aiden asks, and I hear his locker close in the background.

"I think so? I told them." My words trail off as I sink into the sofa.

Aiden pauses, and when he speaks his voice is hesitant. "You told them what?"

"About me, Aiden. They know."

He's silent for a few beats, then, "Are you all right?"

Noah and Mason have started arguing over if I look like a Jessica or not, and a smile tugs at my lips. "Yeah. I am."

"Good. I'll be right there."

When I hang up, Noah and Mason are staring at me. Noah breaks the silence first. "What the hell, not-Amelia, Aiden knew this whole time?"

I shift self-consciously. "Not the whole time, but for a while, yeah."

"Are you going to tell us your real name?" Noah asks. "I have ten bucks on Danielle."

The two of them are looking at me, waiting patiently for me to tell them all about myself. "Wait, so you guys believe me?"

They glance at each other. "Yeah," they say simply.

I eye them suspiciously. "And you're not mad at me?"

"No," they say again, and Mason adds, "You're not supposed to tell people you're in witness protection. Why would we be mad at you for following the rules?"

A laugh bubbles up my throat. All this time I spent panicking about what they'd think if they found out the truth about who I am, and worrying about how I was lying to my friends, for nothing? They just understand? It seems so easy I want to cry and thank the universe for giving me friends as understanding as Mason and Noah.

My laugh turns into a sob and Mason and Noah share panicked looks.

"We broke not-Amelia!" Noah stage-whispers to Mason.

I wipe the tears away and try to regain my composure. "I'm sorry. I came here to apologize to Mason and make sure he was okay and turned it into a whole thing about me."

Mason waves me off. "I'm fine, really. Pissed at my dad, sad for my mom, but it's not my marriage. My mom knows now. My dad took one look at me yesterday and knew I knew, so he told her everything. He really loves your mom, I think. I don't think it was a random affair, Amelia—er . . ."

"Thea," I supply, and Noah swears.

"That wasn't one of my guesses, was it?"

I ignore Noah for the moment, thinking only about sweet Natalia, and how now she knows the truth. "How did she handle it?" His other words sink in my jaw drops. "Are you saying Brian is leaving your mom for mine?" The words are a shock even as I say them. I had suspicions before, but when Mason hesitates and nods in confirmation, the rug is ripped right out from under me.

"I think that's what's going to happen, yeah," he says and his jaw ticks. "Mom's okay. She didn't seem that surprised. My parents talked for hours last night, locked away in their room. When they were finally done, Mom came to see me. She's going to stay with my aunt for a bit, but their marriage is over. There's no saving it."

"I'm—I don't know what to say." I really don't. Mason's parents' marriage is over, and my mom is going to start a relationship with someone who has roots here, in King City. What's going to happen if we really do get relocated? Is she willing to walk away from Brian after he ended his marriage for her?

"So, I know that this is an important thing for you guys to discuss, but is *no one* going to address the fact that *Amelia is really Thea*?" Noah exclaims, staring at me as the doorbell rings, and Mason gets up to let Aiden in.

As I fidget with the sleeve of my sweater, Noah shifts closer to me. "Is that a real beauty mark on your cheek?" When he reaches out to poke me I swat his arm away, even though I appreciate his attempt to break the tension.

"Yes, it's real."

"Hey," Aiden says, putting his arm around me as he drops onto the couch beside me. I instantly feel comforted by his presence. "You okay?" He frowns and wipes a stray tear from my face.

"Yeah. Better than ever," I reply, and it's not a lie. I feel better now that the truth is out.

"What have you told them?" he asks.

"Not much," Mason answers. "We kind of got sidetracked."

"We know her name is Thea, *not* Amelia." Noah grins, then it falters. "So how much do *you* know?"

Aiden looks at me, then back at Noah and shrugs. "Everything."

"What! I can't believe you knew that whole time and didn't say anything! That's a huge secret to keep," Noah says, then adds, "But it's totally one you can trust me with."

Mason's face pales as he regards Aiden. "At the beach house when you said I didn't really know Amelia, you meant . . . ?" He leaves the question open for us to fill in the blanks ourselves.

We still haven't addressed the other elephant in the room, namely Mason's feelings for me. Maybe one thing at a time.

"What's important is that you guys know now, and you know to keep it a secret," Aiden says, and we all subtly look at Noah, who realizes a beat too late.

"What? I said I'd keep it a secret! This isn't like the time Mason couldn't make it to the bathroom and pooped his pants in class in third grade."

"Dude!" Mason exclaims, and when the realization hits Noah, he laughs.

"That secret's different! And if it makes you feel better, I kept that secret for, like, nine years, so I can totally keep secrets. You can trust us, Amelia—not-Amelia—Thea."

I shake my head but a laugh still escapes me. Did I make a mistake? I'm not sure, but I feel better now that everything's out in the open. "I'm just glad I don't have to hide it anymore. I've hated all the running and hiding and lying and losing control."

"What were you saying about a man trying to kill you?" Mason asks, concern shining in his eyes. His face is hard, serious, and reminds me so much of Aiden in that moment.

The weight of Aiden's arm around my back is reassuring, so I take a deep breath and do the one thing I never thought I'd do, but the thing they deserve: I tell them everything.

>> <<

Mason and Noah barely said a word as I told them my past: about me as Thea, as Isabella, as Hailey, and now, as Amelia. They asked a few questions, but otherwise they let me tell the story uninterrupted. When I'm done and wiping the tears from my eyes, Mason and Noah quietly sit there, processing everything I said.

"I know it's a lot," I say.

Noah and Mason look at each other, and as if sending a silent signal, both get up and jump on me, shoving Aiden aside in the process. We're dog piled on the couch, and their arms come around me in a hug. I laugh at the ridiculousness of it all.

"We knew you were badass, but whoa," Mason says from somewhere on top of me, and Noah's sound of agreement comes from somewhere above me as well.

I shove them off me with a laugh. "Thanks, guys. Now get off me, you're crushing me."

They flop off me and Noah lands on the floor with a thud. "Ow!" He stands and rubs his butt, then sits back down on the couch beside me. "Are we going to set up a trap to catch him or what?"

My breath hitches. "What are you talking about?"

Mason's nodding. He hasn't bothered sitting back down, instead choosing to pace back and forth in front of me on the other side of the little coffee table. "Yeah. Yeah, you know, I think Noah's actually right, for once. Let's take the control back."

I'm frozen to the spot, my mind reeling with what they're saying. "We can't do that!"

Mason frowns and stops his pacing. "Why the hell not? It's weird Agent Dylan and friends didn't do it in the first place. This all would've been over and you could've lived your life."

Aiden shifts beside me. He's been quiet this whole time, silently assessing the situation, but his body is tense. "I don't think that's legal, using a minor as bait," he says.

"Well, good thing we're not law enforcement," Noah says, then turns to Mason. "Do you think Tony would notice if we put you in an Amelia wig and used you as bait?"

My spine straightens. "Are you guys being serious right now? Stop it. We're not creating a trap."

"Why not?" Mason's still standing on the other side of the coffee table, directly in front of me. "You're not alone now, or at least, it's not just you and Aiden. You have me and Noah on your side now. We all have your back, and we can finish this once and for all so you can move on with your life."

"I'm in! Let's take him down!" Noah exclaims.

I'm too shocked to speak.

"No." Aiden's voice is clear and authoritative. His hand on my waist tightens. "This isn't a game. It's too dangerous. We're not putting Amelia in danger."

I find my words. "I'm not putting any of *you* in danger! It's enough that you know, but to actually seek him out? No way. Plus, I don't know if I can fully trust Agent Dylan, so I don't want to get him involved."

"Wait, why don't you trust Agent Dylan?" Mason asks.

Aiden and I share a glance. Can we really tell them *everything*?

Noah gasps. "There's more secrets!"

Mason sits, leaning toward us. "What aren't you telling us?"

Aiden's eyes search mine, and I know he's leaving the decision up to me. I take a moment to process the revelations of the day.

Fuck it. They already know everything, might as well go all in.

"We have a theory," I start, cautiously, "that I was placed here in King on purpose, because there's increasing pressure to catch Tony, and while using me as bait isn't legal, they can technically place me somewhere Tony would want to go on his own and happen to come across me."

"Why would he want to come to King?" Noah asks.

I take a breath, gathering confidence. "Because I'm pretty sure Anna is his biological daughter."

The room is quiet—so quiet I can hear the ticking of the clock on the wall in the kitchen all the way from here.

Noah's jaw has dropped open, a look he's sported multiple times today, and Mason's wearing a similar shocked expression on his own face.

"Wow . . . his daughter." Mason leans back on the couch and shakes his head. "Okay, so shady ethics aside, we can still end this. Ourselves. We've done riskier shit."

My throat tightens. "No, Mason. I'm not putting any of you at risk."

They were already handling this better than I expected, but I *really* never expected them to try to set up a Scooby trap to catch Tony. That's way out of our area of expertise, and even if I trust these boys with my literal life, there's no way I want to put them in danger. I wouldn't be able to live with myself if they got caught in the cross fire.

Mason tugs at his hair. "But it would be so simple. We won't even need to get the sketchy government agents involved. You said you think Agent Dylan doesn't actually want to keep you hidden, and that you feel out of control. So let's create our own control. Create an S-Live Time account under your real name and post a picture of yourself. He'll contact you."

"No," Aiden states, his voice trembling.

"She should put her phone number under so he can just contact her right away and skip the games," Noah adds, ignoring Aiden. "He'll call her, we know he will."

"No!" Aiden snaps, louder than last time.

"Don't you want your life back, Thea? We can help you! We want to help you," Noah pleads, his eyes boring into mine.

Mason's standing again, pacing in front of the coffee table. "You wouldn't even have to leave King! Your mom's clearly attached to, well, my dad, so she wouldn't ship you back home. You won't be scared of leaving anymore."

I move my mouth but no sound escapes. I do want my life back. I want to go to school and only worry about passing calculus, not keeping a man from killing me. I want to take pictures with my friends and post them to social media without fearing repercussions. I want to have a decent night's sleep without popping sleeping pills because I'm worried about Tony breaking into my bedroom. I want to be just like everyone else.

I pick up my phone sitting on the coffee table in front of me.

S-Live Time is still loaded from when Charlotte borrowed it and I used it against Andrew and Harvey. It would be easy to make an account, post a picture, and wait for Tony to call me. He'll be curious. It'll be a chess game, him waiting to see what my next move will be.

"Let's say he does call me . . ." I start, my voice small.

Aiden straightens beside me, his body tense. "Thea, you can't be serious."

"What then?" I continue, looking Mason in the eye. "What would I do?"

Aiden growls in frustration beside me and throws his hands in the air. I know where he's coming from—he doesn't want me to get hurt—but I hate this. I hate sitting and waiting for the other shoe to drop. I'm taking my life into my own hands. But maybe I'm not done lying to my friends. Not yet.

Noah hoots and pumps his fist in the air when he realizes I'm relenting, and Mason's lips tug into a victorious grin. "We set a trap, and we end it. Tell him about Anna. Tell him he's her daughter. With what you told me, he'll be curious enough to agree to meet up."

"No. We're not involving Anna," I state, trying to put authority in my voice.

The fewer people who know and want to help means fewer people who can get hurt. I place my phone back on the little coffee table, and Aiden stares at it, probably willing it to disappear through sheer willpower alone.

"We'll figure that out later. First things first." Mason plucks his phone from his back pocket and before I realize it, there's a flash.

My heart stops. This is going too fast. I jump up from where I'm sitting. "Mason! I wasn't ready for a picture!"

"The sooner we get everything set up, the sooner we can end this."

He walks into the kitchen and I follow him, stepping around Aiden, who's got his elbows on his knees and his fingers rubbing circles on his temples, the tension rolling off him in waves.

"If anyone's going to post my picture, it'll be me. And I don't want Noah or Aiden in it!" I grab the phone from him and examine the picture. I feel Noah standing over my shoulder, looking down at Mason's phone. I start to delete it, but Noah stops my hand.

"No. Don't delete it, we look good."

We do not look good. I look confused. Noah looks like there's smoke coming out of his ears from thinking too hard, and Aiden looks pissed. Hot, but pissed.

"Fine," I relent. It won't matter if I have pictures with my friends soon anyway. "But don't post this. I'll post a picture of just myself. *Only* if Aiden's on board."

We all turn to look at Aiden, who's just joined us in the kitchen, my phone in his hand.

I don't need his permission to do anything and he knows it. But I've got a plan forming in my mind, and I need Aiden on board if this is going to work.

His face is hard, his jaw set. He stands in front of me and lowers his head so he's looking right into my eyes. "Are you sure this is what you want to do? That you're ready for this?"

Am I? I'm not sure. But I am ready for the running and hiding and lying and stress to be done with. I'm ready to just live my life. It's time I *do* something about it.

Without taking my eyes off his, I nod, and determination washes over his face.

"I hate this. I really, really hate this. But if it's what you want—"

His jaw works for a moment as he reads the determination on my face. "All right then," he says, handing me my phone. "We do this. Together."

>> «

After running through a plan and forcing the boys to swear not to tell anyone, including a pinkie swear so I know they're serious, I create an S-Live Time account under my real name, Thea Kennedy. I post a lone picture of me, and the caption is simply my phone number. As I drive home around noon and make a stop at the hardware store, all I can think about are the things that can go wrong. I don't want my friends to get hurt but I can't stay here and wait for them to eventually get hurt anyway. I'm just so tired of running and hiding and keeping secrets and looking over my shoulder. I'm taking back control and handling this by charging headfirst into my problem. I will end this. One way or another.

The store is in a plaza with other stores, one of which is a coffee shop. As I walk to my car, I spot a familiar Porsche sitting near my car. Kaitlyn must be on lunch break from school.

She exits the coffee shop and notices me standing near her car. She pauses before sighing and continuing toward me.

"Are you stalking me?" she asks, opening her car door. "Did you forget what I said about us not being friends?"

"Yeah, yeah, not friends, got it. Have you told your mom about Anna?"

The plan might not work out, but at least I'll know that Anna's reputation has been righted and she can come back to King City High with her friends, even if she's pissed at us.

Kaitlyn huffs but doesn't make any move to get in her car and drive away. "Yes. She can't come back until the end of the week, though—some paperwork thing."

"Good. And Ryan?"

"Ryan was arrested, like, two hours after I got home last night. I think he's been charged and let out on bail, but he'll have a hearing. My mom thinks he'll have to do court mandated community service and anger management or intimate partner violence counseling or something."

He deserves it for what he's done to her, and knowing she's getting justice makes me happy. "I'm glad. I deleted the video I took of you, by the way."

She shrugs like she couldn't care either way. "Whatever. My coffee's getting cold," she glances at the hardware store supplies I'm holding. "And I don't really care to get mixed up in whatever you have going on right now, so bye."

She gets in her car and I let her go. It was weird, having an almost normal conversation with her, like two mature people, instead of trading insults. I'm also glad that I had the chance to catch her before the plan with Tony, in case it doesn't work out and I'm not the one who walks away from it. Even though I can't personally make things right with Annalisa, at least she'll know I didn't betray her for Kaitlyn. But for now, I clear my mind of all those thoughts. Right now, I need to focus on the task at hand, on confronting Tony and not letting my friends die because of me.

27

Mom's flight left at one today, leaving me alone for an hour before my phone rings. It's a gut feeling I have as soon I hear my ringtone. I know it's him. There were a few other random calls from kids who saw my number and wanted to prank me with stupid stuff, but I know it's Tony as soon as I see the undisclosed number flash on my screen.

Sharp shivers run down my spine as I force myself to bring the phone to my ear, to answer it. "Hello?" My voice sounds weak even to me.

"This was dumb of you."

I'm too shocked to say anything. I wasn't expecting *him*. The sound of his voice makes my skin crawl, and I force the memories not to come back to me. I don't say anything to his statement because I can't even disagree with him.

"Why are you calling me? How did you get a cell phone in jail?"

Andrew chuckles humorlessly. "Dumb girl. I'm out on *bail*. It wasn't cheap, and it's house arrest, but that's the system for you."

How did we not know Andrew was out on bail? I feel like that's something Aiden should've been notified about. To Andrew, I don't say anything, instead letting Aiden's biological father say his piece. I was expecting *something* to happen from posting online, but not this.

"I always knew something was off about you, *Amelia*." He emphasizes my name. He knows the truth. "I even hinted that to Aiden. Before you screwed everything up for me, I had my investigators look into you, and we were all shocked when we found you didn't exist before this year. No school photos, report cards, hospital visits, social insurance number, nothing."

I sink onto my bed. I don't like how this is going. My control is slipping from my fingers.

"I'm broke again. My wife is divorcing me, and any money I have is for lawyers. You've really fucked me here, Thea."

My heart beats loudly in my ears; my name feels gross in his deep voice, but I still find the will to say, "You fucked yourself, Andrew. I hope you rot in prison."

"Funny you say that. My investigators found out about you before I was arrested, and we found something pretty interesting about your past. Apparently, you piss off a lot of people."

My breathing stops. All the shadows in my room look suspicious, threatening. I don't feel safe here, I don't feel in control.

"I don't know what you were thinking or what the plan was by posting your phone number," he continues, "but the area code gives your location away. If I hadn't already told Tony where you were, that certainly would've given it away. He should be in town by now."

I jump from my bed to peek through my blinds. My street looks calm, the complete opposite of the turmoil of emotions swirling through my body.

I remember I'm holding the phone in my hand, and even though Andrew isn't saying anything, I can practically see his vicious smirk through the phone, his gloating righteousness that he's won. *Tony's coming. He's here.* I'm trying really hard to stay calm. This is what I wanted, wasn't it? To finish it? Everything in me is so used to running in the opposite direction from Tony. Every time he's appeared has ended in pain. I force myself to stay calm even though I feel like pulling all my hair out or crying or screaming or closing my eyes and pretending this is all a dream. But none of that will fix this problem. None of that will make this go away. Only I can do that.

"Rot in hell," I say to Andrew, then hang up and throw my phone on the opposite side of the bed.

Think. I have to think.

Mom is on a flight, so that's one less person to worry about. I run my hands through my hair and force myself not to rip it out by the roots. I need to figure this out. It's ending *today* even if it kills me.

Pouncing on my bed, I scramble back to my phone and call Aiden.

He picks up on the first ring. "Are you okay?"

No. "Yes. It's on. Where are the twins?" The first part of the plan stays the same. I'm protecting my friends.

He swears. I hear a car door open. "I just pulled them from school. I'm bringing them to Mason's house now. Brian's home. We'll be there right away."

I force myself to stay calm, to not give away my panic. *How far away is Tony?*

"Don't do anything without me, okay?" Aiden demands, and when I don't answer, he prompts, "Thea?"

"Yes. Yes, I'll be here." *What am I going to do?*

"I love you, Thea. It's going to be okay," he says, and I hear him talking to the twins on the other end of the phone.

"I love you too," I say, meaning every bit of it.

Tony's here.

We hang up and I pull on a dark sweater and my good running shoes. There's a chill in the air today, and it's not just because of the weather. Leaving the room, I check to make sure all my supplies are prepared, and every squeak of the floor or settling of the house makes my pulse race faster and faster.

Tony's here.

What do I do? How am I supposed to fix this? To win? I feel like banging my head in frustration. Maybe it's time I call Agent Dylan. I may not trust him but at least he's not trying to get me killed . . . probably.

As I pull my phone from my pocket, the screen lights up. An unknown caller is calling me. My blood turns to ice in my veins. Is it Andrew again? Calling back to gloat? To get the final word?

The curiosity gets the better of me. I answer it. "Hello?"

There's no response on the other end, and for every second that passes in silence, my heart rate increases. Just when I think he's not going to say anything, he speaks.

"It's been a while."

Tony.

"What? You have nothing to say? I traveled all this way."

I try and fail several times to voice my thoughts, but they're all jumbled. I don't have the upper hand here. I don't know what I was thinking, how I could possibly have thought I could control this situation, control anything. All I'm thinking is that I want it all to *end*.

I force words out. "I'm tired, Tony. Let's end this once and for all. You and me. Only one of us walks away."

He's silent for a moment, then, "You know, you're almost taking all the fun out of this. Almost."

"Meet me in thirty minutes at Sweetie's Ice Cream Parlor. It's in town."

He laughs. It's a gross sound that's humorless and makes my skin crawl. "How dumb do you think I am? First, I'm not meeting you anywhere public. And second, I'm not meeting you anywhere you choose."

My voice comes out steady even though I feel anything but. "Then what do you propose?"

There's background noise wherever he is, and even though the sounds are familiar, I can't make out any distinct place. "I made a friend."

"Congratulations. That must be hard for you."

His frustration is evident even from over the phone. "Shut up," he snaps. "My friend doesn't like you, and besides letting me know where you are, his investigators told me something interesting. Want to know what that is?"

I want to throw up. "No."

"I have a daughter. Her mother, Elizabeth White, listed me as the father on her birth certificate almost eighteen years ago, but she never contacted me. She only had my name, so I suppose it's not her fault. But Andrew sent me pictures, and wow . . ." He sounds like he's talking more to himself now than to me. "She has my Sabrina's eyes. Same as my mother. And her face, the shape . . . it's just like Sabrina's," he says almost reverently, as if he's looking at the picture now and is transfixed.

A bell rings in the background, and it's then that I realize where he is. My breath hitches at the rumbling of school buses starting up. *He's outside school. He's near Annalisa.*

"I can't wait to meet her," he continues. "School's getting out now, and I've heard she's a good friend of yours."

I was not prepared for this. Nothing could've prepared me for *this*. No one is supposed to get hurt for me.

"Leave her alone!" I exclaim, the desperation in my voice clear as day. "Meet me and leave her alone. This is between us and about finishing what we started."

"Abandon any ideas about whatever silly plan you had when you created a social media account and posted your phone number, a phone number I already *had* because of Andrew, mind you. Meet me alone. No cops—and I'll know if there are cops—or I hurt Annalisa. Or maybe I hurt your other friends. Aiden, his brothers, the other boys you hang around with . . ."

Even the way he says their names make me sick. The way he talks about my friends like he would relish their pain, would hurt them just to hurt me—this is my worst fear come to fruition, all because of Andrew. All because I pissed him off enough to make him dig into me, to have him doubt who I was, to go searching for the truth and uncover a secret that gives him the one thing he wants to accomplish most: payback on me through Tony.

I've always known that no one was going to get hurt for me. I may feel out of control, but I can control who gets caught in the cross fire, and it won't be Annalisa or Aiden or Mom or anyone else. My resolve is set. Any worries I had before are melting away with the realization that I always knew it would come to this. Just me and Tony.

"Where?"

"There's an abandoned factory off forty-two. Know the place?"

I search my mind and an image of the place he's talking about pops up. It's chained up, so there's no going inside, but it's in the middle of nowhere, surrounded only by trees.

"Yes," I state.

"You have thirty minutes to get there. You don't show and I'll visit one of your friends."

He hangs up before I can say anything else, and I clutch my phone in my hand so hard it hurts.

"Fuck!" My yell is answered by silence, and I rack my brain for something, *anything* to come to me.

I stare at my phone's screen, the time glowing up at me innocently. It's 2:30. Tony said school just let out, but that's the time *King* ends. Commack Silver High gets let out early.

And Annalisa's still a student there.

Yes! I feel like pumping my fists in victory. Annalisa's nowhere near Tony, at least for the time being. For the first time ever, I'm grateful that Kaitlyn got her expelled.

Before Aiden, Mason, and Noah get here, I make one last phone call, and pray Annalisa answers.

28

I'm expecting Aiden, Noah, and Mason when they pull up beside my car a few minutes after my call with Tony. I usher them in and give each of them a hug. Even though I may hold on for just a stitch longer than normal, my face is schooled into perfect calmness, my emotions hidden away. I'm sticking to the plan.

"Are you all right? How was the call?" Aiden asks me, grabbing my hips and pulling me close.

"I'm fine," I say, only somewhat believing it. A part of my brain has shut off, as if trying not to fully process everything. If I do, I'll break down.

"And you stuck to the plan? Told him about Anna? Offered him to meet her?" Mason asks, his eyes as intense as Aiden's. It was fun, thinking we could control the situation, could control bad men capable of worse things.

Moving out of Aiden's grip, I lead them up to my room. It's not a lie when I say, "He knows about Anna."

Aiden stops me just before we enter my room. He looks tired, like he hasn't slept in weeks. His gaze is intense and pierces straight to my soul. "Hey. You don't need to do this."

Aiden's always been against this, and I know why. But it's time we end this. I'm not putting anyone in danger anymore. Besides, it's too late to change anything. It was always going to come down to this.

"It'll be all right," I say, for myself as much as him.

His jaw tightens as his eyes roam over me. *Stick to the plan.*

Finally, he nods. He turns to follow Noah and Mason into my room, but I grab his wrist and pull him back to me, drawing him against me and laying my head against his chest. I let his steady heartbeat calm me for a few moments. His arms come around me, his hands clutching fistfuls of my sweater, holding me close.

I pull back and bring my lips to his, kissing him with every-thing I have, since it may be the last time. It's desperate and rough and communicating everything I wish I could say. *I love you. I'm sorry. I'll never forget you. Please forgive me.* I pull away just when I think my heart can't take the pain of what's about to happen.

He plants a kiss on the top of my head and lets me go when I pull away. He clears his throat and enters my room.

"Ew. Get a room," Noah says, even though I know he doesn't mean it. He looks around my bedroom and quickly adds, "But not this one. We're in here."

Mason says something to him, but I'm not listening.

"Hey, give me your phones. I'm going to make sure our times are synced up," I say, holding out my hand for them.

They pass me their phones without hesitation, then start going over their plan.

Before they notice, I back into the hallway and pull the door to my room closed, leaving them in there alone. Swiftly, I close the door to the spare room that's directly in front of mine. The sturdy rope that I picked up from the hardware store today is already tied to that door, and within a few seconds, I have the rope tied to my own door handle, the rope taut across the hallway.

"Thea?" Aiden's voice calls hesitantly from the other side of the door. "Thea, what are you doing?"

Instead of answering, I triple-check the knot I tied. I spent a while searching for videos to find the most effective knot, and practiced to make sure I could do it perfectly and quickly when I got home today.

Stick to the plan.

"What's going on, Thea?" Aiden's voice is louder now, more panicked as he tries to pull open the door, only to be met with resistance.

I wipe away the only tear I'm allowing myself to shed today, forcing myself to block it out, to be strong. My voice comes out calm, detached. "I'm sorry, Aiden."

"Very funny, Thea. Open the door." Noah laughs, but it's weak and hesitant.

"This isn't the plan, Thea!" Mason exclaims.

The doorknob keeps turning and the door is trying to be pulled open, but it's not giving.

"This was always the plan, Mason. My plan."

Step one was always to make sure my friends were kept out of it, to keep them safe. This is *my fight*. Step two is a bit more complicated now with the *no cops* thing and with Tony having already been made aware of Annalisa, so I'm going to have to wing it.

All three boys are talking to me from the other side of the door, trying and failing to get the door open.

"Don't do this, Thea!" Aiden's voice is loud and clear, and there's an edge of desperation leaking into his words. "Don't meet him alone! Stop this!"

My resolve falters for only a moment before returning tenfold. I will never be able to live with myself if something happens to my friends, and I'm ensuring they won't sacrifice themselves for me, not this time. I can live with whatever happens to me—I've made peace with my decision—but I can never live with myself if my friends, my *best* friends, are harmed because of me, not when I can do something to prevent it, to protect them.

There's banging on the door and I jump at the harsh sound. It sounds like the wood's going to splinter apart under the pressure. "Thea, open this door! Thea! Don't do this!" Aiden continues banging on the door, the calmness in his voice completely abandoned for desperation. There's a pressure on my chest as I back away from the door. I've never done what I'm told anyway, why start now?

Stick to the plan.

"I'm sorry, guys. I love you."

"*Thea! Thea!*"

I turn and race down the stairs, ignoring their calls, the despair in their voices, and the frenzied banging on the door. I don't know how long that rope will hold, or how long the door will stay intact, but it'll buy me time.

I drop their cell phones on the kitchen table, grab my car keys, and lock the front door behind me. I don't want to take their phones with me in case there's an actual emergency. Plus, I don't need to keep them hostage, just make sure they don't follow me.

Aiden's car sits innocently in the driveway and Mason's is parked at the curb. As I open my car door, I hear the boys yelling at me. They've opened my window, and for a quick moment I panic. Will they actually jump from the second story? No. They wouldn't.

"At least tell me you're still going to Sweetie's," Mason calls down to me.

I pause right before I get into my car and look up at all of them. The three of them are crowded around my window, staring down at me with concern and horror. My eyes meet Aiden's, and my heart breaks when I realize he's looking at me with a stoic impassiveness, like he did when he first met me.

I wrench my eyes away from him.

Stick to the plan.

Without answering, I hop in my car and drive away, all the while forcing myself not to look in the rearview mirror, to block out the memory of their voices, to ignore the breaking of my heart, to harden myself to the fact that this might be the last memory they ever have of me.

>> <<

When I pull up outside Luke's apartment, Annalisa's already standing there. I'm almost shocked that she actually showed up since her tone wasn't encouraging on the phone, but I'm just so relieved that Tony decided to meet me instead of track her down—relieved that he's nowhere near her. I pull up beside her car and cut my engine, checking the time.

Twelve minutes.

I'm cutting it close but the meeting place isn't far from Luke's apartment.

She's leaning against her car when I emerge, her eyes lined with the dark eyeshadow and eyeliner that make her glaring blue eyes pop. *Eyes that are apparently like Sabrina's.*

"Thanks for meeting up, Anna. This won't take long."

She crosses her arms across her chest. "I only came because on the phone you said it was life or death, and by your tone I believed it. But I'm still pissed at all of you."

I have to do this quick before I chicken out. "I know, and that's fine, and I'm about to piss you off even more, but I don't care because you deserve the truth and I don't have much time. I don't know how this is going to go but I may never get the chance to tell you." *Eleven minutes.*

I hold out a file, the one that's caused so many problems. "I found this in Luke's apartment, and I didn't tell you because, well, a lot of reasons. But Luke thought this man, Anthony DeRosso, is your biological father. It's a long story, but apparently he's listed on your birth certificate as your father too."

The angry expression on her face transforms into a confused one. She hesitates as she reaches out to take the folder, and I force my heartbeat not to speed up.

"Also, as if that wasn't enough, my name isn't Amelia. I'm in witness protection and my name is really Thea Kennedy. Everything about me that you knew is the same except my name. I never meant to lie to you, but I did it to keep you safe, to keep everyone safe."

Ten minutes.

"Your father is not a good person," I say, getting closer to her. "I wrote the name he currently goes by, Tony Derando, on the file. Google him and you'll find everything you need to know. If I fail and he seeks you out, you need to run when you see him.

Aiden knows the whole story, he can tell you more if you have more questions if I . . . if I'm not able to. But don't get in contact with him. Don't get near him. If you see him, run in the opposite direction. Okay, Anna? Do you understand? Promise me you'll go nowhere near him!"

It must be my frenzied tone that causes her eyes to widen and her to quickly nod. Even though I'm probably not making any sense, I feel a bit better knowing she knows how serious this is, how much this means to me.

"Good," I say, backing off with the intensity. "Good."

I step backward until I reach my car, the door already open from before. I place a hand on it. "You and Char have been the best friends I could've asked for."

Annalisa's eyes narrow. "Why does it sound like you're saying good-bye?"

Nine minutes.

"I've gotta go. Bye, Anna."

Before she can say anything else, I hop in my car and pull a U-turn, glancing in my rearview mirror to see Annalisa standing there, file in her hands, staring after me with confusion.

I don't have to go. Technically, I just warned Annalisa, and she'll know to stay away from Tony, and then he has nothing against me. I can tell all my friends, and together we can go to the police. We'll all be safe if we're all together. He technically has nothing against me *now*, and we can avoid him. I don't have to see him. I don't have to meet him. But then what? Live the rest of my life on the run and in fear? Be paranoid all the time? If I go to college I can't be transferring every two months. And what of Annalisa? Have her run too? Have her *connect* with Tony? No. There's no more running and hiding and lying. I want my life back and I want it back *now*. I am taking control of this situation; I'm taking control of *everything*.

I've been hesitant to do this because I've had a hard time trusting the adults in my life lately, but I don't know what else to do. I'm going to meet Tony, and I have no plan except part one, which was lock the boys in my room, and part two, which was tell Annalisa. Now I'm making it up as I go, so I guess part three is to call Agent Dylan. A little later than I probably should have, but it's better than nothing.

Eight minutes.

I use Bluetooth to call Agent Dylan, and the phone's rings are loud on my car's speakers. With every ring that passes, my pulse beats faster and faster, and my hope that he's actually going to answer diminishes. It goes to voice mail and I hang up my phone and redial, trying not to panic. The phone's rings fill the car and I grip the steering wheel, praying that he'll answer. I don't have a plan. I don't know what I'm doing. I should just turn the car around.

What am I *doing*?

Agent Dylan doesn't answer again. I hang up and bang my hand against the steering wheel until it stings. As if I already didn't have a reason not to trust him, he decides not to answer when it's most important, when it's *literally* life and death.

The trees are getting less sparse and the buildings are basically nonexistent. I turn onto a back road and an eeriness creeps up my spine at how alone and deserted I feel.

Seven minutes.

I should turn around. I'm literally walking complacently to my own demise right now. Yes, I want to end it, but what do I think meeting up with Tony will accomplish? I have no plan and

I have no weapon. He has nothing to force me to meet him other than the promise to meet Annalisa, and Annalisa is currently not near him. What do I realistically think is going to happen when I meet him? We'll have a tea party and a little chat and decide to go on our merry little ways?

This is plain idiocy. This isn't me; it must be the pure panic, the helplessness, the adrenaline.

I don't have a plan.

I'm turning around. I'm going to turn around and regroup and maybe sit in the police station for a while until I can figure my shit out. What the hell was I thinking?!

Just as I decide to turn around, something on the road catches my attention.

What's . . . "Oh shit!"

It's too late. I notice it too late.

I drive right over the spike strip and barely register the loud popping noise of all four of my tires over the rushing in my ears. The car spins and I have no control over righting it. The trees rush past me in a blur and my body's thrown against the center console until the car finally comes to an abrupt stop. My head is pounding even though I didn't bang it against anything, and I somehow register the flashing of various warning lights on my car's dash. I blink over and over and over again, trying to sort through everything, trying to force my brain out of shock.

What just happened?

I ignore the sensors yelling at me that I have flat tires and realize my car stopped on the grass just off the road. Rubbing my forehead, I open my car door and place a foot on the ground, freezing when I look up.

Directly in front of me, on the other side of the road, is Tony.

No matter how many times I imagine him, no matter how many times I told myself I was ready for this moment, nothing could've prepared me for all the emotions I feel at seeing the man I'm most terrified of only a few feet away from me.

"Thea," he says from where he stands. Not moving closer, but not needing to for me to feel threatened. The road is quiet. The line of trees behind him stand at attention. "Been a while, but I always find you, don't I?"

He's gloating; proud of himself. I force myself to breathe and step out of my car. It's useless now anyway. I have nowhere to go, nowhere to run, no one to come save me.

"How long have you been in town?" I try not to let my nerves show. I need to be in control of this situation. I can't let him affect me like he wants to.

I have no control.

"I got in this morning. My friend didn't send me this information about you and my daughter until recently."

This time he does move closer. Just a few steps, enough to send my heart rate up, to steal the air from my lungs.

I force words past my lips. "Well, we're here. What now?"

He takes a step closer to me, still on the opposite side of the road, but still way too close for comfort, close enough to send shivers down my spine. I take a few steps back to put more distance between us, the tall grass coming up to my shins.

"Now?" He smiles, but it's a malicious smile, one that I know isn't good for me. "Now, I win."

The look of rage on his face is one I'm familiar with, but not one I'm ever ready for. Before I can process anything, he pulls a gun from behind his back, and aims it at me.

My breath hitches. I turn to the side, trying to get away, trying to put more distance between us, when I register the sound of the gunshot. I don't feel anything at all. Did he miss? He aimed right at me and missed? As I move, though, I realize something's wrong. I touch the side of my chest, right under my arm, and pull my hand away to reveal blood.

I stare at my hand for a moment, words lost to me, not processing what this means.

I've been shot.

It doesn't hurt. Is it supposed to hurt? I collapse to my knees on the grass.

I've been shot.

I'm forced onto my back and register that Tony is on top of me, straddling me. A sadistic smile is plastered on his face. He's waited a year for this moment. He's followed me across the country and dedicated all his time to finding me for this exact moment. To see me in pain. To end me.

I've been shot.

He pulls a knife from his boot and traces the tip of it lightly over my throat. "You were right before when you said we were finishing this today. *I'm* finishing this today."

I've been shot. I'm in the middle of nowhere all alone. I've locked my friends in my room. I didn't ask any adults for help. Agent Dylan didn't pick up. The last thing I told my mom was that I'd order out for dinner. The last time Aiden looked at me was with a stoic impassiveness, like he didn't even know me. Annalisa knows the truth, but I never got to say good-bye to Charlotte, to Chase, or to Julian. This is how it ends. It really is finishing today, and I didn't win.

He raises his arm and I close my eyes, not wanting to see the end coming, not wanting to give him the satisfaction of watching the life drain from my eyes, when I feel a pain so intense radiating from my thigh, it makes me dizzy. A scream escapes my lips as my eyes pop open.

He holds the now bloody knife between the two of us, and the sight of it makes me sick. All I can do is gasp in pain, wishing things didn't end like this.

"It was all worth it, just to see you like this. Suffering. To—"

There's a blur and Tony's weight is pulled off me, tackled to the ground beside me. I don't bother moving, I'm too busy breathing.

Am I dying?

"So, you're the asshole who raped my mom, huh?" The voice is new, familiar, full of rage.

The fog of shock clouding my mind clears a bit, and I register Annalisa beside me. She punches Tony in the face. I don't know where the knife he was holding landed. I don't know where his gun is. I don't know how against all odds, Annalisa is here, looking like an avenging angel, all porcelain skin and dark hair and red lips and a raging expression on her face, one filled with pure, undiluted hate.

"Anna?" I ask, staring at her beside me. What is she doing here? She's not supposed to be here.

Tony shoves her off him with a curse and pins her to the ground. Annalisa's kicking and screaming the entire time. She claws at his face, drawing blood, and lands a bunch right on his nose, but he's bigger, heavier, stronger, and angrier than her. He manages to get her restrained, holding her arms down and placing his knee on her chest. I try to stand, but I catch a glance of the sea of red under me and suddenly all my limbs feel heavy and the world spins, so I let my head drop back on the tall grass around me. I try not to look back at the patch of red grass slowly expanding under me, try to ignore what that means.

"Amazing," he says, staring at Annalisa as if he's transfixed. "Your eyes really are the exact same shade of blue as my Sabrina's. I never got the blue eyes, but my mom had them."

This isn't supposed to be happening. Annalisa's not supposed to be here. She *promised* me she wouldn't go anywhere near Tony. I made sure she knew how dangerous he is. I showed her the folder, gave her all the information about him, and still, she came. She must know who he is, what he's done, because I can see all that hate she's radiating toward him, and yet she's still here. I wish she wasn't. I was supposed to either win or die alone, leaving my friends out of it. Leaving them *safe*.

I slowly sit up, and the realization that I *can* helps clear more of the clouds in my mind.

Annalisa spits at him, hitting him right in the face. "Fuck you." She manages to kick him and topples him off balance, but he's faster. He grabs her, and in one swift motion grabs his gun, rears back his arm, and whacks her on the top of her head with it. She collapses onto the ground, unmoving. Blood seeps from her head.

I'm paralyzed. Time freezes around me as my heart stops.

Is she . . . ? No. *No*. Not Annalisa. Not because of me.

"You stupid bitch," I hear that voice say, the one that haunts my nightmares. He's on his feet now, pointing the gun at Annalisa, lying helplessly on the ground. "You're not my daughter."

There's no time to think, but suddenly everything is so clear to me. I let what feels like a lifetime's worth of fear and rage fuel me. I've wasted enough of my life scared of him. I've lost enough hours of sleep tossing and turning from nightmares. I've lost enough people I love because of him. This ends now.

With all the strength I can muster, I move the few feet to him and grab his leg, pulling it out from under him. The shot goes wide, somewhere in the trees, and he lands on his back. The bang makes my ears ring, but I don't care, I barely acknowledge it. The need to end this for good is taking me over, rising from within me and consuming every fiber of my being.

I'm going to kill him. I need to kill him. I need him dead.

I look around for the gun and see it just a few feet away. It must've been knocked from his hand when he fell. I reach for it but a burning pain erupts from my leg, from the one Tony stabbed, almost in the same place he stabbed me the last time I encountered him. He's got his hand on the wound and is pressing hard, making the pain feel brand new over and over again.

"Why won't you just *die* already?" he growls, and I ignore his rhetorical question, trying to kick him away from me, to get his hand away from the blood oozing out of my leg.

The gun's out of reach; it's so close but so far. My leg's on fire. I've been shot. Annalisa needs medical attention. I don't want to die.

I need that gun. I don't have the strength in me to overpower Tony by myself. I need a weapon, and there's one sitting there, taunting me, just a few feet out of reach.

I stretch my body as much as I can, still kicking at Tony with whatever strength I have, ignoring the burn of my thigh, of my chest, focusing only on my fingertips, which might as well be miles away from the gun. As I reach, something slips out of my sweater, dangling from around my neck.

My necklace.

Aiden.

I stop struggling against Tony and reaching for the gun, and instead rip my necklace from my neck. As if I've done it a million times, I click the button that releases the switchblade, lean over, and stab Tony right in the throat. It's not a big blade, but it's sharp and pierces right through.

His eyes widen and he releases his grip on my leg, letting my breath come a bit easier now that the pressure's let up. Aiden's not even here and he's still saving me. I scramble away from Tony and toward the gun, and he's on his feet, hovering over me, the small blade still in his throat, the chain dangling down his neck in the direction of a small stream of blood coming from the wound. It wasn't big enough to kill, but was big enough to hurt him, to distract him, to give me time to get away. Somewhere in the back of my mind, I register cars crunching on the asphalt, but right now I'm focused on Tony. He reaches out to me, his face screwed up in fury as I grab the gun, look him right in the eye, and shoot him in the chest. I pull the trigger two more times. Then a third.

He stops in his tracks and it's like time is paused, as he's suspended there, our gazes clashing, until he collapses in a heap, unmoving. I release a shaky exhale and drop the gun with equally shaky hands, as if I just realized it was *me* who pulled the trigger, *me* who stopped Tony in his tracks, *me* who created the pool of blood slowly forming around Tony's body. It's huge, much larger than the one from my leg or from my side. I'm too busy trying to breathe to actually make sense of anything that's going on.

Annalisa's still lying on the ground, her eyes closed and face serene, almost like she's taking a nap. I use the last of my adrenaline to crawl over to her and collapse on my back beside her.

The sounds of cars are louder now. I find Annalisa's hand on the ground and grasp it in mine without looking at her. She came for me. She may have been mad at me, she may have thought the worst of me, but in the end, she had my back. She saved me from Tony's killing blow. I'd be dead if not for her.

As I stare up at the blue sky, my eyes focusing and unfocusing on the random smattering of clouds, I swear I hear my name being called.

"Thea! Thea!"

It must be my imagination, because it sounds just like Aiden, but not like Aiden. My Aiden is confident, his voice unwavering and deep and commanding the attention of everyone around him. This Aiden doesn't sound like that. This Aiden sounds frantic. Desperate.

As the edges of my vision become blurrier and the feel of Annalisa's hand in mine weakens, the sound of Aiden's voice gets louder, closer maybe. I don't even get to answer him before I give in to the darkness.

29

The next little bit is fuzzy. My eyelids feel so heavy. I remember waking up in the hospital, seeing Aiden talking to some doctors in the hallway. I remember my mom sitting beside me, crying. I remember seeing the flowers that filled the room. But I don't remember much else.

When the grogginess clears and I pry my eyes open again, I'm met with darkness. I'm lying in a bed that's not mine, and when I turn my head I see Mom, sleeping in a big reclining chair beside me, illuminated by the moonlight coming through the window.

"Mom?"

My voice is rough, and I reach up to rub my throat but stop when there's pulling on my arms. Needles and tubes are stuck in my hands and arms, and I'm grabbing one to try and pull it out when a hand stops me.

"Thea?" Mom removes her hand and rubs the sleep from her eyes, and she immediately tears up. "You're up! How are you feeling? Oh honey, you had us so worried. You've been in and out for a few days." She pulls me against her for a hug but it's a bit awkward because of all the stuff in my arms.

"A few days?" My throat is still sore, and I try to clear it again.

Mom notices. "Let me call the nurse, she'll get you some ice chips. It's from the tubes they had in your throat during surgery. But don't touch any of the needles in your arm, you need the IV."

Surgery? Mom scurries around the bed and is out the door, the light from the hallway leaking into the room.

I lie there in the hospital room, letting the memories come back to me, and as the events of that afternoon flood my mind, my heartbeat increases and the beeps on the monitor beside me speed up. I remember the call from Andrew. Locking Aiden, Noah, and Mason in my room. Meeting Annalisa. My tires being popped. Meeting Tony. *Shooting* Tony.

Where's Annalisa?

Mom enters the room with a cup in her hand and sets it on the table beside me. She notices the heart monitor's loud beeps and her eyes widen. She rushes to me and smooths my hair away from my face. It's almost odd, seeing her so worried, so concerned.

She must be reading my thoughts because she says in a soothing voice, "It's okay, Thea. Tony's dead; I identified his body myself. And your friends are all okay. Annalisa's fine."

Tony's dead. He's *dead.* Annalisa's fine.

Maybe if I keep saying it over and over again it'll feel real.

Tony is dead.

I don't have to hide anymore. I don't have to be scared anymore.

I don't have to be Amelia anymore.

Mom hands me the cup of ice chips and I greedily suck on them, wishing I could chug water instead.

"What happened? I was shot?" I ask around a full mouth.

Mom continues stroking my hair away from my face, the gesture oddly comforting, motherly. Her lips wobble as she tries not to cry. "Maybe we should wait for the doctor."

"Mom. I was shot." It's not a question this time.

She takes a shaky inhale. "It hit your chest cavity. They said you were incredibly lucky it didn't puncture your lung. They fixed you up. You lost some blood from your leg, but help came before you lost too much."

Help came? I hadn't told anyone where I was. Agent Dylan didn't answer his phone, and I was too scared to call the police. I remember a voice before everything went blank. Aiden? Was he really there or did I imagine him?

Mom's stopped touching me and is now wringing her hands in front of her. It's then, as my eyes continue to adjust to the dimness of the room, that I notice her face is makeup-free, her eyes are red, and there are dark circles under her eyes. Her hair isn't styled and she's in rumpled sweats. Has she been here the whole time?

She continues talking. "The police told me after that he used a nine millimeter. Those bullets stay intact instead of . . . exploding in you . . . so it could've been that much worse . . ." She trails off, her jaw working, her eyes watering.

She's really affected by this, seeing me here in a hospital bed, and my eyes water on their own at the thought. I was *shot*. It was a 9 mm. My mom's been by my side the whole time, crying at the thought of losing me?

"You should get some rest, Thea," Mom says, her voice weak, tears lining her eyes again. It's almost weird having her call me Thea. We never used our real names at home, always using our new names in case we got too comfortable and slipped while others were around. It's been a long time since I've heard my actual name, the one *she* gave me, voiced from her lips.

Despite having tons of questions, I settle back into the pillow. "Where's Annalisa? How did she find me?"

Mom's fussing over me. Fixing the blankets and fluffing the pillows and pushing my hair behind my ears. She sets the ice-chip cup on the bedside table. It's all so strangely comforting, and my eyelids grow heavier.

"Annalisa's fine. She had a minor concussion, but she's okay." She leans back and exhaustion seeps into my bones.

"I'm—" Mom's lips are quivering again. "I'm so sorry, Thea. I haven't handled any of this the way I should've. I've been terrible, and I thought I was doing the right thing and protecting us, but I made you feel like you couldn't trust me, like you had to do everything alone, like you couldn't come to me when Tony called you. Things"—she sniffles back her tears—"things could've been different. They *should've* been different."

Despite being tired, her words hit me right in the stomach. I try to form my own words but I'm too overwhelmed by what she's saying to properly process anything.

"I'm sorry we've been fighting so much," she continues when words fail me. "I'm going to do better, okay? We're going to work on our relationship. I quit my job, too, so I'll be around more."

All I can do is stare at her with wide eyes. It took a near-death experience to *finally* get my mom back, but I'm not even mad about it. I'm just happy she's trying, that we're trying. That maybe, after all this time, I'm going to have a healthy relationship with my mom because we'll both put in the effort. She hasn't made the best decisions in my opinion, but I haven't made life easy for her either. But together, we can fix our relationship, and I'd really like that.

I'd like that more than I ever thought possible, more than I thought I'd ever care.

"I'm so proud of you," she whispers as my eyes close. "Get some rest, we can talk in the morning."

As my eyes shut of their own accord and calmness takes over me, Mom's sob of "*I'm so sorry,*" is the last thing I hear before I welcome sleep.

>> <<

When I wake up again, the sun is shining through the open window, and Mom's beside me, sipping from a coffee mug. I feel much better than I did last night.

"Hi, honey." My mom greets me, setting her mug down. "The doctor wants to see you. I'm going to call him."

She leaves the room as I orient myself again. There are flowers on every surface, and a few stuffed animals. Mom returns with a doctor who has kind eyes and a warm smile.

The doctor says something to me, and I only mostly listen to what she's saying. Something about antibiotics and stitches and aftercare, but I'm only half listening. Mom's paying enough attention for the both of us. Nodding attentively, asking questions, and taking notes, though I'm sure this isn't the first time she's been told about my aftercare instructions. Mom's here now, *really* here, and I trust her to listen to the important stuff, to take care of me, to remember what to do, because as I sit here and watch the doctor's lips move, all I can think about is Tony.

He's dead. It's over.

The doctor checks me over and removes some of the tubes, then talks some more to Mom.

I don't have to hide anymore. I don't have to be paranoid or look over my shoulder or be terrified of screwing up or hide who I really am.

As the doctor leaves, there's a knock on the door, and my breath hitches. It's Aiden.

Mom leans down near my ear. "He's been here every moment he's been allowed. Your other friends have been popping in as well, all harassing me for updates."

I feel giddy as I take in his handsome face, the concern etched into his features. He enters the room, and as his broad frame shifts, I see Annalisa following him.

"Thea," Aiden breathes, rushing over to me.

He takes my face in both hands and leans his forehead against mine. It's sweet and tender, and even though I'm not usually a crier, my eyes begin to tear. I never thought I'd have a moment like this with Aiden again. I thought I would never see him again, his betrayed face the last thing I would see. But it's not. He's here; he's still with me.

"I should yell at you for being so damn stubborn and doing this all on your own, but I'm just too fucking happy that you're okay," he says, his deep voice filling me with warmth. "You really had me scared there for a bit." His eyes stare deep into mine, searching.

"How are you feeling?" Annalisa asks from where she's standing beside Aiden, and he straightens up, but our connection is still there, even though he's not touching me. I can feel him everywhere.

Mom clears her throat. "I'm going to get more coffee. I'll be back in a bit."

"Okay," I murmur, grateful that she's giving me some time alone with my friends, and soon she's out of the room.

I try to sort through all my emotions and feelings so I can express them properly. "Anna, how are *you* feeling?" Last I saw her, she was unconscious, bleeding out, her hand cold in mine.

"I'm fine, just a concussion and some stitches." She waves me off. "But seriously, are you okay? I saw you get *shot*!"

"How—" I glance between her and Aiden. Aiden's jaw tics. I continue. "How did you see that? How were you there? You saved me."

She shakes her head. "No. You saved me. I did a shit job saving you."

I disagree with that, but I press on for answers. "How did you find me?"

She's not wearing any makeup, and it's so weird to see her eyes without the smoky black eyeshadow and eyeliner enhancing them, her lips without the blood-red tinge. She looks okay. No noticeable bruises or cuts anywhere on her face, though she seems paler than usual.

"I followed you," she says without a hint of remorse. "You were acting all weird and the stuff you were saying about witness protection and my father and that weird good-bye made me suspicious and worried about you, so I followed you from a distance. It was easy since you took back roads. No one really takes them, and the trees hid me a bit. I had just turned the corner when I saw him shoot you."

Tears well in my eyes. She didn't stop to think, didn't hesitate. She jumped from her car and saved me, stopped him from killing me. She was worried about me even though she was mad at me.

"You were so brave, Anna. I'm sorry about all the secrets."

She waves me off again. Something's different about her and it's more than just a makeup-free face. She seems more vulnerable.

"Don't be sorry. *I'm* sorry I was being a bitch, and I shouldn't have reacted that way when I learned about the twins and you and Kaitlyn. I never gave anyone time to talk before jumping to my own conclusions. I apologized to Mason for telling him about his dad the way I did too."

She grabs my hand and it's so different from the last time I held her hand. It's warm and her grip is strong, reassuring. "I know we've had a rough few days, but you know I love you, right?"

I almost laugh but it hurts my chest. She literally tackled the man hunting me down, her biological father, and saved my life. Of course I know she does.

"Always. I love you too. And we'll sort everything out with the twins and Luke. It'll all work out."

Annalisa and Aiden exchange a glance.

"Actually," Aiden starts, "Luke's been cleared. Remember my friend who works at the gas station, Ben? He found video footage of Luke."

Annalisa smiles. "It showed him passed out on a bench from five thirty to seven thirty. They were ruling it as a murder because it looked like Greg was killed in a fight with Luke, but since Luke has an alibi from five to seven, it obviously wasn't him. Forensics was forced to take another look at all the evidence and are ruling it an accident, technically death by misadventure. Now they think Greg didn't die from a fight but instead tripped and hit his head." Her smile grows bigger, her joy infectious. She seems years younger. "Luke's free."

Her words feel muddy in my mind. They're ruling it an accident? "What about the twins?"

Annalisa and Aiden glance at each other again. "We decided to take that secret to our graves. Coming forward won't do anything now that Luke's free, anyway," Annalisa says, and I can feel the weight behind her words, the significance in their meaning. She's forgiven us for keeping that secret, forgiven Aiden for not wanting to turn the twins in, and is promising to protect them as well.

"Everyone promised not to say anything," Aiden adds.

"I won't say anything either," I vow. I never would've, but I promise it anyway. I speak it into existence because it's important to me for him to know I'm with him, I have his back, I'll protect the twins. I'll take this secret to my grave; my friends will as well.

Maybe we really have won. Luke's free. The twins won't be a media sensation or face penalties for keeping the accident a secret. Tony's dead. Annalisa's happy. My friends are safe. Hell, even Kaitlyn and I are on speaking terms. Is everything finally *normal*? Is the craziness and secrets and lies and drama finally *over*?

Aiden and I haven't glanced away from each other, our eyes saying everything we wish we could. Annalisa clears her throat. "I'll give you guys some time. I'll be back later, Amelia—er—Thea."

Then she's gone, leaving me alone with Aiden. He sits in the chair beside my bed, not once breaking his gaze from me. "While I'm mad at you for what you did, and wish with every fiber in my being that I was there with you, I can't say I'm all that surprised."

The memories of taking his phone and locking him and the boys in my room make my cheeks heat. I should apologize, but I'm not sorry. I'd do it again. I'd do anything to keep my friends safe, to prevent them from being in harm's way because of me. So no, I don't feel that bad for keeping him out of the fight with Tony, but I do feel bad I had to lie to him to do so.

Aiden leans closer to me. "I cannot believe you *Ethan Moored* me, though! Really, Thea?" A smile tugs at his lips, and I let one pull on mine as well. It feels like that was forever ago.

"I locked him in the closet to take his phone, though. You were in a bedroom. Totally different."

A chuckle escapes him as he shakes his head, but then his expression grows deadly serious. "When I found the two of you, lying there unmoving, it nearly killed me. I thought I was too late."

Aiden really *was* there. It wasn't an imaginary Aiden my mind had conjured up to comfort me. "How were you there? How did you get out of my room? How did you find me?"

He grabs my hand, holding it in his. His hand is warm and strong and my hand feels right at home.

He lifts a shoulder in a shrug. "I broke your door down as soon as you left the driveway," he says calmly, like it's no big deal. That was a sturdy wood door. It shouldn't have been so easy to break.

"And how did you know where I was?" He was *there*. He came for me.

His hold on my hand tightens. "At Mason's, when you were arguing with Mason and Noah about the picture he took of you, you left your phone on the table. You were so dead set on not getting anyone involved, and I don't know, I just couldn't let anything happen to you. I turned the Track My Friends on your phone on so that I would know where you were if anything happened. I also copied down Agent Dylan's number."

I'm speechless. I can't even be mad that he tracked my phone because he saved me from bleeding out by finding me in time. "Did you know I wouldn't stick to the plan?"

He shakes his head. "*I* wasn't going to stick to the plan. I was going to drive you to the police station and call Agent Dylan anyway. Noah and Mason were acting like vigilantes, trying to rush into something without a solid plan, acting like they were invincible.

You just strayed from the plan before I had a chance to. I really should've seen it coming; you *never* listen to me, and you gave in to Mason and Noah way too quickly." He smiles at that last part, not mad about it like he probably should be. "I called Agent Dylan as soon as we got out of your bedroom, and then hopped in my car to track you. Agent Dylan also has your phone tracked, by the way. I only got there a few moments before he and the others did."

"It was stupid, so stupid of me, to rush to meet Tony." I just wanted my *life* back. I was fooling myself into thinking that if I agreed to meet him instead of waiting for him to find me, I was taking control back. "I was turning around but he had set up a spike strip."

His hand squeezes mine. "I know, I know, it's okay." His other hand comes up to rest on my cheek, and I lean in to his touch.

"You saved my life, you know," I whisper, and he tenses.

"No, no, I really didn't. I should've done a better job protecting you. But I didn't save your life, you saved your own life."

His words make my stomach tighten. Deep down I never thought I'd be strong enough to do it on my own, never thought I'd find the strength to pull the trigger when it really mattered. "I used the necklace you gave me for Christmas. If I didn't have that, I don't think I would've been able to get out of there. Plus, you knew where I was; you got there before I lost too much blood."

"I'm just glad you're okay." Aiden's voice is soft, his eyes shining with emotion. "I love you, Thea. You're the strongest, most beautiful, and most badass person I know."

I laugh at that. Even though I don't particularly feel strong, beautiful, or badass, I know Aiden means every word. "I love you, too, Aiden."

"Knock, knock," comes a voice, and I'm shocked when Agent Dylan walks into my room. "How are you feeling?" he asks, setting a little stuffed teddy bear down on one of the counters beside a vase of pink lilies.

I shift, not knowing how exactly to feel at seeing him. On the one hand, he sent me here on purpose, to be near Annalisa, and he didn't answer my calls. But on the other, he came through when I needed him. He answered Aiden's call, and showed up when I needed him.

"I've been better, but I've been worse. You know, the usual."

Aiden stands from the chair, giving my hand one last squeeze before letting it go. "I'll be back a bit later, okay, Thea?"

I nod and he kisses me, quickly, chastely, and not for as long as I want.

Once he's out of the room, Agent Dylan is at my side. He gestures to the chair Aiden just vacated. "May I?"

"Did you send me here as bait?" I blurt, skipping any pleasantries. The curiosity has been killing me. "Did you put me with Anna in case Tony sought her out and ran into me too? I know people have been putting pressure on you to find him after the last time he got away."

Agent Dylan pauses, hovering over the seat, his eyebrow quirked, before slowly settling into the chair.

"That's an interesting theory."

"Is it true?"

Agent Dylan sighs. "You're right that there was pressure on us to find him. But we didn't put you here as *bait*. As we learned more about Tony, we found out about his daughter. We figured it would be easier to watch over the both of you if you were together. We don't like using kids as bait for dangerous men like Tony or we would've done this a long time ago."

The wind is knocked out of my sails as I process what he's saying. I guess it would make sense, not having to divide assets and agents if we were near each other.

"Plus, we didn't know you would become friends," Agent Dylan says, "and we certainly didn't think this whole thing would end with two of our charges taking on Tony by themselves. But you guys did great. Barely needed our help."

I shift, holding up the hand with the IV in it to make my point. "Well, we could've *used* some help."

I drop my hand. He seems somber but still raises an amused eyebrow. "And we would've given it if you had called us. If Aiden hadn't called us we wouldn't have gotten there in time. You and Annalisa would've been a lot worse off if we hadn't gotten you in that ambulance."

I grumble in agreement since I can't really argue with that. I didn't call him when I should've. I didn't give him enough time to get there or give him the chance to come up with his own plan, one that probably would've avoided everything we went through. But we can't change any of that, and what matters is that he came through, that they saved Annalisa, that they got me help before I bled out.

His face grows serious and his body stiffens. "But I'm sorry we weren't on top of it. I'm sorry we failed you. I saw your missed calls as I was rounding up people to find you, and you didn't answer when I called back. You really had me worried. We should've been there."

I scan his face and register the genuine remorse he seems to feel. It's not his fault, it's really my own. Everything was going to shit around me and I assumed that included him as well.

"It's not your fault. Thank you for showing up when you did."

We sit together, both of us silent, lost in our own thoughts. He honestly does seem to hate the way things played out, and I wish I had put more faith in him.

"So is he really dead?" My voice comes out in a whisper.

I've been in shock about everything this whole time, thinking those words but too afraid to voice them.

"He really is. You don't need to worry, ever again."

Something I've been holding on to in my chest cracks with those words. I saw the bullets lodge in his chest, Mom said she identified the body, and Agent Dylan is confirming it, so it must be true. *He's dead. For real.* But do I really never need to worry again? I remember the other phone call I had that day and am going to voice my thoughts but hesitate. Can I trust Agent Dylan if I tell him?

He notices and leans forward, his analytical gaze roaming my face. "What aren't you telling me?"

My breath hitches, but then I let go of the hesitation and tell him about Andrew and how he called me, about his role in sending Tony to me, about how he tried to kill me on New Year's Eve. He listens attentively, and promises me he'll take care of it, and this time I believe him.

He stands and buttons his top suit-jacket button. "I'll get out of here and let you rest. But we've started the process to release you and your mother from witness protection. Your mom just has to sign some stuff and you're officially Thea Kennedy again."

My eyes tear up, but I force myself not to cry. My voice comes out high and cracks when I thank him. He nods once and strides from the room, leaving me staring at him in wonder.

I'm Thea Kennedy.

≫ ≪

Two weeks after I'm discharged from the hospital with some meds and care instructions, Mom lets me invite my friends over. They all visited me in the hospital, and Charlotte, Julian, and Chase were given the full story. They were surprised, but eventually understood that I'm still me, just with a different name that they're still getting used to, and now I'm allowed to be in pictures.

I'm relieved they're not mad at me for keeping such a big secret from them, but they were understanding and knew what I was running from and why it was so important to keep my secret a secret, especially after seeing me in the hospital.

My friends crowd around a board game on the floor, where we have been for hours, arguing over unofficial rules. It's weird to be myself around them, but it also seems completely normal. I'm glad everything is out in the open and I can finally just *be* with the people I was most worried I'd hurt. We're all here together: Annalisa, Charlotte, Mason, Noah, Chase, Julian, and Aiden. I have love for all of them. I basically stumbled upon them by accident, but that accident was probably the best thing to happen to me.

The television is on in the background and I hear someone say, "Ew, I hate Siren of the Heart, who would even go to their concert?"

I look up from my cards. "Hey, they're, like, my favorite band, don't trash them."

An incredibly loud gasp comes from Noah as his head slowly turns to look at me.

"You're a fan of Siren of the Heart? How did I not know this?"

"Um, yes. They're my absolute favorite!"

"Me. Too." Noah stresses each word. "Did we just find our thing?"

I feel a slow smile spread across my face. "You know what, Noah. I think we just did."

"*Ha!*" he exclaims. "In your *face* Mason. I have a thing with Thea! Hey, do you think if we tell them you were in witness protection they'll write a song about us? Or invite us up on stage?" Noah asks, arguing with everyone else when they say that would never work.

It took us a while, but it looks like we finally found our thing. I hear the front door open and soon Brian is standing in my living room with Mom.

"Hey, guys, you think we can get some time with Mason and Thea?" Brian asks, standing with Mom, his arm around her back. She looks happy, her features relaxed, her shoulders not holding their usual tension.

Mason's told everyone about his parents' impending divorce, about how Natalia has reclaimed their house and kicked Brian out, and how Brian has basically moved in here. It's weird seeing him around every day, in the kitchen for breakfast, at the table for dinner, in the living room in front of the television with Mom at night, acting like it's always been this way, like he's right at home in our lives. It's weirder still when he offers to help me with the calculus homework I've missed and am trying to catch up on, when he picks up my favorite smoothie for me "just because" on his way here from work, when he reminds me to take my medication on time. It's like he *cares*, like he wants to be my ... father? Or at least a father figure? I'm not sure, and it's weird to even think about, but I can't truly say that I hate it. Mason's always gone on about his dad being a good father, and in the short time we've been living together, and the times he visited me at the hospital, and even before all of this with Aiden and his brothers, I can't disagree with Mason. Brian may have done something terrible with the affair and how he treated Natalia, but I'm learning not everything is always as it seems; not everything is all the way right and all the way wrong. Sometimes there's a middle ground.

Everyone but me and Mason gets up to collect their stuff. "I'll call you later," Aiden says to me before giving me a quick kiss. To Mason he says, "I'll see you at home."

It's still weird for Aiden to say it, and I'm not sure that he'll ever get used to it, but after everything we went through, Aiden decided to sell his house and take Natalia up on her offer to move in with her and Mason. Apparently, this is something she's talked to him about multiple times, and after making sure Mason and the twins were okay with it, Aiden took her up on the offer. I know he likes to appear strong and like he always has his shit together, but I know the relief of not having to worry about bills and money and all things adulting is a huge weight off his shoulders. He gets to just be *Aiden* now, though he is still filing for custody of his brothers.

He and Mason do their handshake thing and Aiden heads to the front door with everyone else.

Noah walks backward to the door, mouthing to Mason, "I have a thing with Thea," then very maturely sticks his tongue out at him before disappearing from sight.

Mom leaves Brian's side to walk my friends out and close the front door, and Mason and I awkwardly stare at Brian, then at each other.

"Why don't you guys sit on the couch? We just want to have a talk with you," Brian says.

Mason gently helps me off the floor, conscious of my healing wounds, and we sit beside each other on the couch, our backs straight, looking at Brian, who's sitting on the couch across from us.

When Mason confronted his father about the affair, he was pissed at him, but now they're on speaking terms. Their relationship isn't perfect, and Mason is rightfully upset about how Brian treated his mother, but Mason hasn't written him off completely. It'll take time for them to heal, to get back to where they were before, and Mason needs time to process, to accept what's happened and fully forgive Brian for hurting Natalia and lying to the both of them. But for now, they're able to be in the same room as each other, to speak civilly to each other, to acknowledge that this may be the new normal.

Mom comes back from closing the front door and joins Brian on the couch across from us, and they both just sit there, staring at us with these weird little smiles.

Mason leans over to me, speaking in a hushed tone. "You think this is creepy, too, right?"

"Totally," I answer, and Mom and Brian share a look. It's almost gross how happy they look, how *domestic* and at home they seem together. They cuddle up on that very couch before bed every night and watch their show.

Brian clears his throat. "There's really no easy way to say this—" he starts, and Mom exclaims, "I'm pregnant!"

The ground drops out from under me and Mason's frozen beside me.

"No," I say after picking my jaw up off the floor. "No. I saw the pregnancy test. It said you weren't—it said Not Pregnant."

Mom looks guilty, and it's then I notice she has her hand on her stomach. She's done that a lot lately, hasn't she? "I wanted to tell you, but with all our fighting and then your recovery, I never found a good time, and then I didn't want to stress you out."

Mason and I look at each other, and I'm sure we're both wearing the same horrified expressions.

"But the test was negative!" is all I can seem to say.

"I know when I'm pregnant. You were a false negative too. That's why I went to the doctor and did a test. I'm pregnant, Thea. Brian and I are going to raise this baby together. We're going to stay here, in King City," she says as Brian places his hand on hers and looks at Mason.

I'm going to stay here. I'll be with my friends. I was too scared to ask Mom about what we would do, where we would go once my injuries healed. I didn't want to go back to the place I grew up, the place I lived for the majority of my life until I was forced to relocate, because that place doesn't seem like *home* anymore. Home is here, in King, with my friends. And now I'm staying here, I'll never have to fear leaving them before I'm ready again.

"We're really happy, Mason," Brian says. "I know this is all a lot and you two have been adjusting really well, considering, but we want you both to know that this isn't going to change how we feel about you."

I don't know what to say.

She seems happy, Brian seems happy, and Mason just looks confused. I'm not sure how Natalia feels about it, but it can't be good.

"I—uh. Congrats?" I say, nudging Mason to see if he's broken.

He clears his throat. "Yeah, um. Congrats."

"Do you have any questions?" Brian asks, watching us patiently.

Tons. Mason and I shake our heads at the same time.

"Okay, then. Why don't we leave you two alone to process this?" Brian suggests, taking Mom's hand and drawing her from the room. "We're always here to talk. We're not going anywhere," he adds before they disappear from the room completely.

Mason and I sit in silence, staring at the spot they just vacated. *A sibling? I'm going to have a sibling? Is Mason going to be my* brother *now?*

Mason snaps out of it first. "Just wait until Noah finds out about *this*. We share more than a thing, we share a *sibling*."

A laugh bubbles out of me, and he sends me a crooked grin, any tension now gone and letting us fall into our natural camaraderie.

"What do you think?" I ask Mason. "About all of this?"

"I—I don't know. Does this mean you're my sister now?"

I shrug. "I guess?"

Mason nods thoughtfully. "You know I've always loved you."

My eyes widen. I'm about to interrupt him, but he keeps talking. "Wait, let me finish. You know I've always loved you, but I know you'll always be in love with Aiden. And I'm at peace with that, I genuinely am. I thought he didn't know you, but turns out, he's actually the only one who *truly* knew you. You were meant to be together. I'll always have love for you, but it's the love I have for a sister, especially since you might actually *become* my sister."

He gives an awkward laugh at that last part, and I say, "Mason, you know I've always considered you my brother. Whether our parents make it official or not, I'll always love you too."

>> <<

When I walk through the halls of King City High for the first time since before Tony, I have a new appreciation for it all. For the beige lockers, the chatter of kids packing the hallways, the fading GO LIONS! mural in the hall. I even spot Kaitlyn talking to Makayla in the hall and it doesn't dim my good mood.

I am Thea Kennedy.

Aiden's by his locker, his shirt stretched across his broad shoulders, his handsome face set in concentration as he checks his phone. I stride over to him as he closes his locker and bump into him, much like the first time I met him, except I keep hold of all my belongings. He reaches out an arm to steady me. "Did you just walk into me on purpose?" he asks, raising an eyebrow.

I can't resist, he left it open for me. "Well, maybe if you didn't bulldoze down the hall in a straight line, I wouldn't have to jump out of your way to avoid destruction."

Aiden's eyebrows draw together but the corners of his lips pull up. "What are you . . . ?"

I hold up the brand-new schedule, the exact same as my old one, but now with the name *Thea Kennedy* printed on the top. Excitement bubbles through me. I'm here, at this school, with Aiden and my friends, as *me*. Not hiding secrets. Not using a fake name. Not trying to solve a murder. Not trying to bring down a corrupt politician. Just two kids going to class. Two kids living their everyday, boring lives.

I never thought I'd see the day.

My life may never exactly be *normal*, and especially not *boring*, but if these last few months have taught me anything, it's that I have people who love me, and together, we can face anything.

I peek up at him through my lashes. "Sorry. I'm Thea Kennedy and it's my first official day here. You wouldn't happen to know where room 341 is, would you?"

The End

Acknowledgments

Ending a series is always hard, but trying to write this acknowledgments page without forgetting everyone who's helped make this series possible is even harder.

As always, the first people I want to thank are you, the readers. Thank you for picking up this series and joining Amelia and friends on their journey. I never thought I'd be a writer, but as I started writing for fun on Wattpad and you found my work and encouraged me, I started realizing that writing is something I *could* do. Thank you for following me on this journey, and if you never heard of me on Wattpad and picked up my books recently, thank you as well! I hope you loved the story as much as I loved writing it. I am forever grateful for your love and support.

Thank you to my amazing parents, Carmela and Bruno Cunsolo. I hid my writing from you for years until Mom found my book and "sneakily" started reading it (I totally knew, Mom, that's why I came clean). It was and always will be petrifying to have your *mom* read your stories, but I know you'll always support me.

Thanks for staying up to 3 a.m. proofreading for me, encouraging me to keep writing, and introducing me to the love of stories when I was a kid. My dad's not a big YA romance reader, so he's never read my work (at least not that I know of), and *please* keep it that way (don't read the kissing scenes!), but he's never needed to know the details of the book to believe in me and tell all his friends. He brags about me all the time, and when people asked him if he's read the book, he always replies "I'm waiting for the movie." Now Sony Pictures Television is developing *She's With Me* for television, and even without reading the book, my dad always knew it would happen. He believes in me wholeheartedly, and I'll always be grateful. You're the best parents ever.

Thank you to my brother, Michael. You didn't read the book, but you still supported me in your own way.

Thank you to my grandparents, *zias*, *zios*, cousins, neighbors, family, and friends. It intimidates me but also means so much to me when you guys read my stories. Thank you so much for all the love and support.

Thank you to my boyfriend, Mario, and his family. You guys have always supported me from the first moment I told you about this story. Thank you for believing in me and my story, and for always sharing it with others. I'm still positive you guys hold the record for most copies of a book bought by a single family.

Thank you to Wattpad Books for picking up this series and sharing it with the world. Thank you to the whole team for working so hard to make this book so successful. Thank you to the marketing team, the designers and typesetters, the social media team, and everyone else behind the scenes. Also thank you to everyone at Wattpad HQ in general for supporting me and my book, and Wattpad Studios for reading my book and pitching it to Sony. Also, thanks to Sony Pictures for seeing the potential in my story and picking it out of millions.

Thank you to my amazing talent manager, I-Yana Tucker, who's been with me for five years (since August 30, 2016)! Thanks for everything from fighting for me to running around putting out fires to being on top of all the small details like what color flowers I'm sent. I couldn't imagine this experience without you.

This series has come a long way from how it started when I first started writing it at seventeen years old, and that's thanks to all the amazing editors who've had their hands on my work. Thanks to Adam Wilson, developmental editor extraordinaire, and Rebecca Mills, copy editing queen. Special thanks to Deanna McFadden. I've trusted your edits and suggestions wholeheartedly and it shows in the final product. Thanks for believing in me even when my perfectionism gets the best of me and I frantically email you at 3 a.m. asking for an extension on the edits (LOL!). I really appreciate all your hard work.

Thank you to my author/writer friends. You've made all the difference this year. Writing is already an isolated activity, and quarantine has only made it worse. However, I've never felt alone while typing away because I've always had you to talk to, laugh with, share ideas with, and sprint with. It's gotten to that point where I don't even remember what writing without sprinting feels like. It's crazy to think we used to sit alone in a dark room from when we woke up until when we went to bed and didn't talk to another soul. Thank you to my friends on #TeamNoSleep: Jordan, Sydni, Kenadee, SJ, Laylaa, and Lauren. On top of the fact that I've talked to you every single day since meeting you, I literally forced you to stay up with me to 2 a.m. every single day for weeks straight while I rewrote this book. You kept me sane.

Thank you to my friends on #TheATeam: Andi, Van, Emily, Ava, and April. No matter what time of day it is, one (or all) of you are always there to sprint with me. Thank you to Rodney V. (the V is for "*Vampire!*"), for not only sprinting with me, but being a source of knowledge on literally everything and being willing to share with any writer in need. I know I can always turn to you for advice or a good pep talk. Also, thank you to the many other writers who are always happy to help another writer in need, and to all my writer friends who promote my story and exciting news and announcements. I couldn't possibly name all of you or we'd be here all day, but I appreciate you all so much.

Since this is the end of a series that I know people have been following for years, I wanted to do something special for my readers. On March 13, on Instagram, I asked readers to share what they loved about the story. I was originally going to share some of those thoughts, but I received over three hundred (!) comments! So instead, I'm going to randomly list a bunch of your names from that post as thanks for following along and for all the kind words you left. I can't include everyone's name because there's way too many, but know that I read all the comments and loved and appreciated every single one of them. Thanks to: Lucy, Yashvi, Katie, Leah, Sherry, Cassidy, Dinisha, Jen, Janvi, Samara, Ananya, Nishi, Claire, Nicki, Kayla, Nandika, Juliana, Ella, Cristina, Brianna, Jensen, Madisyn, Emma, Stephanie, Kruthika, Khulood, Revati, Gillian, Hannah, Breyanna, Alefiyah, Alexia, Ruby, Andromeda, Andrea, Freya, Mai, Mahek, Jamie, Zero, Amy, Liberty, Sierra, Reagan, Scarlett, Amirah, Sidney, Chloe, Heather, Aysel, Mary, and *so many others*. Seriously, if I could sit here all day and list your names I totally would.

Thank you to everyone who picks up my books. Seriously, you guys are the best.

about the author

Jessica Cunsolo's young adult series With Me has amassed over 140 million reads on Wattpad since she posted her first story, *She's With Me*, on the platform in 2015. That novel has since won a 2016 Watty Award for Best Teen Fiction, and has been published in French, Spanish, and English. The story is also in development for TV with Sony Pictures Television. Jessica lives with her family and dog, Leo, just outside of Toronto, where she enjoys the outdoors and transforming her real-life awkward situations into plotlines for her viral stories. You can find her on Twitter @AvaViolet, on Instagram @jesscunsolo, or on Wattpad @AvaViolet.

Thank You!

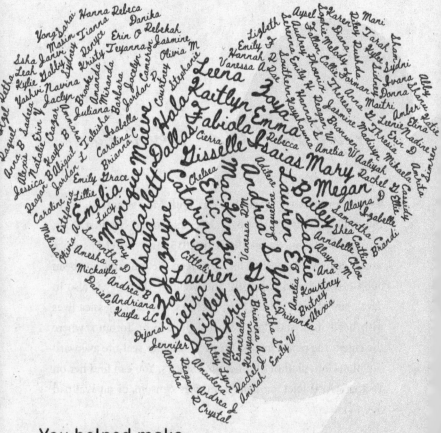

You helped make
this dream possible.

With love,

Jess

Buy the stories already loved by millions on Wattpad

Collect the #OriginalSix Wattpad Books.
Now available everywhere books are sold.

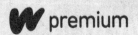

wattpad W

Where stories live.

Discover millions of stories created by diverse writers from around the globe.

Download the app or visit
www.wattpad.com today.

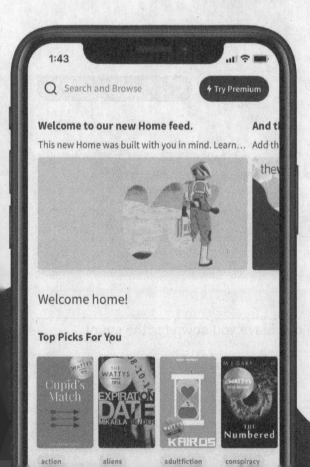

Want more? Why not try . . .

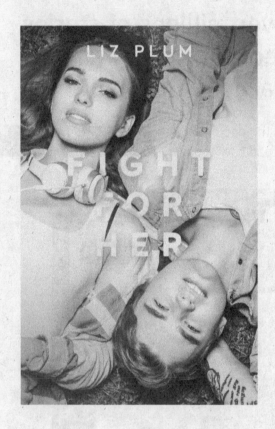

Love can leave you down for the count.